CHRIS FORMANT, who got his start in rock and roll in his early "garage band" days, never dreamed he would one day hold a seat on the Board of Trustees of the Rock and Roll Hall of Fame. Today he is still a student of rock and roll and an avid collector of rock memorabilia.

As an executive in a leading global company, running a multi-billion-dollar business, Formant is the unlikeliest of authors of a murder mystery.

However, the continued unanswered questions surrounding the deaths of our most iconic rock legends led Formant to first speculate and then re-imagine what would happen if cutting-edge technology were applied to these famous cold cases.

By conducting research into the archives of the Hall of Fame, studying advanced forensic techniques and gaining creative insights from top doctors, FBI investigators, and a former editor of Rolling Stone magazine, Formant has crafted what is being referred to as "*The DaVinci Code for Rock and Roll Fans.*"

Gregg Fienberg, award-winning Producer and Director of hit television series including 'Deadwood', 'True Blood' and 'Twin Peaks' writes:

"Bright Midnight is an unexpected gem of a story. From the moment the mysterious clues surfaced, I was immediately drawn into Gantry Elliot's world, as the ageing Rolling Stone writer discovers that a long established rock and roll myth is actually something much more sinister. Chris Formant is so adept at crafting the intrigues of his novel that one can't help but come away questioning what is the real truth behind the deaths of some of our most-beloved artists. The ingenious weaving of "historical "accounts and clever vignettes with descriptions of advanced forensic technology unlock a set of startling revelations that will leave readers reeling at the end. Bright Midnight is Rock and Roll's DaVinci Code!"

CHRIS FORMANT

Bright Midnight

*For those who heard the music, like they never heard
the music before.*

ASTOR
+BLUE
EDITIONS

Published in 2016 by Astor and Blue LLC,
Suite 23A, 1330 Avenue Of The Americas, New York, NY 10019, U.S.A.
www.houseofstratus.com

Typeset by Astor + Blue

A catalogue record for this book is available from the Library of Congress and the British Library.

ISBN (Paperback): 978-1-941286-92-0
ISBN (EPUB): 978-1-941286-93-7
ISBN (EPDF): 978-1-941286-94-4
ISBN (Mobi): 978-1-68120-004-0

1. Speculative Fiction—Cold case murder mystery of classic Rock and Roll Stars—Fiction. 2. Investigative Journalist seeking the truth behind Myth of 27th—Fiction. 3. Secret Cult controlling the Music Industry—Fiction .4. American Crime and Police Procedural—Fiction. 6. FBI and Journalist team up to uncover massive corruption and murder of famous Rock Stars—Fiction. 7. New York City, London, England, Quantico, VA—Fiction I. Title

Acknowledgments

I would like to acknowledge the advice, insights and assistance from the various friends and associates who encouraged me and helped bring Bright Midnight into the sunlight. There are many: my Agent, Lisa Queen, Publicist Meryl Moss, Business Manager Angela Virzi, and my social media muses, Tamara and Michael McCleary. Also, the insight and professional support received from Raphael Tamargo, Jim Henke, Gregg Fienberg, Robert Woodcox, Robert Astle, and David Lane.

A special mention must be made of The Rock and Roll Hall of Fame, particularly the incredible archive research staff, and to the encouragement and support of my family: Libby, Cooper, Chris, Virginia, Angelina, and Cindy.

Lastly, and most of all, to the beautiful musicians who made the legendary music that continues to haunt us and inspire us.

Chris Formant
July 2016

Cover Art: The stunning cover art is by one of the artistic geniuses of the psychedelic era, legendary Fillmore poster artist, David Singer. It depicts the joy and sorrow of the young "minstrels" and musical poets of 1960's rock and roll along with the harrowing suspense of a 21st century murder mystery. Singer is well known as one of the early psychedelic poster and album cover artists, and the artist that made collage art popular.

List of Sources

PART ONE

10 PM, November 17, 1967

Reading, England

The opening chord exploded like a thunderclap, silencing the raucous late night crowd in a nanosecond as it reverberated off the walls and ceiling, almost shaking the beer and wine glasses off the flimsy cocktail tables.

Nearly every head snapped toward the stage in unison straining to see, through the smoky club atmosphere, just who was playing with such power and precision.

The unmistakable dominant seventh sharp ninth chord of "Purple Haze" and the tamed fuzz buster distortion could only announce the arrival of Jimi Hendrix.

The crowd went wild and surged toward the stage.

Only this was not Hendrix.

This otherworldly sound was coming from a scraggly teenager with a forty-year-old whiskey voice.

He moved effortlessly from hard rock to sing-along English folk ballads, the crowd silenced as he channeled the best of Hendrix, then segued to the Beatles, then Stones, then his own catchy songs.

They were in awe as he played with their emotions, drawing them in and twisting them around his finger with each song.

He owned the room full of stylish mods and black leather rockers and everyone instinctively knew that this kid and his group from Wales were destined to explode onto the music scene.

He was good. Really good.

Unfortunately, he was too good for the record company

representative in the audience, who stormed out before they were even finished. Wheezing and coughing, he hurriedly waded through the Vespa scooters, past the Norton and Triton motorcycles, to the beaten up old red phone booth on the edge of the parking lot. Gasping, he leaned against the phone booth and pulled out his inhaler and took two deep breaths.

Calming himself, he dialed a familiar number. "Boss," he said slowly, "we have a big fucking problem..."

Present Day

Rolling Stone Magazine Offices, NYC

Early Afternoon

"No one's gonna give a shit about where we place the Rock Hall piece," the new staffer curtly commented. "Our readers don't really follow stuff like that anymore. The latest focus groups suggest that we need more current and diverse material, like EDM...or Electronic Dance Music, for you Gantry." The new staffer condescendingly looked at the older men, and went on. "*Grammy's*, yes. *Oscars*, yes. But our readers weren't even alive when most of these groups were popular. Maybe the AARP might be interested?"

The young staffer laughed at his joke.

Gantry stared at the staffer with a perplexed expression, like a spoiled teenager. Alex sat back and rolled his eyes. He knew what was coming next.

"Young man, do you know the derivation of the metered heartbeat, the backbone of EDM?" Gantry asked in a slow Texan drawl as the smiling staffer shook his head. "It was introduced by Greg Errico, the drummer for Sly and the Family Stone. Inducted into the Rock and Roll Hall of Fame in 1993. One of the most influential drummers in rock history."

The kid sunk down in his chair as Gantry continued.

"It's the basis for much of Rock, Funk, Hip Hop, and EDM... electronic dance music for us old timers."

Alex smirked at Gantry.

A soft knock on the glass conference door interrupted Gantry's lecture. It was Dave Grohl of The Foo Fighters. In awe of the rocker that they'd idolized since they were young, the staff jumped up as if the president of the United States had walked in the room.

"Hey Alex, sorry to barge in, but I'm in town for a show at the Garden and thought I'd stop by and say hello," he explained as he stuck his head in.

"Anytime," Alex responded as he introduced the rocker to his staff. They were star struck.

"And here's the MAN," Grohl exclaimed when he spotted Gantry, and ran over to shake his hand.

"Hey, can I ask you a question? "Alex interjected, "Do you know Greg Errico?"

"You've got to be kidding! He's one of my idols…the father of modern drumming. I learned to play by imitating him. Why do you ask?"

"Ah, no reason. No reason at all." Satisfied, Alex slyly glanced over at Gantry, who couldn't help but smile.

Gantry Elliot was a tough son of a bitch, but always fair, and much smarter than his appearance let on. Now at age sixty-five, he looked as out of place working in *Rolling Stone's* Manhattan offices as "a centipede at a toe-tappin' contest," a term he liked to use in the rare instances when the opportunity presented itself. His well-worn, dark crocodile cowboy boots were always propped on his desk when he was deep in thought. He'd come a long way since leaving Irving, Texas, but Gantry never lost the boots. They meant home to him.

He had joined Alex Jaeger, *Rolling Stone's* publisher, more than four decades earlier. He was a wunderkind when he first came on in the late sixties—a smash investigative reporter—but now he was just a relic to the rest of the staff. Holding the title of "Classic Rock Editor," Gantry had been relegated to commenting on rock & roll stars, writing the occasional article on the "classic" era, or reviewing the Rock and Roll Hall of Fame induction ceremony every April. Though he tried to pitch substantial stories, lately he had been shut out of every promising lead. Frustrated, he seldom left his back office.

Gazing out the window at the bright rays of morning sun over the East River, Gantry made his first cup of strong coffee and settled in for the day. He'd been thinking about his life lately. Turning sixty-five tends to focus a man on what's important, what he's accomplished, how he'll be remembered. He tried not to dwell on the writing opportunities he was losing to younger staffers, but it nevertheless ate at him, as his boredom grew month after month.

After taking a large gulp of coffee, and with little else to do, he began to reorganize his file drawers which were filled with stories dating back to 1968. Occasionally, Gantry liked to read his old copy to remind himself he really *was* a writer. He pulled out an article, dated July 1999–skimming the coffee stained paper, his eyes softened as he read the opening words.

> *I believe we are moving toward a new age in ideas and events. Astrologically, we are at the end of the Pisces Age...soon to begin the Age of Aquarius, in which events as important as those at the beginning of Pisces are likely to occur. There is a young revolution in thought and manner about to take place.*
> — Brian Jones

It all came rushing back to him as the words triggered memories of a time when a new form of music filled the air. The unusual blended dissonance of sitar and guitar was still fresh in his mind. He could almost hear it...Inspired by creative bands, a devoted following of avid disciples actively searched the music and lyrics for the signposts and symbols of peace and love. A new musical religion emerged. It was truly the dawning of the Age of Aquarius.

Gantry's adrenaline started pumping, remembering the familiar hum and feel of the perfect keyboard of his beat up IBM Selectric 11 typewriter—the little golf ball whirling and punching the paper... he sped through the old article.

Juxtaposing this free love culture was the "us vs. them" militaristic stance of the government and local authorities. Musicians, singers, poets, and songwriters became enemies of the state. It became almost a form of "rock and roll McCarthyism."

Damn fine quote, he thought to himself. Then, smugly, *These fucking Millenials can't write four sentences in a row without adding a link to Wikipedia*. His eyes lingered on the page, and with a sharp cold inhale of his breath, he felt the tragic reminder of the untimely death of a great artist...

Because of an unwritten code, when a rock & roll star suddenly died, generally of what was called "excess" (drugs and alcohol), investigations were grossly inadequate and superficial, leading to wild speculations and urban legends that have persisted over time.

Then darting to the conclusion, he recalled rewriting the last line about sixty times. *It was a killer line...worth a Pulitzer.*

"Electricity was in the air. Everything was in a state of upheaval and chaos. It was reflected, even inspired by the music. It *was* a renaissance."

Suddenly his office door swung open

—a major affront and an unpleasant surprise. No one ever came into his office without knocking first. *Who the hell was this?*

His heavy boots hit the floor with a thud as he looked up at the tri-colored, spike-haired kid standing before him.

"Hey, *Mr.* Artifact-oh!" the kid said in an irritating voice, with a heavy emphasis on the last syllable. The kid had called him this once before, and Gantry had told him if he ever did it again, he'd find his multicolored head on a spike.

"What the fuck do you want, rainbow head?" Gantry retorted, turning back to his computer as if busy with something important.

Rainbow head was the first thing that had popped into his mind, and he wished he'd been cleverer. Of course now, seconds later, he could think of at least ten good retorts. Perhaps something about the large black plug that was stretching the kid's earlobe to the size of a quarter. "Ubangee freak" would have worked well.

"Hey, Gantry, I heard you covered the classic-rock show over at St. Agnes Retirement Home last night. Did that Beatles cover band really drive up in a paisley, psychedelic VW Microbus?"

The kid waited, his left hand propping him up in the doorjamb, his right hand fingering the plug in his ear.

"I told you what I would do if you ever called me that again, you little Ubangee freak," Gantry said without turning, his fingers working his keyboard, typing *xjglskpg fstxpmonc, flhghfkdl, xtufrohpzzid.*

"Yeah, yeah," the kid murmured, knowing when to quit.

When the kid finally left, Gantry had to get up and close his door again—*they* never did, another sign of youthful disrespect. But he had to smile as he sat back down, thinking of all the shit he pulled during the halcyon days of the late sixties and early seventies back in Texas and, later, in the magazine's home office in San Francisco.

What a trip that place had been. Especially Haight-Ashbury. *What these kids do now pales in comparison.* With Alex as the ringleader, it was as if the inmates had taken over the asylum.

"Did you know there is a town in Texas called Useless?" Gantry had opened his unsolicited query to Rolling Stone with what he thought was a little-known fact about his home state.

He was a college junior living in Austin, and Buddy Holly was a favorite of his. Holly was a Texan from Lubbock and was later one of the original inductees into the Rock and Roll Hall of Fame. Together, Holly and the Hall of Fame comprised Gantry's two favorite subjects.

He knew back in 1968 that Alex, and by extension *Rolling Stone,* shared his interests because Alex's thoughts permeated those pages, and Gantry had read every word. He wanted desperately to get published in *Rolling Stone* because it was the only magazine of its kind. Nothing before or since compared, and with only five issues out that first year, getting into it would be like winning a Pulitzer.

He poured himself another cup of coffee, remembering with a silent laugh the way Alex had responded to the grabber line in his query.

Gantry had proposed a creative and unusual sort of obituary for Buddy Holly in his query letter. It would be a post-epitaphic, wherein he would write something about Holly, that had been whispered, but never written about: the possibility that the plane crash that killed him,

Ritchie Valens, and J. P. Richardson, the Big Bopper, might not have been an accident.

Gantry's letter had caught Alex's eye.

Why not? He thought.

Alex responded to Gantry with a surprise phone call. On that day, Gantry had been engaged in a protest and was working on a report about it, which he'd hoped to sell. As a student he was so poor that he was living on whatever leftover condiments were still in the refrigerator and visiting hotel happy-hour bars three nights a week for free buffets. He had perfected the art of ordering one beer and nursing it until he'd had his fill of appetizers.

So when Alex called that day, Gantry was speechless. When the voice on the other end of the line said, "Hello, is Gantry Elliot there? This is Alex Jaeger calling from *Rolling Stone*," his hands began to tremble.

"Shit," he remembered saying, covering his mouth too late to grab back the word he had now flung out into the world and into Alex's holy ear. This was the *man*. This was *Rolling Stone* magazine. He could barely breathe as he pulled himself together, the receiver in his left hand, a cowboy boot in the other—he'd been caught dressing.

"Uh, umm, yes, this is Gantry Elliot," he said.

"Got your note. Do you know you spelled 'Euless' wrong? It's "you less," he said phonetically. "Not useless." This became a running joke for years.

Before Gantry could reply, Alex laughed and said, "That's okay. I like your idea about Buddy Holly's plane crash. I like it a lot. I'd like to talk to you about it."

Gantry didn't know how to respond. He was paralyzed. Not only was he talking to the publisher of the country's premier rock magazine, but said publisher liked his idea a lot.

He took a deep breath and got into gear. "Yes. I'd like that. I'd like that very much. You're in San Francisco, aren't you?" He tried to sound worldly, having never been out of Texas.

"Yep. Give me your address and I'll send you an airline ticket. Next Monday okay with you?"

A meeting tonight in a woodshed would be just fine. Are you kidding?

Gantry closed his eyes and savored the memory. So many years had passed since then.

The respect and admiration cut both ways. Alex knew that first month that he'd found a diamond in the rough. Gantry's obsession with the integrity of the music, his detail-oriented stories and his creativity were the perfect complement to Alex's tough-minded business style.

One of his Hendrix favorites was softly drifting out of his vintage Emerson radio…"There must be some kind of way out of here said the joker to the thief…" Hendrix's cover of Dylan's "All Along the Watchtower," voted the best cover of all time. So good that Dylan was now covering Hendrix's cover in his concerts.

Bam!

A loud thud awakened Gantry, who, despite multiple cups of coffee, had dozed off, his feet up on his desk, his disheveled salt-and-pepper hair scattered across his face. Anyone passing by might have thought he was just in a state of deep concentration. A shard of bright sunlight had filled his office through his east-facing window, pouring across his dark, old oak desk and illuminating a credenza, a worn brown-leather couch, and a bookcase filled with old LPs.

The afternoon mail had arrived, as always, piled in a cardboard box on his side of the wall, under a small opening he'd asked maintenance to cut so the mail boy could leave it without disturbing him. Glancing over, he saw that the envelopes were piled higher than usual, a sign that it was time to rummage through a week's worth of unread mail. He did it in a hurry, giving only a passing glance to most of it as he fanned through the envelopes, promptly trashing them.

Rarely did anything catch his interest. He figured, as he did with his e-mails, that if something was important enough, it would resurface or someone would call to follow up. He was known to ignore e-mails for weeks, and then just clear out his inbox and let it start all over, which drove his colleagues crazy. But what they hated more was the fact that he rarely answered his antiquated cell phone, one of the few remaining not-so-smart phones in Manhattan. Only Alex knew how to reach Gantry most of the time, knowing that he would either be in the office, at home, or down at Marty's for an after-work whiskey.

The sound of mail hitting the bottom of the box was followed by a knock on the door.

"Yeah, what is it?" he yelled out.

"Mr. Elliot. There is one more package. It's too big for the slot. Someone left it downstairs at the mail room counter."

Gantry swiveled around and opened the door and took the large manila envelope from the boy. As he began to close the door, he could hear the kid muttering sarcastically as he walked away, "*Thank you* Dustin, for picking up the package for me."

Gantry took the envelope to his desk and grabbed a letter opener out of a coffee cup. The opener was lethal looking, with a sharp blade and a heavy knob on the top embossed with a black-and-white skull and crossbones; a gift from Keith Richards for a favorable review of his solo album back when Richards and Jagger were having problems.

He turned the envelope over to see who the sender was, but there was no name or return address, just a handwritten message scrawled with a Sharpie, that read: *To Gantry Elliot. Personal and Confidential.* Now he was intrigued. It was the first piece of mail worth opening in months.

He reached in and pulled out a single sheet of paper. He slipped on his readers and read the short typewritten note:

Brian Jones was murdered. It was not an accident. There were others. Look and see.

Suddenly all the mystery and fun was gone. It was obviously a prank. Jones, the founding member of the Rolling Stones and their lead guitarist, had been found floating facedown in the pool behind his country house outside London in 1969. His death was the first casualty of the Age of Aquarius.

Gantry started at University of Texas the year before Jones died. Everyone had read the media reports—death by drowning—and heard the flood of rumors and conjecture that followed for years, just like the reports of all the other stars who had died, usually of an "excess" of alcohol or drugs.

He'd heard all the wild conspiracy theories before. So not giving it a second thought, he tossed the note into the wastebasket and thrust his prized letter opener back into its coffee cup sheath. As he did, he flashed back to 1965.

That year the Stones dominated the airwaves. "(I Can't Get No) Satisfaction" from the *Out of Our Heads* album was the number one song in the country and was the first song on the flip side (Track 7). The opening eight note guitar riff exploded from Keith Richard's Fuzz Box. It *was* the most electrifying sound anyone had ever heard. When Gantry and his friends heard that the Stones would be playing at the Will Rogers in Fort Worth, they had to go.

The show was sold out, their seats sucked, the sound system was unbalanced, and the venue was hot, humid, and filled with smoke, some of it from cigarettes. Still, Gantry and his friends were in heaven. In fact, when it was over, they were uniformly speechless: it had been their first real rock concert.

Starved for a beer and food, they piled into Randy Melendi's El Camino and drove to the famous Cattlemen's Steakhouse. Squeezing through the huge throng, they saw with stunned amazement that the Stones were now holding court at the bar, and Brian Jones was the center of attention.

Gantry had never seen anyone dressed like Jones...His outfit was like a costume out of a Renaissance fair, a multi-colored coat...his blonde hair glowed, seeming to turn different colors under the lights; a life force unto himself.

Gantry and his friends pushed their way through the crowd for a closer look, but couldn't make it past the fourth row of tightly packed bodies. Disappointed and needing to pee, Gantry squeezed his way in the direction of the men's room. When he finally got to a urinal, next to him, another guy unzipped his pants...He could not believe his eyes...Peeing next to him was Brian Jones...Holy Shit!

Gantry swiveled in his office chair, laughing at the memory of almost pissing on Brian Jones. He remembered the incident in minute detail.

"Mr. J-Jones, you and the b-band were fantastic tonight. It was the best concert I have ever been to."

Jones laughed. "Cheers mate! 'preciate that."

Pausing in silence, they both zipped up.

"You from Fort Worth, then?" Jones asked.

"No. Austin. We're all at the university... going back tonight."

"Well then, let me buy you and your mates a drink before you leave."

Gantry was dumbstruck as he and Brian Jones walked out of the men's room together...then a sea of women descended on Brian and he was quickly swept away.

They never did have that drink.

Gantry was startled from his daydream when a red light began to blink on his phone, the Alex hotline, as he liked to refer to it, which usually meant trouble, personal or business.

"Hey, Alex, what's up?"

"Hey, buddy. Did I wake you?"

Gantry pulled his boots off his desk and straightened himself.

"Naw, just going over that copy for the induction ceremony. Guess I'll never get used to watching it on TV."

"Okay. This is a pop quiz...Who were the inductees?"

"Do I get a bonus for the right answer?"

"Nope, no bonus, just testing your short-term memory, old man."

Gantry rocked back in his chair clearly stung by the comment. "Oh, now you're gettin' on me with the old-guy shit, too? Just like the mail boy and the other adolescents here."

"Come on Gantry, quit stalling."

Gantry smiled. "Do you want 'em alphabetical?"

"Yeah. That's good."

"Last name or first name first?"

"First."

"Alex, that's too fucking easy: Albert King, Donna Summer, Heart, Lou Adler, Public Enemy, Quincy Jones, Randy Newman, and Rush."

"Gantry, you are good. You even put the two R's in the right order. Bravo."

"Cut the shit, Alex. You know I could do that for every year if I wanted. What are you looking for, buddy?"

"I've got something I need to talk to you about. Marty's at six."

"Sure, six…Marty's…"

That was it. The phone clicked in Gantry's ear and went dead.

Odd call, why not talk now?

He looked at his watch. It was five—still too early to leave the office. Gantry caught himself glancing down at the mysterious envelope and note he had tossed in his wastebasket.

Remembering his crazy reverie about Brian Jones, he bent over to pick out the note and envelope when he noticed a small, thin piece of paper caught inside of the envelope. Gently tugging so as to not rip the vintage waxy paper, he extracted it, and squinted hard to read the faded words. He was immediately struck by a major *deja-vu* taser.

My Little One. What the fuck? There can't be more than a dozen people who know about this recording. And most are dead. My Little One. Brian Jones and Jimi Hendrix. Exceptional. 1960s psychedelic gem. The very best of both artists, recorded shortly before Brian Jones died.

Collecting his journalist thoughts, Gantry spun his chair and opened the file cabinet, then flipped to his Jimi Hendrix file and read with a need to know interest:

Hendrix died in September of 1970 in a hotel in London. The official reports listed asphyxiation with a note, choked on his own wine-induced vomit.

Brian Jones died just a year earlier to the month.

Gantry spun his chair back to the desk, now staring at both notes fanned out between his fingers. There had been murder allegations at the time of Hendrix's death that involved a management contract dispute, but nothing was ever proven, and the case closed.

Both twenty-seven years old when they died. Part of the Myth of 27.

"Naw, probably from some weirdo whack job…but Jesus…My Little One," he said under his breath.

He felt his heart rate speeding up a bit as he stood up and gazed out the window at the traffic below. He totally lost track of the time as he fixated on the stalled cars and the weird message. He checked his watch.

"Damn, Alex at Marty's in twenty minutes." He grabbed the envelope and a couple of overstuffed files titled: DEAD ARTISTS and ran out.

The room at Marty's Bar and Grill on Fourteenth Street was right out of a Hemingway novel, everything was made of mahogany, including the booths. The ornate mirror behind the bar was framed in the same wood and featured hand-carved figures in the style of Michelangelo.

Gantry took his seat in the well worn red-leather booths in the back, nodded and smiled to Marty, who was already walking over with his drink, two fingers of Booker's, neat. Surprising to newcomers, Marty was a woman, the granddaughter of Marty Boyle who'd opened the New York establishment more than fifty years before.

Gantry loved the authenticity and the quiet of his surroundings. On any other night, he'd be home in his rent-controlled apartment on Twenty-Third Street by 6:30, pulling one of the hundreds of dusty, cracked cardboard LP jackets off his shelves and gingerly placing its contents on his Technics turntable. Then he'd start to type on his IBM Selectric, just the way he liked.

Because his was in a pre-war building, the insulation was excellent, which allowed him his musical passion and kept the clamor of the streets and neighbors out.

He'd been in the booth for almost twenty minutes when Alex walked in, squinting and trying to find Gantry in the dark. Dressed in a black suit, no tie, and a crisp white shirt; his wavy hair was glistening, and he wore his perfected "say cheese" photo-op smile. When he slid in, Gantry smiled and held out his hand.

"Hey, pardner. Late as usual."

"Late for what? Where are you in such a rush to get to? It's not even Friday night."

"Ah, they're all the same to me."

"That's depressing."

The waiter returned, immediately recognized Alex, took his order, and quickly disappeared.

"So, what's up, your phone call was pretty weird?" Gantry asked. "Business?"

"No," Alex said, nervously smiling from ear to ear.

"Must be fun, whatever it is."

Alex said, "We go way back Gantry?"

"Hey, we go back to my college days, brother."

"I know. Believe me I know, and that's one of the reasons I want to talk to you," Alex said, as the waiter returned with a vodka martini.

"I don't know how to say this," Alex said, fidgeting uncharacteristically.

"Oh, come on. You can tell me anything. What's up?" Gantry suddenly became worried that this may be the "it's time to move on" talk.

"Gantry, I want you to be my best man." Alex took a large gulp of his drink.

"Holy shit! You're getting married *again*? Who's the lucky girl?" A relieved Gantry blurted.

"Well, buddy, that's just it. It *isn't* a girl. His name is Daniel," Alex said, taking another swallow of his drink. He waited for his friend's reaction.

There was an awkward silence.

"Well, now, ain't that some shit," Gantry said lamely.

"Come on...What do you think?" Alex asked nervously.

Another pause, but longer this time for affect. Gantry took a slow, thoughtful sip of his drink, put it back down on the table and looked his friend squarely in the eye.

"Buddy, I think it's fantastic. Of course I'll be your best man. I'd be honored."

A smile creased Alex's face. "I'm glad. I didn't know how you would react."

"Are you shitting me? I've known you were gay since we were kids. It never bothered me. I'm surprised you'd think I'd judge you."

Gantry held up his glass. "Here's a toast to you and Daniel."

Alex raised his glass.

Gantry was truly surprised because he'd always assumed that Alex knew that *he* knew Alex was gay. "Pay no attention to what critics say," Gantry said in toast. "There has never been a statue erected to a critic. May you both live long, happy lives together. Amen."

The two men clinked glasses vigorously, downed the remainder of their drinks, and headed out into the clamor and rush of New York City.

"Hey Alex, one more thing?"

"Sure, but you still don't get a bonus."

"You ever hear of a secret recording by Hendrix and Brian Jones called "My Little One"...sitar and guitar...psychedelic...?"

"Can't say I have...But maybe your old vinyl record guy might know?"

"Dennis? Maybe...probably too obscure."

"G'night pardner."

At that, they gave each other a bro hug, and Alex jumped into his waiting limo.

Just as Gantry was spinning on his heels to head home, Marty came rushing out.

"Gantry, glad I caught you. Did you leave this on the table, got your name on it... Personal and Confidential?"

Gantry caught himself taking a step backward, emotion draining from his face, as he stared at the manila envelope–then exhaled. "Shit. "

"You OK, Gantry, looks like you seen a ghost...need a drink?"

"Naw, it's OK Marty, some crank is sending me love letters–did you see anyone drop it off?"

"Nobody but you and Alex in the back booths tonight."

Grabbing the envelope and carefully inspecting it, he looked Marty in the eyes, and gave her a sly, "you're not shitting me look."

His name was clearly written on the envelope with a Sharpie. Same as the first one.

"Must be a special delivery, from Alex…maybe it's your retirement package…?"

"Don't think this old cowboy is going out with a package…"

"Come on then…drink is on me, Gantry."

"No thanks…G'night Marty."

Gantry was certain that Alex did not have a package with him, although in all their years together he'd rarely known Alex to act so … tentative…so vulnerable, if that was the word to describe him. Gantry had never judged him. To the critics, Alex was arrogant and even tyrannical when he wanted to be. To Gantry, he was just Alex, the same friend who'd given him a chance more than four decades ago, and the same Alex who still believed in him and still needed him.

He stared at the envelope again and thought out loud,

"Alex, if this is a fucking prank…"

Gantry kicked the door open to his apartment–junk mail and old copies of Rolling Stone were caught on the transom, and he brushed those out of the way with his foot. The whole place was his man cave…so clean and tidy came in bi-annual purges. He dropped the manila envelope onto the dining table that doubled as storage for his vast record collection and noticed that there were four messages on his answering machine, none from Alex, so he clicked the off button without listening to any of them and fixated on the offending envelope.

This was getting a little sick, he thought, *two envelopes in one day, and whoever made the drop, knew of my meeting with Alex. Must be a Stone insider.*

He ran through a list of possible culprits.

The mail kid? A staffer at the editorial meeting…? Naw, these kids are too self absorbed to pull off this prank. Alex's weird behavior at Marty's. He could've slipped the envelope on the table…

Gantry felt himself getting a little nervous, as his heart rate picked up ever so slightly. He cleared a couple of albums off his "dining" table and sliced open the manila envelope with a leftover dinner knife. He almost didn't want to look inside. Without reaching in, he turned the envelope upside down, and the contents floated out: He read:

No drug overdose. Murder. There were others. Look and see. It didn't stop.

This one was typewritten, just as the previous note was. But this time there were two other objects. One was the size of a dollar bill and had dark ink smudges on the back, almost like carbon paper had rubbed off on it. Maybe an old ticket receipt of some sort, the kind that were filled out by hand. The other was smaller, without smudges, a printed piece with clearer letters that looked like "Sup," followed by "70 conc," and then "970," but the letters were either rubbed raw or had faded over time.

It was beginning to feel like a weird and sick joke. Like something that Alex might try to pull off, that would lead to a complicated ruse or maze of some kind.

The first message felt random, but this one seemed more specific, yet still arcane. He pulled on his reading glasses and looked more closely at the dollar-bill-sized piece. In the corner was what looked like a corporate logo, perhaps a globe with some lettering. Next to that was a word, "Date," and then a line, which obviously had originally been meant to contain a handwritten date.

Neither piece made any sense, but then neither did jigsaw puzzle pieces if you didn't have the box art to go with it. The pieces were so old that the writing could barely be discerned, all except for the broken letters on the small piece of paper.

He had two messages, or parts of messages. The title of a very obscure song, "My Little One," possibly on a label of some sort, and two pieces of paper, maybe a ticket and possibly part of a poster, or even another label.

This is not some random, game playing weirdo, he thought to himself; *someone wants me to connect these.*

Gantry needed to see what he could find. He opened a bottle of

Chianti, poured a glass, and booted up his laptop. He began searching combinations of the enigmatic letter code on the piece of paper until finally a bright light went on over his head. He began to fill in the letters like a game of hangman.

SUPer Conc**ERT** 70. Berlin, September 1970.

He felt proud. Now he had something to go on. He Googled the full phrase and date and unfolded the files he'd brought home from his Dead Artists folders, as the options were listing. Now, like finding the corner of a jigsaw puzzle made entirely of blue sky, he was mildly elated. Taking his eyes from the screen, he re-read the newspaper report he'd kept in his file as background about Hendrix. The opening quote still amazing him:

> I want to do with my guitar what Little Richard does with his voice.
> — Jimi Hendrix

At the end, he was the world's highest paid rock & roll performer, headlining at Woodstock in 1969 and the Isle of Wight Festival in 1970, before dying from what English investigators said was barbiturate-related asphyxia. He was twenty-seven.

Gantry still found it hard to believe that Hendrix went from playing at Army dive bars to sold-out crowds at the largest rock venues in the world in only nine years. *What a small world it was...*he thought to himself as he scanned the article...

Keith Richard's girlfriend was so overcome by his explosive energy that she recommended him to Chas Chandler, who immediately signed him and flew him to London. Jimmy became "Jimi," bassist Noel Redding and drummer Mitch Mitchell were recruited, and the Jimi Hendrix Experience was formed.

Gantry remembered the iconic sixties image of Hendrix burning his guitar, then smashing it to bits, transforming rock and roll into performance art and propelling Jimi Hendrix to the pinnacle of rock and roll. But his legend was sealed at Woodstock...

His psychedelic version of "The Star-Spangled Banner" at the end of the Woodstock Festival forever burned him into sixties zeitgeist. An exhausted Hendrix collapsed as soon as he walked offstage.

Gantry knew that there had been no lack of speculation on the cause of Hendrix's death. All of them, including official police reports, were unclear and widely disputed.

According to the coroner, Hendrix aspirated his own vomit and died of asphyxia while intoxicated on barbiturates. The words were there in black and white, as he read them slowly:

"Insufficient evidence."

"Murder was plausible."

"It seemed as if he drowned in a large amount of red wine," came from the doctors who tried reviving him.

Gantry put the newspaper story down and looked at the first page that came up on his Google search; a poster printed in sepia tone with a bare-chested Hendrix standing in the foreground. The photo was taken with a wide-angle lens, and his legs spread apart as he loomed upward from the bottom of the frame. Between his legs and behind him were three young women, girls actually, also bare-chested. In the far background were two men. The image might have been a handbill, but there was no type on it, nor any mention of the concert and no other identifying information.

At the bottom, the words: *Super Concert 70. Berlin, September 1970* were printed.

Gantry leaned back and pulled on the ends of his mustache. *This is a piece of that poster. Same typeface. Super Concert 70.*

Hendrix, Canned Heat, and even a surprise appearance by Janis Joplin, he remembered. None of them had ever performed in Germany.

Gantry jotted some notes on a pad and continued to scroll through references to the concert—and then it hit him like a punch. *Holy fuck, all three of them—Hendrix, Joplin, and Al Wilson of Canned Heat, were dead less than thirty days after that concert.*

He took off his glasses and rubbed his eyes.

All within thirty days! What the hell is the connection? He stood up and backed away from the computer, and turned down the stereo just as "Riders on the Storm" was ending.

Who would know about that concert? Who could he bounce this off of? He needed to talk to someone about this?

Maybe, Dennis…yeah…right…He lived in London then. Maybe he remembers it?

It was almost 1:00 a.m., but he knew that Dennis was a night owl. He took a shot.

Dennis answered the phone on the third ring.

"Gantry, what the fuck do you want at 1:00 a.m.? Are you in trouble?" Dennis snapped.

"No Dennis, but I have a question straight out of left field. Do you remember a concert in Berlin in 1970 called the Super Concert?"

"You have to be fucking kidding me. This couldn't wait until the morning?

Gantry didn't answer.

"Well then, my friend," a calmer Dennis said, "yes, I do as a matter of fact. I actually got over for part of it. It was the biggest event ever held in Berlin. Huge buzz in Europe about it at the time. Everyone tried to go. And thank you for waking me up, asshole, to answer your Trivial Pursuit question."

"Dennis…sorry. Really sorry. But what else can you tell me?"

"Well, I do distinctly remember the event and the entire scene because the stage and lights were set as usual, but the promoters lined up all the speakers to face the Berlin Wall. The local radio station broadcasted most of it live, and I was told it was the single biggest day of defections ever. Why do you want to know all this at one in the morning?"

Gantry was reluctant to share anything beyond what he'd already told Dennis.

"Umm, I…"

"Oh come on, spit it out. What's up?"

"Well, someone is playing a game with me. I got a package. It contains a piece of paper that I think is part of a poster for Super Concert 70.

"Jesus, Gantry. A piece of a poster...*a poster*? Probably a fucking prank. Go to sleep! After all, you *do* work for *Rolling Stone* magazine. Wackos must send you stuff like this all the time. I'll tell you this, though, it was a magical event, and with the surprise appearance of Joplin, well, it was pretty special."

He jotted down "Brian Jones, Al Wilson, Jimi Hendrix, and Janis Joplin."

"Thanks, Dennis. Sorry to bother you."

Gantry was now too worked up to sleep, so he lit up a joint and floated back with the Doors music, recalling the August 1970 opening party at Hendrix's state of the art, Electric Lady Studios in Greenwich Village.

"God, what a talent he was..." He sighed as he began to reminisce.

Eddie Kramer, the chief engineer, gave Gantry a personal tour that evening. The highlight coming when Hendrix walked in on them in the control room and pulled Kramer aside to discuss an idea for using their new multi -track tape recorder to create a unique sense of depth on a piece he was working on.

"Jimi is such a perfectionist," Kramer said to Gantry, "he remembers every note he ever played. By the way, Jimi, meet Gantry Elliot from *Rolling Stone*."

"What do I have to do to get on the cover again...drop dead?" Hendrix laughing at his own joke, as he shook Gantry's hand.

"Hey Eddie, let's get out of here and get something to eat; too many posers here. Gantry, come on with us." They headed out the back door.

"Stage Deli," Hendrix barked to the cabbie. "If we're going to pig out, that's the place. Best strawberry shortcake on the planet."

Gantry remembered the trio feasting on gigantic corned-beef sandwiches, monstrous onion rings and six-inch-high shortcake. Never mind the looks Hendrix got from the after-theater patrons.

"Do you know that I was kicked out of my first group, at our very first gig, at a synagogue in Seattle? Can you imagine? They said I was too flamboyant! Me, flamboyant?"

"I know, and you just wanted to make the guitar do what Little Richard does with his voice," Eddie said, predicting where Hendrix was going next.

"We're like an old married couple," Jimi said.

The crotchety old waitress gave them a dirty look as she dropped the check on the table. Eddie picked it up. "Almost twenty dollars! Jeez, New York prices. Jimi, you have any money?"

"No wallet, señor," Jimi retorted.

Gantry was stuck offering only a shrug and a nervous smile.

Hendrix laughed. "Well, I guess we are going to have to resort to the old chitlin' circuit credit card."

"What's that?" Gantry asked.

"Well, you get up and nonchalantly walk around a bit, and then walk out. You first, then me," Hendrix said to Gantry. "And then finally, Eddie walks out."

"Oh great, so I'm the one who gets caught?" Eddie said, irritated.

"Don't be a pussy," Hendrix scolded him.

"Go, Gantry. Let's meet one block south," Hendrix ordered. Gantry was glad to be a part of the moment and did as he was told. Hendrix showed up like clockwork, and then the two waited. And waited. No Eddie.

"Uh oh. He musta got caught. He's gonna be so fucking pissed at me tomorrow. The ole 'CCCC' worked again." Hendrix threw his arm around the young writer as they meandered off down the street.

A month later, Hendrix was dead.

Gantry stayed up all night going through his Dead Artists materials, reading article after article about each of the four artists, including a newspaper account about Al Wilson of Canned Heat.

Blind (Owl) Al Wilson Dies

Alan Christie Wilson died on September 3, 1970, at the age of 27. He was the founder, lead singer and primary composer for the group Canned Heat.

Canned Heat gained worldwide attention and secured their niche in rock & roll history after their performances at the 1967 Monterey Pop Festival and Woodstock in 1969. The band's hit, "Going Up the Country," sung by Wilson, became the festival's unofficial theme song. Wilson died in Topanga Canyon, California of acute barbiturate intoxication. Reported as a suicide, his friends suggested that he was extremely distressed about management issues.

Gantry took a deep breath. The kicker was in looking at his playing dates. Wilson never showed up for the concert in Berlin. Canned Heat went on without him, not knowing that he'd died the night before.

After another glass of wine, he fell asleep on the sofa while mentally toggling back and forth between the 60's rock stars. "Just a fried out hippie…"

Gantry woke up early, still in his clothes. He'd gone to bed restless and awoke in the same state. He could see the sun peeking through the buildings across the street, as he walked over to start a pot of coffee.

This entire thing is taking up too much thinking. If it was a joke, it would eventually run its course and the sender would move on to someone who'd react to the notes. After all, that's probably all the sender wants anyway, to get a rise out of someone, get some attention.

Gantry took a large swallow of coffee and walked into the bathroom. It was so small he couldn't use the toilet without closing the door. He ran the water as hot as he could stand it and stepped into the stall and closed the tattered plastic shower curtain.

Letting the hot water run over his head and down his spine, he relaxed and let the always-stiff morning muscles go limp. He relished his morning showers. He put his hands on the tile in front of him, arched his back a little, and felt the hot water run over him. *Getting old is a bitch.*

His mind drifted, and he began to realize just how isolated and insular he had become. He was bored beyond belief, and he was tired of pretending he was still important to Alex, to the magazine, to the culture. He lived in a small, one-room apartment, alone, with only two close friends and no girlfriend.

Sad…sad. Maybe he was making too much of this.

Gantry stepped out of the shower, toweled himself off and started to get dressed.

As he pulled on his boots, it hit him. *Super Concert 70…The other piece of paper is an airline ticket!*

Gantry flew over to his dining table and spilled out the three pieces. He picked up a notepad and began to make notes.

What were the harmonies here? The concert was in Berlin. Anyone coming from the U.S. would have to fly, including Wilson. But Wilson died the day before the concert. The dollar-bill-sized paper was an airline ticket with a faded Pan Am logo—a globe.

He pulled a magnifying glass out of the drawer in the small cabinet next to the dining table. Lining up the large lens, the small, smudged type became more legible. It read, "September 3, 1970."

The day before the concert.

Gantry couldn't scribble fast enough. He wrote each thought as a bullet point one after the other.

- *Super Concert 70 Berlin.*
- *Canned Heat, Joplin and Hendrix there.*
- *Wilson, Hendrix, Joplin dead within 30 days of the concert.*
- *Brian Jones dead the year before.*
- *All dead at age 27.*
- *Someone is claiming they were all murdered.*

Maybe his decision had been made for him. Whoever was sending these messages had to either have been present or had to have been at the concert. On the other hand, the sender could have stolen these items, or gotten his hands on them in some other manner. Maybe it was someone from a studio. God, how many people knew all four of these artists well enough? Too many to count. An unused airline ticket meant that the sender had either taken it off Wilson's body or gotten it from among Wilson's personal belongings.

Gantry began to think of the possibilities: management, friends, deranged fans, ex-lovers…He realized his list of potentially common connections was bewildering, but it was very possible that this could be the work of one person, and that person wanted him to connect the dots. Someone was trying to tell him to make the connections.

But why the games? Why make it difficult? It didn't make sense.

Rolling Stone Offices

The Next Morning

Groggy from the wine and poor sleep, Gantry unlocked his office door at 10:00 a.m. and immediately made a strong pot of coffee and turned on his computer. Standing over his desk, he found himself oddly relieved. But then, on top of the mail stack, he saw a now-familiar large manila envelope with his name. It was hand-addressed with a Sharpie.

"What the fuck!" he shouted, loud enough for everyone on the floor to hear.

"You've got to be fuckin' kidding. This can't be happening..."

For a moment he didn't want to touch it. *The mail boy must have brought it in with the late delivery yesterday.* He sat down and reached for his crossbones opener, slit the top, and turned it upside down over his desk. This is the third package in less than twenty-four hours, all anonymous. Someone was very eager to get his attention and his immediate focus.

He shook the envelope and the contents including a glossy paper slid onto his desk.

"Hendrix—High, Live and Dirty" was commercially printed in dark ink on a red background.

Gantry picked it up and stared at it, trying to place the title. It took a couple of seconds for him to remember the jam session at the Scene Club and the rare bootleg recording that had been made of it, "High, Live and Dirty."

Like the two previous clues, this one contained more than just the printed paper. There was a folded and stained bar napkin with the logo

29

of the West Forty-Sixth Street club. It was neatly creased and folded twice. Turning it over, Gantry wasn't surprised to find a handwritten note. The edges of the letters had gotten wet, and the handwriting had grown some watery veins outward, but he could still make it out:

"To Jimi—Let's do a record together. It would be great — *J.M.*"

Gantry took a deep breath and released the paper. "Now what…?" He then dialed an old friend's number. The phone rang several times, and a deep male voice answered, "Yeah, it's Lenny."

"Lenny, it's Gantry Elliot. For a second there, I thought I was talking to a message machine."

There was a second's pause, and then Lenny Kravitz said, "Oh, Gantry. Hey, how the hell are you? Been a long, long time, buddy. What's up?"

Though well known as a musician, not many knew that Lenny Kravitz had a world-class collection of Jimi Hendrix memorabilia and an even greater knowledge of Hendrix history. Years ago, Gantry had written "An Old Soul in a New Body" as the headline for his interview with Kravitz after his first album. Lenny loved the review and never forgot Gantry, and the two had kept in touch.

Gantry needed to catch up before asking a favor.

"Lenny, good to hear your voice. The question is, what are *you* doing? Any new work on the horizon?"

"Funny you should ask. I was just at the Rumpus Room in Brooklyn recording a new song. It's a retro sixties psychedelic number, very cool. Mellotron, Leslie amps, recording on tape, the full monty!"

Old soul, Gantry thought.

"That's great, man, just fantastic. I'd like to hear it sometime. Hey, I don't want to take you from your psychedelia, but I have a question only you could answer."

"Shoot, brother. Anything."

"Have you ever heard of a Hendrix recording called 'High, Live and Dirty'?"

Kravitz laughed. "Of course," he replied. "The Scene Club, down on 46th. A drunken affair."

"Yeah?"

"Oh, Gantry, I'm surprised you don't remember. It was really more of a party. The recording was pitiful, almost incoherent, and sad, really. Someone in the audience taped it on a little cheap cassette deck and then managed to get it published...Are you still there, buddy?"

"Absolutely. Just taking some notes."

"Must be important. Where are you going with this?"

"Nowhere just yet," Gantry said, already formulating a lie.

"Okay. Well, Johnny Winter had some blistering riffs on the recording, and Jim Morrison was drunk on his ass, not really singing as much as he was cussing throughout the entire thing. In my opinion, it was the low point for Hendrix, real low, and even lower for Morrison. Boy, what a waste of talent. Did you get a copy or something?" Kravitz asked.

"No, and I didn't know Morrison was there."

"Yes, and he was out of it—on his ass. I was surprised, really."

"At what?"

"That it took two more years for him to crash and burn. Truly sad. He could have done so much." Kravitz sighed.

"Are you there, buddy?" Kravitz asked again.

"Yeah. Sorry, Lenny, I was just thinking. I appreciate your help. Send me a demo when you're done. I have to go."

"Okay, Gantry, will do. Don't wait so long to call again."

"I won't. Thanks again."

Morrison...the note was from Morrison.

The conversation sparked a memory of Jim Morrison in 1970 Los Angeles.

It was one of Gantry's first assignments for *Rolling Stone*; an interview with him to uncover his musical influences. They met late one afternoon at the Hullaballoo Club on Sunset Strip.

The legend around the singer had already swelled. He was referred to as a mystic, a drunkard, and either a genius or a waste. Gantry wanted to expose the real person as best he could.

When Gantry got to the club, Morrison was already there, nursing a Coke. The surroundings were dark and somber, the pungent smell of crushed cigarette butts floating in ash trays of spilled whiskey and beer added to the morning-after ambience. A beat up jukebox in the corner was turned off in deference to the group about to take the stage.

Morrison told him that he'd come to the club to listen to a group, JK and Co., as a favor to a friend. The group was just starting its first song. They were so young; he was surprised they were playing where alcohol was served. Jay Kaye, the leader and vocalist, was only fifteen, Morrison pointed out. They'd gotten a little buzz on the underground stations for an album they had just recorded in Vancouver. He was impressed by the band's complex layered psychedelia and mature poetic lyrics.

"They have a bright future," Morrison said. "Listen to the texture of the harmonics and the lyrical interplay. I think this song is called 'Fly.' Close your eyes. Don't you feel the air under you?"

Gantry was genuinely surprised with how articulate Morrison was. He explained over the next hour how he had been influenced by Huxley, Blake, Rimbaud, Moliere, and Norman Mailer. He mentioned only poets and writers.

When Gantry asked why he hadn't mentioned any musicians, Morrison replied that he was a poet, not a musician.

"I only sing to bring my poetry to life," he said staring at Gantry.

Then he broke up laughing, "I guess I do have one musical influence…Frank Sinatra."

His parting words still haunted Gantry:

"I see myself as a huge, fiery comet, a shooting star. Everyone stops, points up and gasps, 'Oh look at that!' Then whoosh, and I'm gone…and they'll never see anything like it ever again…and they won't be able to forget me, ever."

Gantry wiped away a slight tear, not for Morrison, but for himself, as he thought about how much time had passed since then. He couldn't remember where, but he'd recently read that "knowledge is better than ignorant dread—though not always more pleasant."

Gantry was now completely wired and fixated on the increasingly intimate collection of clues. He needed to talk to someone he could trust, to help sort out what to do. He called Dennis.

"Dusty Records," the voice said.

"Dennis, it's Gantry."

"Eh, mate. Sorry about the blow out last night, to what do I owe the pleasure of a call?

"That's all right. Can we talk? It's kind of urgent, in a very weird way."

"Urgent and weird, now that sounds like a man with a story to tell. You know Dusty Records, home of total classic recall. I'm here 'till ten tonight."

"Dennis, I'm jumping in a cab…see you in thirty minutes."

Dennis Briganty was originally from the West End of London. He grew up surrounded by music. His father had worked for EMI, the British record company, and was transferred to New York in 1975. He had been involved in the production of the Beatles' *White Album* in 1968 and Pink Floyd's *Dark Side of the Moon* in 1973. Dennis grew up surrounded by music and the business of making it. Dennis claimed he went to Columbia University for three years, but ended up dropping out to try his hand at creating an independent label, which quickly failed. During that time, he'd met Gantry, and their mutual interests helped forge a friendship. Gantry was working for *Rolling Stone* by then, and Dennis's failure in the record industry was the reason he started Dusty Records, where he bought and sold collectible albums and, later, tapes and CDs.

Every several years, Dennis would return to his old haunts in the West End, where many of his friends still lived, including an old flame that never quite burned out…a cheeky and spirited Irish gal.

Dennis was muscular, about six-feet-two with a narrow face and a mop of thick, fading red hair that sat on his head like a plate of crispy hash browns. His appearance and his occasional lapse into a cockney accent made him an odd but friendly fixture in the neighborhood.

Dennis saw Gantry standing at the windowed front door and buzzed him in, just as they do in jewelry stores filled with expensive gems–which was exactly how Dennis felt about Dusty Records. His records *were* his gems. The store was musty, dark, but somehow perfect, like the bargain bins in the used bookstores on Bleecker Street. There were row upon row of two-sided shelves with tapes, 45s and LPs.

This place and this man were the safest, most comfortable environment Gantry knew outside of his apartment.

"Ya know, Dennis, I never asked you, but what do you think all these are worth, to the right people?"

"Never added it up, just too busy buying and collecting," Dennis said. "Some of these I got at a street bazaar down in the village years ago, when they were practically throwing them away. Some are worth thousands now. I used to collect them when they were new, when I was young, living in London. My pops used to bring them home in a wheelbarrow. I don't know…maybe a quarter million altogether, maybe more to the right person. But you and I know that's not the point."

"Amen, brother."

"So, what's up?" Dennis took an old Stones album out of its pristine jacket and placed it on the turntable as delicately as he would maneuver a vial of nitroglycerin, using only his fingertips, and careful not to allow his oversized Celtic cross ring to touch the record. The music filled the store, muffled by the tons of cardboard LP's on the shelves.

Dennis reached behind the counter. "Here we are mate—two Macanudos, not Cuban, of course, but sufficient for today."

The two men puffed away, smiling at each other for a few silent moments, until unexpectedly interrupted by Dennis's coughing spell.

"Sorry, the price I pay for the pleasure of your company," he laughingly said.

Gantry particularly loved the smells here: the rich aroma of the Macanudos, the musty odor of so much cardboard pressed closely for so long, and the almost damp smell of the orange shag carpet. Nirvana.

"So what about the urgent and weird?" Dennis asked.

Ever since Gantry and his wife had divorced, he and Dennis had spent years of good, quiet times sharing just one subject–classic rock & roll. But this would be a first, Gantry sharing something other than lyrics or riffs.

"Oh, you know, I'm so fucking bored in that place," he started, but then interrupted himself. "But don't get me wrong, I couldn't have a better job. It's just that, well, you know, these days all I do is pretend to be *relevant*, as Alex puts it, and to be his friend. Sometimes I wonder if he just keeps me around because we go so far back. But then again, I *do* get one glorious day each year to report on the inductees' ceremony," he said with a note of sarcasm.

"Sounds like you're feeling sorry for yourself," Dennis observed. "I think I know how you feel, mate. But, I've been independent all my life, you've worked for Alex most of yours. I only need to be relevant to people who want old rock and roll albums. You need to be relevant to an entire generation. Problem is, your expertise and your relevance are stuck in the 1960s, and your audience is *today*. That's why it bothers you."

He moved his chair in closer to Gantry. "Try thinking of it this way: you don't have to be a leader or one of those uber-high-earning executives; you only need to be relevant to *yourself*. Alex wouldn't have you working for him unless he really needed you. He needs your history, your knowledge and—hah—your wisdom, mate."

"I guess you're right, it's probably just the boredom talking. Makes me feel like the world is racing past me sometimes," Gantry said, pulling the pieces of paper from his pocket. "These came to the office the other day," he said, holding them out.

"What are these?"

"You tell me."

Dennis took the slips of paper from Gantry. He read:

Brian Jones was murdered. It was not an accident. There were others. Look and see.

He gave Gantry a quizzical look.

"Read the other one," Gantry said.

Dennis squinted. "Doesn't look like anything to me."

"Look closer."

Dennis put on a pair of cheap reading glasses and looked again.

"Hmm. I don't know. Where did you get these?"

"They came in the office mail. I didn't give them much credence other than some curiosity until that bit about Jones started me rummaging through my old Dead Artists file. You know, the one I started when that Myth of 27 thing got going."

"Yeah. I'd almost forgotten about that."

"So I ran across an article about Jones drowning in his swimming the pool. It seemed real strange that whoever sent this *chose* Brian Jones."

Gantry pulled the Jones article from his valise and handed it to Dennis.

Dennis began reading out loud as he skimmed though it:

Brian Jones found dead...singular emblem of 1960's sex, drugs and rock and roll...Prince Valiant-coiffed founder of the Rolling Stones....Brian Jones was rock and roll.

"Dennis, he was the one who contrived their unique weaving guitar sound...Paint it Black....Under my Thumb," Gantry explained, "Read the last paragraph?" Gantry added.

Dennis read slowly, "In August of 1969, a devastated Jones was replaced by Mick Taylor......less than a month later, Jones, an excellent swimmer, was found motionless in his swimming pool.....dead at the age of 27." He put the article down.

"Now look real close at the other paper," Gantry asked.

Dennis squinted again.

"It looks like it says, 'My Little One.' What the hell does that mean?"

Gantry filled his friend in on the story.

"I'd say that's pretty damned *obnubilate,* wouldn't you?"

Dennis grinned. "You know what this looks like?"

"What?"

Dennis held the slip of glossy paper under a light.

"See this?" He pointed to the back corner. "Printed very faintly, it looks like it says, 'O Studios.' That would be short for Olympic Studios, where the Stones used to record. Damn, this is an old demo tape label! The kind they used back in the sixties."

"Hey, let's hear the song?" Dennis said, "Let's Google it."

"I don't think…" Gantry stopping himself as Dennis sat in front of his monitor.

Dennis punched out, "My Little One, Brian Jones," and up popped still pictures of Jones in his Prince Valiant haircut and Hendrix, his hair tied back in his ever-present bandana, sporting one of his many jackets with brocade buttons and braid.

"No song?" Dennis said.

"Nope," as Gantry pulled an old cassette tape out of his pocket.

"You must have a cassette player somewhere in this museum?" Gantry asked.

"Of course," he grabbed the tape and popped it in an old GE cassette player in the tape section and the psychedelic treasure started playing.

"Wow," Dennis said. "Un-fucking-believable! Listen to how Jones's sitar and Hendrix's guitar riffs imitate each other and then weave in and out like a jazz jam. They're using the old Rolling Stones' weaving guitars formula."

"Who else is playing with them?" Dennis asked.

"Dave Mason and Mitch Mitchell."

"I can't believe this has been buried all this time!" an excited Dennis blurted.

"Yeah, somethin' else. Now if I could only figure out why someone would send these."

"I wouldn't spend too much time on it, mate, probably just a hippie nut case. You know how that shit always recycles every time one of the stars dies." Dennis reminded him.

"But, don't you think it's a little spooky that they would send me a bit of a demo tape label from an obscure collaboration. This isn't some random kook. They had to have been there, or something. How else would they have gotten that tape label?"

"Come on Gantry, get real man. Let it go. No reason to get your bowels in an uproar," Dennis said in a dismissive voice.

"I guess you're right, but…on the other hand, then how would you explain this?" he said dumping out the second message and contents.

"This envelope was left on the table that Alex and I were having drinks on at Marty's last night." He spread them out in front of Dennis and explained what they were. "And then this envelope was delivered to my office this morning."

A speechless Dennis's eyes widened.

"Still think it's a random kook?" Gantry asked. "I think I should head uptown to show these to Alex."

"But you were first on my list, for anything that is urgent and weird," Gantry added.

"Thanks for thinking of me," a still stunned Dennis answered.

Dennis watched Gantry's cab move slowly around the corner and then out of sight. His phone rang a unique ring three times, then stopped…Then rang two times, then stopped…

On the third ring, Dennis grabbed the phone, and listened.

In the uptown cab, Gantry called Alex's private line on his cell.

"Christ, Gantry, do we have to go over this now?" Alex complained into the phone propped between his shoulder and ear.

"I need your opinion on something important," Gantry insisted.

"It better be. All right, come over, but I don't have much time."

Gantry took the cab to Alex's Upper East Side apartment. The traffic was unusually heavy, even for Manhattan, so he had time to think. *Two mysterious clues delivered to his office, one to Marty's and two of them claiming a star was killed. Was it just coincidence that the famous dead stars were all twenty-seven, just as the old myth contended? If Jones was killed—if they all were killed—the question was, why?* Clearly someone wanted him to see this as a string of murders.

The cabbie pounded on his horn as another taxi ran the red light not inches from his bumper. Not even the sudden braking and honking could tear Gantry from his thoughts.

The taxi pulled up at Park Avenue and Fifty-Ninth Street. Gantry paid, grabbed up his small, tan valise filled with the messages and files, and exited the cab. When he reached the seventh-floor penthouse he found Alex sitting quietly with a glass of scotch and a cigar. He'd visited several times before, usually for parties, but was always amazed by how huge the apartment was; it seemed as vast as a warehouse, albeit with better furniture.

Alex's, "Hey, buddy" belied the mood Gantry had anticipated.

"Come on in. Have a seat. Want a scotch?"

"No. I'm fine," Gantry said, sitting down in a large, purple goose-down chair beside Alex.

"My man, you have a look of concern. What's up? Did someone steal your only copy of 'Purple Haze?'...Just kidding. Really, what's on your mind that brought you uptown at this time of day? I hope it's not about being best man. I can't get another best man now, buddy, nor would I want to. Don't tell me you can't come," Alex said in rapid fire.

"No. It's not about that," Gantry said, pulling the zipper on his valise and carefully putting the pieces of paper on the immense, glass-topped coffee table. Gantry could hear stirring in another room, which he assumed came from Alex's soon-to-be-partner in marriage. Somewhere music was playing, a light, nondescript jazz ensemble, not Alex's style.

"What are these, buddy?"

Gantry sat quiet for a second. Waiting for Alex to crack a smile and admit his weird joke.

"These are clues," Gantry said, not knowing exactly how to start.

"Is it a game? I'm supposed to guess what they are clues to?"

Just then Daniel came into the room. He smiled and nodded, then sat down in a red leather and chrome chair facing Gantry and Alex. Daniel and Gantry had met several times at Alex's gatherings, though Gantry didn't know much about him other than he'd been involved in a successful hedge fund and made an obscene amount of money.

"No. You're not supposed to guess, and it isn't a game. I'm serious. I need your opinion about something I know you're going to dismiss at first, or at least you'll think I've gone over the edge. But hear me out," Gantry said.

"Hey, buddy, anything for you. You know that."

Gantry nodded and immediately launched into his story: The packages at Marty's and his office, the intimate contents, his talks with Dennis and Kravitz, and how it seemed someone was trying to get him to investigate the myth, or at least these particular dead stars.

Alex and Daniel listened silently and intently.

Gantry wanted Alex to pay particular attention to the napkin with Morrison's note to Hendrix, the demo label for "My Little One," and above all, the unused Pan Am ticket. As he explained his theories about the clues, he suggested that it was becoming clearly evident that someone was building a case, so to speak, from simple to complex, each clue providing intimate proof that these could be murders. To Gantry it seemed obvious that each clue revealed more and more that the person sending them was an insider of some sort.

But Alex was more into solutions than conjecture. He wasn't one for jigsaw puzzles. He looked at Daniel and took another drag off his cigar. He looked serious, almost contemplative. A wide and facetious smile crossed his face and he said, "Sounds like you have a crazy one on your hands."

Relieved, Gantry was about to continue his hypotheses when Alex added, "Did you connect the torching of Michael Jackson's hair to these four yet?" He laughed out loud at his own joke.

Gantry groaned under his breath and saw that Daniel wasn't joining in with the laughter. In fact, he looked quite serious. Gantry quickly gathered up the slips of paper and put them back in his valise.

"Thanks for your interest, Alex," he said coldly, standing up.

He'd half expected this reaction. *This was a mistake*, he thought, *and maybe all this is just as ridiculous as Alex felt it was. Maybe the whole thing was a lame joke and I'm gonna wind up being incredibly embarrassed.*

Almost to the door, Gantry heard the two men arguing behind him in low voices. He had no idea what they were saying, but at this point, he didn't really care. He was embarrassed and angry. But then Alex spoke.

"Wait." Alex shouted, as Daniel tried to hold him back.

Gantry continued walking to the door.

"No, seriously, Gantry, wait. I mean it. I'm sorry. That wasn't fair. Let's talk some more. I didn't mean to piss you off."

Gantry turned, a look of relief crossing his face as Alex smiled at him and walked him back. An irritated Daniel sat down, lips taunt, twisting his ring.

"Sit down," Alex said. "Let's think about this. We don't have anything to lose. Suppose you call the cops. I mean, if this is as serious as you obviously think it is, it's not something for us to unravel—better yet, call the FBI."

Gantry hoped he wasn't being set up for another joke.

"No, seriously. It makes sense. If someone was trying to send messages about rock stars who died of overdoses or whatever, that were actually murdered, who else would be more qualified to do something with the evidence? The only thing that's weird is if this guy is serious and really has something, then why not just tell you what it is? Why send vague anonymous clues? Why drag it out and make it difficult?"

"Good question, Alex. Why make a game of it? I asked myself that same question last night. Still, I can't shake it. These clues are things that even a die-hard fan wouldn't know. I mean, 'My Little One?' Come on…he knew that I would know. I'm just saying…"

"Of course he did…the Robert Langdon of rock," Alex gestured as he responded now staring at Gantry.

"The thing that *is* obvious," Gantry continued, "is that the sender doesn't want us to know who he is. Maybe he's the one who murdered them all. Maybe he's trying to confess. Think about it. Don't you think thirty-eight celebrities of any kind dying at the exact same age is beyond coincidence? I used to keep track of these just for that reason, and I've heard all the other explanations, mostly that they were prodigies that burned themselves out in their late teens and early to their mid-twenties, so that by the time they reached twenty-seven, the drugs and stress had taken their toll. I've heard it all. But this is different. This guy wants my focused attention, right now."

"Well," Alex chimed in, "if we assume this is real, and I use the term *assume* deliberately, what you're proposing is that all of these stars were killed. They did not overdose by accident or commit suicide. That right there is a monumental story. Now, if you add the fact that they all died one way or another at the age of twenty-seven, then you truly do have a mystery on your hands— maybe one worth pursuing." .

There was a pause in the conversation as Alex stood up and walked to one of the large, south-facing windows. The other two men sat waiting while Alex stood staring out for what seemed like ten minutes. Gantry glanced at an expressionless Daniel, his ring catching his eye, just as then Alex turned to face Gantry and Daniel.

"Gantry, I'll make you a deal. If you'll go to the FBI and tell them your story, and if *they* think it's worth pursuing, then you'll have my permission to run it down. You can use the magazine's time, and I'll give you some expense money. At least enough time and money to see where the feds lead you or you lead them. What do you say?"

Gantry smiled. *Yes!* He thanked Alex and nodded to Daniel, then turned toward the door, impatient to get started.

"Good luck, amigo," Alex said. "Keep me posted."

Gantry was exhilarated, with Alex's words ringing in his head as he walked out…" right there is a monumental story."

As he exited the building, he dialed 411 and connected to the office of the Manhattan FBI. The receptionist told him he'd have to call the Academy in Quantico, Virginia. She said that the "kind of agents" he needed to talk to worked at the Behavioral Analysis Unit in Quantico, Virginia and not in New York City.

Gantry stretched out his arm to hail a cab, just as it came to him… *Melendez*.

Raphael Melendez had been the lead FBI investigator on the John Lennon murder case. Lennon's killer, Mark David Chapman, got twenty years to life, and in 2012 he was denied parole—for the seventh time. Gantry remembered reading that Melendez had testified for Chapman's continued incarceration at the parole board meeting. He had originally met him while on the assignment and remained in contact for a brief period after the Lennon case.

Melendez? Doesn't he work there? Maybe he's still around… Thirty-three years was a long time, but he had nothing to lose by looking him up.

Elliot Gantry's Apartment, W 23rd Street

When Gantry returned to his apartment, he couldn't find Melendez's contact info, but he did find the Behavioral Analysis Unit's main number. Before calling he wanted to do a bit of research so that he could sound reasonably intelligent, especially if he got to Melendez.

The sunlight dimmed in his apartment and he opened the heavy curtains to allow the last bit of light to sneak its way in as he perused the BAU's homepage:

> *The Behavioral Analysis Unit is a department within the National Center for the Analysis of Violent Crimes (NCAVC). The Unit rose to fame as it led the FBI in solving very high-profile serial killer cases. BAU-trained analysts are considered the investigative elite, and over the last twenty years have progressed from highly intuitive FBI agents to cutting edge data and forensic analytics investigators. The department applies this expertise to time-sensitive and complex crimes that typically involve violence.*

There was no mention of Raphael Melendez on the website, and of course, he might have retired. Gantry turned from the monitor, got up, and pulled out one of his favorite classic albums, carefully slid the record out, and put it on the turntable. The unusual percussion of "White Bird," performed by It's a Beautiful Day, started pulsating through his apartment. The song had been one of Jodi's favorites, but now bittersweet for Gantry since the lyrics spoke of a bird needing to escape her cage.

The tune took him back to the day he'd first spoken to Melendez.

Gantry was thirty-two. Lennon's death was a shock to the national psyche—and also to Melendez. He had interviewed him for more than two hours at a table at Central Park's Tavern on the Green. Melendez recounted the work he'd done during the case, and Gantry was enthralled with the technical aspects of the job and with the man's keen analytical skills. But what really stuck with him was seeing a tear running down Melendez's cheek as he spoke. He'd lifted his linen napkin and slowly wiped his cheek, not even trying to disguise his emotions.

Gantry didn't know what to say—or even if anything needed to be said.

"I love music. I loved Lennon," Melendez had said after composing himself. "It was tragic to me…heartbreaking." Gantry could see that he was re-living a moment that was deeply personal to him, so he put down his notepad out of respect and refrained from taking notes.

"Agent Melendez, what you do sounds almost as creative as it is analytical." Gantry asked to change the subject.

What Gantry didn't know was that Melendez was now the dean of VICAP, the Violent Criminal Apprehension Program. His critical mind and his years of experience with cold cases put him in a unique situation within the FBI. With his expertise and charming manner, he could pretty much do what he wanted, the *way* he wanted, and he had a test lab with the latest technology to help him do it.

It had taken Gantry the better part of an hour to find Melendez's direct number. He hoped he could get through on the first try, but had to settle for leaving a message.

He got up to stretch his legs and opened the window onto Twenty-Third Street. The air was still warm, even in the early evening. He deeply breathed it in, listening to the ubiquitous taxi horns warring with each other, and practiced what he would say to the FBI agent and how he would try to jog his memory of their luncheon thirty-three years ago.

As the first side was ending, Gantry returned to the turntable, flipped the disk over and took another swallow of his, now, room-temperature coffee. He paced anxiously, glancing across the room at the signed poster of Janis Joplin with its touching personal note. Then he stared intently at the picture of his red-headed ex-wife, Jodi, with her arm around their panting, blue-eyed sheep dog, Montana. The photo had been in a drawer for a long time, but recently he had been able to look at it again.

He thought of how it would be sweet revenge, vindicating those incredible artists. He'd be their conduit to the truth. It would be a vindication, somehow, of his own worth.

Shit, maybe she still has it? He suddenly thought to himself as he zoomed in on the picture. Lying beside the dog was a beat up knapsack covered with patches and flags from Gantry's travels. Impulsively, he grabbed the phone and dialed a number he hadn't called in years, but knew it by heart.

"Jodi Randolph, please leave a message." He was a little relieved that it went directly to voicemail.

"Jodi, this is Gantry, do you still have my old knapsack. I think it has some items in it that I need for a big story I'm working on. Let me know as soon as you can." He quickly hung up. He immediately felt awkward and stupid for being so abrupt after so many years. "I'm an idiot," he said out loud.

His phone rang almost as soon as he put it down. Gantry quickly picked it on the first ring. "Jodi, sorry to call…"

"Gantry. How the hell are you? It's Raphael Melendez returning your call."

"Oh, sorry. I was expecting someone else."

"You *remember* me?" Gantry said.

"Of course. How could I forget? You and *Rolling Stone*. I wouldn't miss an issue, though I haven't seen your byline in quite some time."

"Well, that's a long story. But thanks for returning my call. What have you been doing with yourself?"

"Oh, man. The stories I could tell you. But then I'd have to kill you." He laughed at the cliché. "No, really, I've been around the world with Magellan, eaten my own shoes and seen the worst."

Gantry jumped on the joke energetically, "I imagined you dealt with a lot of vicious types, sickos and God knows what else. And you're still at it."

"Yep. Love it more than ever. Obviously you're still with Alex Jaeger."

"Yeah, and that's why I'm calling. I have something that is right up your alley, and I need your help."

"Okay, whaddya got for me?"

Gantry's mind started to race. How to condense all he had to tell? He didn't know much about how the Bureau worked or how the agents went about starting an investigation, but he assumed they didn't jump to conclusions. As a group, he'd read, they were about as serious as a stroke when it came to opening a case, cold or otherwise.

He took a breath and plunged right in. "Are you familiar with the urban legend referred to as the Myth of 27?"

"Yes, of course. When I was working on the Lennon case I ran across it many times—and it *is* just that, an urban legend. Why?" Melendez's voice getting serious.

"Well…" Gantry hesitated. "It might not be a myth."

Gantry heard a muffled groan. He quickly defended himself.

"Agent Melendez, the myth *might* be true. We don't know each other that well, but I think my reputation—and though it was brief and long ago, my interview with you would at least give me enough credibility to warrant a few minutes to explain."

Melendez's silence told him this wasn't going to be easy. However, he was after all, an investigator who specialized in cold cases—*real* cold cases. And this one was about as icy as they got.

"Okay, let's slow down a little. What makes you think it's not a myth? I have to tell you, Gantry, there are many, *many* people who have already spun their wheels on this one. We get calls every month. You must know that."

Gantry said he did, but he quickly went on to explain how he'd kept his Dead Artists file and how he'd followed the myth for many years. And how these clues—the anonymous messages delivered in the last 24 hours, with at least two solid inside connections, had possibly unearthed a surprising pattern.

No response. A good thing, he hoped.

"Agent Melendez, you've got to admit, it's interesting, at the very least. Think about it. There aren't many people who know this history the way I do. You know my work, you know me a little. I read your unit's mission statement, and this is what you do. Someone wants me to figure this out, to connect the clues and artifacts, to pursue this coincidence, if you can call it that. All these rock stars dead at age twenty-seven, all connected in one way or another through the clues I've been sent."

Gantry quickly went through the clues again, not wanting Melendez to get a word of dissent in until he'd hopefully raised his curiosity. He knew that the FBI had its priorities and strict protocol. Their bullshit receptors were finely honed and this was a long shot.

When Gantry was finished, the phone line was silent. Then Melendez said, "Okay, Gantry, I'm going to be honest, I'm mostly listening out of respect for you. I don't really see this panning out. I mean, after all these years, someone would have put the same things together."

"No—not really," Gantry interrupted, "Think about the era they lived in. Rock and roll musicians and their followers were considered almost enemies of the state in the U.S. and Europe. Remember Nixon and his cronies? Remember the culture during the sixties? I know you do. Hell, we had just come out of the McCarthy era not long before that. Most of the time the authorities chalked it all up to drugs and rock and roll. Sometimes they didn't even conduct autopsies. Hell, they didn't even know what DNA was back then, let alone know how to use it in an investiga—"

"Gantry stop, you don't understand the protocol with these kinds of investigations. It's strictly by the book; no room for guesses."

A silent moment passed. Gantry sensed he'd have to be more aggressive, even at the risk of not fitting all of Melendez's protocols. He took a leap.

"How do we start? Should I come down there to Quantico and meet with you?"

A skeptical Melendez breathed a long sigh, "Okay. Come down on Friday. I'll e-mail you the directions and a pass for the front gate. Be here at 10:00 a.m. I have an hour—one hour. I hope this is good. See you then, I have to go."

"Thanks, I'll be there."

Gantry hung up the phone and smiled.

The next morning, a gray and ominous bank of clouds was blowing east, taking its drizzle along. A flood of sunlight suddenly poured into Gantry's apartment. *The more light the better,* he said to himself, looking at the remnants of rain running down his window. *Only this time, I'm going to shine it into the dark corners and see what bugs come crawling out.*

Gantry turned off the coffee pot and put his cup in the sink. He went to the phone and dialed Alex Jaeger's number. When Alex picked up, Gantry immediately starting talking. "I want to remind you, Alex, that *you* told me to call the FBI."

"Gantry? What are you talking about?"

"You told me if I called the FBI—"

"Yes I did. So you called the FBI? What did they say?"

"I spoke to the guy who's the top agent in his field down in Quantico. He's into analytics, cold cases mostly. His unit—" Gantry stopped and forced himself to organize his thoughts. "His unit is perfect for this. If anyone or any group can find out what these messages are leading to, it's them. This is what they do. You told me if they were interested I could purse this on the magazine's dime, remember?"

Alex began thinking seriously for the first time about what could be a wild goose chase— and then a bulb the size of a klieg light cracked on above his head. He could get some real traction out of all of it. Light, as it always does, illuminates and clarifies.

While Gantry was talking about Quantico, he sensed Alex's mind kicking into sales mode. The wheels were turning: an instant spike in readership…higher advertising revenues…

"Gantry, run with this story and call me every day. I wanna know everything that's going on. Got it?"

Before Gantry could thank him, the line went dead.

In Alex's apartment, the mood was also elevated. Alex walked briskly over to Daniel, who was making an omelet in the kitchen.

"What's all the excitement about, Alex?"

"Well, let's say that for now, I believe in the power of a great story. Gantry actually called the FBI."

"He *did?*"

"Yep. I knew he would. He's like that. And I might be able to turn this into some serious money. I know he's trying to redeem himself. He wants to prove he's still important and still a real journalist. And if he actually comes up with something with the FBI, well…"

"How's that?" Daniel quickly interjected.

"He's managed to hook up with some heavyweight agent who's in charge of some behavioral unit or something down in Quantico. He said the guy is a genius with cold cases, and he's going to meet with him tomorrow. This agent is actually going to listen to Gantry's serial-killer theory."

Daniel stared at him, "Alex, you know this is going to end up embarrassing you and the magazine? It is admirable of you to want to help Gantry and I know you feel you owe him. But Alex, get serious. Serial killers…conspiracies. Come on now. This could end very badly if you don't nip it in the bud. Focus on us."

Alex was taken aback by this sudden concern, but felt compelled to defend his support of Gantry.

"Well, I didn't want to share this with him, but I'm thinking there are maybe eighty million baby boomers in the U.S. of A."

"So what's that got to do with dead rock stars?"

"That eighty million—give or take a million or two—were born between 1946 and 1964."

"I still don't see the connection." Daniel looked at him quizzically.

Alex smiled. "How many of those eighty million people do you think read the magazine?

"Not a clue, but I'm guessing not as many as you'd like," Daniel responded knowing where this was going.

"Right! If I could serialize this story like I did with *The Bonfire of the Vanities*, I could increase readership exponentially and add to the subscriber base. Think about it Daniel, our smallest demographic is men and women fifty-five plus. Out of a total circulation of over twelve million, only a million and a half are over fifty-five. Just think what I could do with a flood of boomers starting to read *Stone* again. Jesus! The boomers would stampede to read this!"

Alex looked at Daniel. "You're younger, but you know this audience. These are the same people who trust you with their investments. I just want some of their money too."

Daniel plopped Alex's plate in front of him, but Alex was on a roll, far more interested in talking than eating.

"The Gen-Xers are wondering when the oldies radio stations will start playing music from the 1980s. Hell, all the oldies stations still cater to boomers, but we don't. Our prime target's is the same as television, eighteen to thirty-four. That's half our demo, man. This is a chance to change that, or at least add to it."

Alex was getting more excited and walked toward the living area, talking mostly to himself.

"And it's not the subscriptions, or certainly not the stand sales, it's those beautiful, rich advertisers. That's where the money is!" Alex was practically licking his lips.

Daniel finally joined in. "Yeah. I see it. All you old farts loved Joplin, Morrison, Hendrix. You were raised on that music. A big story about them being killed instead of checking out with drugs would drive gobs of interest. It's brilliant, Alex. Not only would a whole new generation be reading the magazine, you could start fielding a new universe of advertisers—AARP, Viagra, Cialis, bowling alleys, Rascal sales. The list is endless," he said sarcastically.

Alex sat down next to him.

"Are you fucking with me?" he said. "I'm serious. This is serious money, man."

Daniel threw his hands up in disgust. "I'm sorry, I couldn't help myself. You're always fucking with Gantry and saying how he's over the hill. But here he is now; ready to take you on a wild goose chase and you're falling for it like an infatuated teenager."

Alex rolled his eyes as his partner continued.

"And yes, Pfizer and Viagra would be nice, so would AARP, but there are also cruise-line agencies, retirement communities, health-care plans…The list is practically endless."

Daniel paused for affect.

"Very funny," Alex responded defensively. "You'll see. Remember back in 2010, when the media was trumpeting my demise because I started expanding into restaurants and concert promotion? Ha! Who's laughing now?"

"Yes, I remember. They accused you of allowing your magazine's success to go to your head, as I recall. It's funny, though, back then you fired just about everyone. It almost took you under and took you years to recover."

"Why is that so fucking funny?" Alex looked at him defiantly.

There was a long pause, as Daniel stood up and got face to face with Alex:

"Gantry had encouraged you and kept telling you what a good idea it was. And like an idiot, you believed him. Don't make the same fucking mistake again!"

Quantico, Virginia

Early Morning

Three days later, on Friday, Gantry got up at 4:00 a.m. to prepare for the two hundred thirty-mile trip to Quantico, Virginia. He gathered the slips and pieces of paper and the five newspaper accounts he'd pulled from his Dead Artists file on the deaths of Jones, Wilson, Hendrix, Joplin, and Morrison.

Gantry left before the morning rush and drove straight through to the Quantico Marine Base, where the FBI building housing the training facilities for the BAU Academy, is located. The bright and clear day energized Gantry. During the ride through some of the most beautiful country in the U.S., he listened to his oldies station and silently sorted through the clues, rehearsing for his meeting. He knew he would only get one shot. He'd even worn his sport coat, a dark, good-for-any-occasion wool jacket, with black dress slacks. He arrived at 9:45.

Stopping at the gate, he gave the guard his name, along with the pass he'd printed out. The Marine pointed to the BAU building without speaking.

After parking, Gantry walked through the front door of the green-gray cinderblock building, expecting to see banks of computer servers and rows of people in cubicles accessing masses of information projected on giant video screens. But it was nothing like that. This looked more like the interior of a school, with long gray hallways and heavy old wooden doors leading into rooms that might well have been classrooms. He looked in both directions, but seeing no signs, he turned and started blindly walking. Suddenly a man in a dark gray suit approached him from behind.

"Mr. Elliot?"

Gantry was startled. "Yes."

"Come with me, please. Mr. Melendez is in his office. It's just down this hall."

Gantry took a seat in what appeared to be a waiting room, but there was no secretary or any magazines. His escort left, but it felt weird as if *he* were the subject of investigation today. The walls were drab gray with a receptionist's desk sans receptionist, a small lamp, phone, and an empty coffee table. The only things that could be considered decoration were three framed photos on the wall near the inner door. One was of President Obama, the other of Vice President Biden and the third, FBI Director James B. Comey.

Quite the group, he'd thought.

After a few moments, a tall Hispanic man came into the room through an inner door. Gantry recognized him immediately. He rose, smiling, and held out his hand, which Melendez shook vigorously. *His hands are as big as catchers' mitts,* he thought, glancing down to his shoes as all men do when they size one another up. To his surprise, Melendez, though wearing a well-cut black suit, was also wearing cowboy boots. *A good start.*

"Gantry, good to see you again. Come in," Melendez said, gesturing for him to walk ahead and be seated in the large brown leather chair facing the desk. After about three minutes of small talk, Melendez got down to business.

"So, tell me, what do you do at the magazine now?"

Gantry felt himself wanting to be more personal than he should. Hell, he knew very little about this man, but there was something about him. Still, he sensed a formality just beneath the surface.

"Can I call you Raphael?" Gantry asked.

"Of course."

"Okay...but let me ask you something off the subject first."

"Sure."

"This place looks like a high school. I thought you were hot on cold cases and heavy-duty analytics. You know, all the latest techno gadgets. White walls. Humidity control. Slim, attractive assistants."

Melendez chuckled.

"I'm very much involved in cases, but with retirement raising its ugly head right around the corner, I had to work a special deal with the Bureau. If I wanted to keep working, and believe me, I want to, they said I would have to teach here at the academy. The way I looked at it, it was very positive for me. I teach a few hours a day, three days a week, then I'm free to do what I do, which is the analytical side of it all. And I do have a state-of-the-art test lab. I have two very old cold cases that I am working on, but right now I'd like to hear what you have to say."

"I don't write much anymore, to be honest. I've found myself living in the past too much," Gantry admitted frankly.

"What do you mean?" Melendez said. "In my day, you were the pinnacle. No one could touch your stuff and no one knew rock and roll the way you knew it."

"I guess you're right. I just want to, you know, get back in the game. I want to do more investigative work, solid writing, not just covering the Hall of Fame inductions and career retrospectives. I feel like I'm forty-five, and the fire still burns."

Melendez nodded. He'd fought his own battles trying to stay significant to the Bureau.

"'Only the shallow knows themselves,'" Melendez said, quoting Oscar Wilde. "There is always much to learn."

"That's true. I know a lot of folks who fit that description."

"Yeah, think about it. When you don't have much depth, it isn't hard to mine the soil. Never forget your significance, your bearing. If you don't respect what you carry in that noggin, no one else will either. Why should they care? They're all too damned superficial." He caught himself getting too emotional, before adding, "For me, I won't stop doing what I do until they start throwing the dirt on my coffin."

The two men laughed.

Gantry went with the moment. He launched into his thoughts about the case, quickly reviewing all he'd explained over the phone.

He picked up his tan valise from beside his chair and pulled out the mysterious messages, lining them up in front of Melendez.

"I'm sure you know how many rock stars have died suspiciously at the age of twenty-seven, and all since 1969. We talked about that. But these five…"

"Yes, I'm aware," Melendez said quietly. "Again, to be honest, my first inclination when you called was that this is the work of some hippie whack job, probably in his sixties like us, having LSD flashbacks and reliving his glory days at your expense. Didn't cost the guy anything. There's not even any postage on the envelopes."

Gantry looked at Melendez. Did the man think that Gantry was trying to sell him? He didn't know it, but he had just crossed a line he didn't even know existed. And he also didn't know how quickly an agent would shut down any process if he thought he smelled a sales pitch. Bureau agents are not motivated by someone else's motivation, especially if they are members of the media.

Melendez didn't want to reveal that he had a personal interest in the whole Myth of 27 legend, even if his logical mind told him to knock it off. He'd read about the so-called satanic pact, in which members of the 27 Club had supposedly signed contracts with the devil. That particular urban legend owed its roots to the blues musician Robert Johnson, who, according to the tale, heard a voice telling him to meet a large black man at a crossroads who would change his world. The man, of course, was the devil, and Johnson gave his guitar to the man, who tuned it and promptly handed it back. The payoff was that the devil owned his soul, and Johnson became an overnight guitar virtuoso.

Johnson died in 1938 at the age of twenty-seven.

But it was just one legend among many.

"Let me tell you what we do here," Melendez said. "We find patterns and links in seemingly random facts and incidents. We always start with a hypothesis that we try to develop, and there has to be a damned good reason to start in the first place. There's too much money and manpower at stake to chase fairy tales, and too much liability to follow wild-ass legends. I say that with all due respect to your enthusiasm about this. In fact, the way you go about investigating and writing is pretty much the same way we operate."

"How so?"

"Who, what, where, when, and why. The five Ws. With cold cases, that process is just as important to solving a case as it is to you writing an investigative story.

"Murderers usually have very primal motives, like jealousy or anger. Multiple murderers or serial killers usually have something else driving them. To be honest, there is a possibility that you have such a thing here. But more than likely it's just a practical joke. You are almost certainly dealing with someone who's crazy, one way or another."

"Okay, but all I know is that whoever might have done this had to have been at these locations in order to get possession of these items: a napkin, a demo label, and an unused airline ticket. And they knew my whereabouts. You see what I mean?"

Melendez was clearly irritated and was now standing. He began to pace.

"You have to realize the bureau doesn't automatically jump into cold cases unless there is a preponderance of real evidence, some visible inconsistencies and an apparent motive. We follow a process, and we follow it religiously. This is not an improvisational game. There is absolutely no speculation.

"What you have here is a what, when, and where, but those are the easy parts. We know these people died, we know where they expired, and we know when—or at least you do. In very old cold cases, the challenge is the who and the how—the sixth element."

Gantry felt his case was quickly sliding away. He wasn't sure if he was making his points or not.

Melendez continued. "Of course there are the more, shall we say, intimate connections you're talking about. That is a conundrum. This is just hypothetical, but if I were to work on this, one of the first things I'd do would be to look at potential commonalities, like social contacts, doctors, business ties, lifestyle ties, management connections. There are pieces of this puzzle that seem to touch each other, and these artifacts could be—and I emphasize could be—more than rock and roll memorabilia."

Gantry waited. He suddenly felt that Melendez was convincing himself to look into the case.

"What I'm saying, Gantry, is there might be a pattern here that could suggest something sinister. We have some very sophisticated technology and processes; we're able to look at data to discern statistically viable patterns. But even with all you've brought in, this is still just conjecture, even if whoever is sending you these clues would appear to have had access to these stars, to their homes, their belongings—access to their lives. It isn't enough, not the way the Bureau sees it.

"I'm sorry," Melendez went on. "I know you've come a long way and have convinced yourself that this is real. If you had something more tangible, or a bit more implicating, it might be worth looking into."

Gantry slumped in his chair. Melendez had done an excellent job of priming him and then pulling the rug out from under him. What was there left to say?

Both men sat quietly for a few moments, and then Melendez stood up and reached across the desk to Gantry. They shook hands.

"Gantry, I'm sorry. I wish I could help you. I hope you understand."

"I do, and thank you for your time, Raphael. I guess you're right. If there was really something to this, after all this time..." Suddenly he felt tired, deflated. It was time to go. "Thanks again," he said.

Gantry started back down the long, gray hallway, rationalizing to himself that perhaps he'd just saved himself from a real nightmare. As he approached the heavy front doors of the building and saw the Marines standing outside, he happened to glance up into the lens of a surveillance camera. He turned and saw another behind him. More along several locations down the hallway.

Gantry ran back down the hallway to Melendez's office.

"Raphael!"

Melendez came out.

Gantry, a little out of breath, "Surveillance cameras!"

Melendez gave him a questioning look.

"Cameras," Gantry said. "We have them all over the building at the magazine. There are several in the lobby. I never even gave it a thought. So stupid. The mail boy brings our mail up every day after he sorts it downstairs. He sits in a small room where all the mail is delivered from the post office and FedEx and UPS, but more importantly, from anyone who wants to drop something off! All of it goes into that one room first, and there are several cameras monitoring the entrance and the mail room."

Melendez said slowly, "Well, now…that may put a different spin on things."

He liked Gantry, and even if he didn't want to admit it, this was starting to look interesting. Maybe he would give Gantry a little leeway, just enough to check it out a bit more. Hell, he was getting close to the end of another case, and he did have eight months before his retirement. Maybe if he started a new case, he thought, he could stay on the job beyond that date.

"It would be interesting to see who is delivering these items. I'm not promising you anything, but go ahead and get those security images. There are several types of cameras, so let me know which type we're dealing with. Some of them make it much easier to zero in on a frame at a time.

"Oh—and if you get another envelope, don't handle it any more than you have to, and don't open it."

"Okay. I can probably have that footage here by next Tuesday," Gantry said.

Melendez checked his calendar. "Tuesday would be okay. Make it around noon."

Gantry went to bed that night exhausted but exhilarated. Vivid dreams began to crowd their way into his sleep, and he rolled and squirmed through the night with a mix of scenes from old concerts, backstage interviews, and intimate moments he'd shared with Hendrix, Wilson, Jones, and Janis…

Janis Joplin had been a force to reckon with. She'd spoken to him in the visceral language of music, but they also had cultural connections.

He was nineteen and a freshman at UT, majoring in journalism. Joplin, five years older, had gone to UT, but then she left Texas. She returned in 1965 to attend Lamar College and was singing part time, driving to Austin on the weekends to play some of the small, smoky clubs there. Music and writing were Gantry's two passions, and he liked to pretend he was working for some important magazine, reviewing rock stars. He'd go to the clubs and sit in the back nursing a Coke for hours, watching and listening to the second-rate bands on stage.

Occasionally, though, someone with real talent and power would show up out of nowhere, and he would be ecstatic, noting all the subtleties and tonalities that appealed to him. He knew instinctively when a singer or musician was going to catch on, and Janis was most definitely one of those.

He was enthralled. He noted in his journal that she had a "secret energy." It was a raw verve that was unlike any female singer he'd ever heard. On top of that, she was sexual on stage—not in an obvious way, not just sexy, but through the energy she cast out into the audience that went way beyond musical energy. This young, brash, rough-voiced singer had caught his eye several times with a hint of a smile, nothing anyone but he would notice. He always smiled back, both intrigued and a little shy.

He wasn't sure, but he guessed she was in her early twenties. It was unusual in those days for a woman to take over a stage so authoritatively. The industry was dominated by men; women were usually in the background or off to the side. To Gantry, Janis made the room almost smell like sex through an odd-mix of lust, power, and vulnerability.

One night when her set was over, she put the mic down on her stool and walked straight over to his table. She threw herself hard into the chair opposite his, smiled, and without saying a word snapped her fingers for a waiter. When one appeared, she handed him her glass and said, "The same. Make it two." She kept her eyes on Gantry the whole time.

"Hello, cowboy," Joplin purred.

The words still rang in his head; he'd never forget them. He'd been wearing his boots and one of his two Stetson beaver hats.

Within a minute the waiter returned with a tray and two heavy tumblers three-quarters filled with Southern Comfort, neat.

Janis raised her glass. Gantry followed suit quickly.

"May you always have a clean shirt, a clear conscience, and enough coins in your pocket to buy a pint," she said, clanking her glass to his.

He laughed and took a sip of the sweet whiskey, unlike any he'd tasted before. There was no bite to it, and that became the problem, or rather, the hangover, but what a glorious hangover it had been, worth every throb, pound, and ache. He woke up the next morning in a motel room sprawled out in a bed next to Janis. Both of them were naked and uncovered, and she was still asleep.

He felt her stirring as he lay quietly, their backs lightly touching, their legs partly entwined.

She moaned, probably in as much pain as he was. The motel room was filled with the musky smell of sex, Janis's sandalwood perfume, marijuana ash, cigarette smoke, and the sour stink of whiskey.

She ran her foot casually up his calf.

Morning sex, the best kind.

They were both in the haze of half sleep. He slowly rolled over and stroked her shoulder, then ran his hand down her side and over her ass, which was firm and without a blemish. She moaned and stirred, responding to his touch.

He pulled her thick dark hair back and kissed her neck. She stirred again, and he could feel the muscles in her back tense slightly. He slipped his hand around her waist, under her arm and up over her breasts—supple, pear shaped, and with nipples as hard and pink as tightly rolled rosebuds.

The lovemaking was sublime and raw; the smells so intense, the climax like a volcanic eruption with an anodyne ending that just drifted off. He had never made love to a woman like this before. She was like a young tiger you thought would make a great pet, but knew in a few years would grow far too strong and powerful to control.

With the memory-dream sublimely disappearing, the alarm went off, startling him. Sitting up, he remembered the aftermath of their fling.

He'd gone back to see her perform every weekend that she came to Austin. And then, one day, she simply vanished. She never came back.

By the time Gantry graduated, he'd been working for *Rolling Stone* for three months, and by then he was hearing about her all the time. Janis Joplin, his secret memory. Dennis was the only one he had ever shared these memories with.

Getting up, he looked across the room at his one framed photo, his ex-wife, Jodi, and his beloved dog, Montana. For a split second, he let her memory invade his thoughts as well, and he immediately felt that soft but unwelcome feeling of the blues begin to pour over his shoulders. He shook his head and walked quickly to the bathroom to run his shower.

When Gantry spied the red message light blinking on his ancient answering machine, he thought ruefully that he may no longer be able to afford his relative anonymity. He was going to have to start answering his cell phone and his e-mails and paying attention to his answering machine. Hell, he might even treat himself to one of those new smartphones.

He felt motivated again. Melendez had only given him a carrot, and it dangled from the end of a long string, but he had a chance, and it was promising. Putting a face and a body to the mysterious messenger would be a game changer.

He quickly walked over to the table and pushed the PLAY button. He was hoping for a message from Raphael, but all three were from Alex.

"Hey, buddy, it's Alex. Where the hell are you? I didn't have the number of your FBI contact. Hell, I don't even remember his name, a Mexican, I think. You obviously aren't answering your cell, or maybe you didn't take it with you. At any rate, I have big news. Call me as soon as you get in."

Then the second message:

"Hey, buddy. Are you back yet? You said you'd be back today. Call me. Hot news."

The third message was a hang-up, but Gantry knew it was him.

He quickly dialed Alex.

"Hey Alex, it's me. Yep, I forgot my cell. Left it here, and—"

"Buddy, have I got news for you. Yesterday the mail boy called my secretary. He was concerned you weren't in. He said you'd been getting these mysterious hand-addressed manila envelopes, and he was going to drop off another one. Thought it was serious enough to tell me. I haven't opened it, but it must be another one of the packages, so I brought it home with me. So, what do we do? What happened in Quan—"

"Don't handle the envelope anymore," Gantry blurted out. "Don't open it!"

"God, I can't open it? Now you've got me all amped up about this damned thing."

Gantry hadn't seen Alex this excited about anything in years, with the exception of his wedding. Maybe now would be the perfect time to tell him he couldn't make his pre-wedding dinner. He'd have to go back to Quantico if he wanted to keep his momentum going. But he was the best man, and he couldn't be at the dinner and also visit Quantico.

"Alex, wait. Let me call Melendez. I have his cell, and he told me to call him if anything else happened. Let's see what he says."

"Great, I'm at home. Call me back."

After a brief call with Melendez, Gantry called Alex back.

"Alex, we're about to have a conference call with Melendez. We need to both hang up, and when the phone rings, pick up and we'll all be on."

Within a minute, Raphael, Gantry and Alex were talking. After Alex described the envelope and how it was addressed, Melendez began to tell him what to do.

"Do you have any latex gloves in the house?"

"Yes."

"Get them. We'll wait."

Gantry said, "Why the gloves? There are probably already at least five sets of prints on that envelope."

"Trust me. You want the fewest prints possible. We can identify

Alex's and the mail kid's. There might only be a couple of others, and one of them might be from the guy we're hoping to pick up on the surveillance video."

"Okay. I'm back," Alex said. "Do I open it now?"

"Yes, carefully. Don't handle anything inside. Just turn the envelope over on a table and tell us what you find."

Pause.

"It's another note. It's typed."

He read the note aloud:

"Ron McKernan did not die of natural causes. He was murdered. It didn't stop."

"Anything else?" Gantry said. "Any small slips of paper or cardboard?"

"Yes. There is something that looks like maybe a piece of an album cover. It reads, 'Recorded at the Euphoria Ballroom, San Raphael, California, July 1970. Turn on Your Love Light.'"

Alex and Gantry immediately recognized the words, they were the traditional ending to every Grateful Dead concert and had been written and performed by Ron McKernan.

"Do you know what that means?" Melendez asked.

"No, but it's the typical ending to a Grateful Dead concert," Gantry said.

Alex jumped in.

"Mr. Melendez," he said. "Ron McKernan was better known as Pigpen. He and Jerry Garcia were the founding members of the band. Always a jokester, Garcia nicknamed him Pigpen after the Peanuts character because Ron was always dressed sloppily. He died in 1973 of what they said was a massive intestinal hemorrhage."

"Is that about right, Gantry?"

"Exactly. Couldn't have stated it better myself." He was happy to be asked. "Oh, yeah—and Janis Joplin was there, too," he added.

Alex said, "Yes, she and McKernan also dated for a while. In fact, she died less than ninety days later. McKernan was twenty-seven, just like Joplin and the others."

Going back to the envelope's contents, Alex said, "It looks like it might have been a set list, or part of one. On the back of this paper is a handwritten note. Jesus! These are lyrics or a poem or something, written to Joplin, it looks like, from McKernan."

He read:

To J from Ron:
And you know that I believe in my lord.
I believe in everything he stands for.
I believe in my woman too.
I believe in my woman more than you, my lord.

Silence on the line.

"Oh, and it looks like there is one more artifact in the envelope," Alex continued, "a bracelet with a horned steer charm. Maybe a present from McKernan? What do you think Gantry?" he asked.

He didn't respond.

"Let me send you guys a picture of it."

"Okay guys, interesting artifacts," Melendez interjected. "The Rock and Roll Hall of Fame would love this, but it's not a murder clue. I don't see it—*yet*," he said. "But it would help if I could get that video we talked about here on Tuesday. Gantry, bring both and I'll look at all of it. Bring all of the envelopes back."

Gantry interrupted before Alex could speak.

"Raphael, tell me something, and be straight with me. If I bring you the surveillance footage showing someone dropping off these envelopes, and we now have these four artifacts, what can you do?"

"I'll have to wait to answer that," Melendez said shortly. "And then we'll talk. I've got to go. Good talking to you, Mr. Jaeger."

"Likewise. Anything I can do, just let me know."

"Of course," Melendez said, and hung up.

Before Gantry could say anything about the schedule, Alex said, "Wait. Fuck, wait a minute. Tuesday? That's my pre-wedding dinner party and you're my best man!"

Gantry knew he had to bite the bullet. "Alex, I know how important this is to you, but you did say 'anything,' and if I don't strike while this iron is hot, we may never have a story. Raphael wasn't even going to entertain the thought of spending a minute on this until I remembered the surveillance cameras. I have to get those to him immediately."

Alex, clearly upset, paused before responding, as Gantry was one of his oldest friends. "I see…This is important…You're right. I'll meet you at the office tomorrow and give you this envelope. And I'll call security now and tell them you're coming to pick up a file with all the surveillance from the last two weeks. I think the footage is kept on a hard drive for six months and then archived. It should still be easy to get."

Gantry couldn't find words. "Alex, I—"

"Look, I know your heart will be there, and I know you hate these things anyway. Make sure you get down to Quantico early."

He hung up before Gantry could respond.

Gantry set his Dead Artists folder on his coffee table and leafed to the middle to find the Ron McKernan file. He gently unfolded an old article from the 1973 *New York Times*.

Now he had four clues reflecting five artists, each one more intimate than the previous. He sat back, took his time reading the article, and vividly remembered the music scene in San Francisco when he arrived, with the Grateful Dead already defining a "jam band" sound that became the soundtrack for the Haight Ashbury community and for hippies across the country.

Garcia and McKernan met at an open-mic night in a nearly empty coffee house in San Francisco when McKernan walked onstage to play harmonica—blues style and a raspy voice were the perfect complement to Garcia's sweet guitar and vocals.

Funny …Pigpen. I had completely forgotten about that until Alex mentioned it…as he read about McKernan's kooky lifestyle, I bet the peace and love hippies freaked out! He laughed to himself.

McKernan's seductive organ and harmonica defined the Dead's sound for a generation of fans…perfected musicianship contrasted sharply with his disheveled appearance…tough biker demeanor and passion for Thunderbird wine...honorary Hell's Angel.

Same old story, Gantry thought to himself, *not able to handle the demands of performing.*

McKernan missed rehearsals, recording sessions, and concert dates, forcing management to hire a replacement—ultimately fired—came back in a lesser capacity—almost always present for the Dead's signature concert finale, "Turn on Your Love Light."

McKernan's biker lifestyle eventually caught up with him.

Gantry sat quietly, trying to make sense of all of the clues, organizing his archives to hand over to Agent Melendez, adding the McKernan and Joplin files to his package. Obviously, Janis had a special place in his heart, and though her death wasn't among the direct clues, it was insinuated.

He stared at the cover page of an article he'd written years ago:

Joplin was part of a unique group of rock stars who were popular as much for their attitudes as for their music. Second only to Bob Dylan and the only woman of her generation who achieved that kind of stature in a male-dominated music culture. Sadly, like so many of them, her days were cut short.

He had to smile, recalling one of her controversial feminist quotes. In her quest for liberation, which was a much different quest than that of her male peers, she often identified the first principle of rock and roll as, "singing as fucking, and fucking as liberation."

Pulling out the articles about Janis and stacking them alongside the other four, he was overcome with a surge of emotion. This story wasn't all he wanted. Something much more personal was driving him, something much more important. Reliving the tragedies surrounding these young artists who were so talented, so hell-bent on breaking ground and who died so young... he wanted redemption for them... for her.

His lack of sleep was catching up with him, but he couldn't help being drawn into the Joplin article like a moth to a porch light.

On the 4th of October, 1970, Janis Joplin was staying at the Landmark Hotel in West Hollywood. When she didn't show for a Sunset Sound recording session, her manager drove out to the hotel and recognized her unmistakable, psychedelic painted Porsche 356C in the parking lot; driver's door ajar, lights on, engine running.

He found her lying on the floor beside her bed unresponsive.

Gantry put the article down and rubbed his eyes. Reliving it again summoned up a wave of emotions in him.

The cause of death was listed as a heroin overdose. Fourteen needle tracks attested to the medical appraisal. The most famous woman in rock & roll was dead.

He could now see, in retrospect, how prescient his interpretation of the events had really been and what the entire era had spawned over the decades that followed in all aspects of modern day life.

...the movie Easy Rider contemplated the anguish of this generation, and to many it seemed that Joplin's death signaled the flaming-out of a meteoric era...the frame around the Age of Aquarius and its utopian vision...not unlike the Renaissance in Italy when genius seemingly sprang up from primitive origins, later to astonish historians with its complexities.

Gantry got up to walk around. He knew the article by heart having read it hundreds of times. He wanted to put it down but couldn't stop...it was almost religious-like for him...as if reading and rereading it was a way of keeping her irrepressible spirit alive.

Her bold style drew growing attention in San Francisco...Big Brother and the Holding Company asked her to front them...electrifying performance at the Monterey Pop Festival..."most powerful singer in the rock and roll," Time Magazine...Vogue called her "staggering."

..."Piece of My Heart" forever became a quintessential standard for female blues and rock singers.

...Janice left $1,500 in her will to pay for a party in the event of

her death.

Always up for a good time, he said to himself before finally putting the article down.

Gantry told himself not to stay up too late Sunday night. He needed to recharge.

But he couldn't sleep. He was running on adrenaline.

Gantry woke up instantly alert. He'd set his alarm for 5:00 a.m. On his way to the kitchen to start a pot of coffee, he caught a glimpse of a FedEx envelope that had been slipped under his door.

"Jesus fuckin Christ! What now. I never get deliveries here," he said out loud.

Gantry bent down to grab the envelope, already knowing what it was.

"Shit...shit..." he said, unnerved that it was delivered to his home address.

"Of course no fucking sender." He flipped over the delivery slip.

He pulled the small tab that unzipped the top and looked inside. There was a piece of white copy paper. Not yet thinking clearly, he pulled it out with his bare hand and read, to his astonishment:

Peter Ham did not commit suicide. He was murdered.

Gantry dropped both the FedEx envelope and note on the floor, "Goddamn it...forgot the gloves...fuck."

His hands started to tremble and he began to breathe heavily, as he realized that the guy knew where he lived. The more than passing thought he had the other day, however brief, now came back to him like a sledgehammer...a stalker, a killer.

He jumped to his pc and quickly looked up the tracking number on the FedEx website. His face scrunched as he read. The package was sent from his address.

Gantry was angry and alarmed, but also wired. Whoever knew his address might be following him and keeping an eye on him from a distance. He'd now be constantly looking over his shoulder.

He quickly dialed up Melendez, but got his voicemail. "Raphael, I got a Fedex package with another message. This one is about the death of Peter Ham. Leaving now," a breathless Gantry quickly explained.

On instinct he walked into his bedroom and pulled the hidden key from beneath his end table and slid it into the heavy lock on his footlocker. Under a pile of papers was a black alloy Smith and Wesson .44 magnum with six high-pressure hollow points in the cylinder.

"*OK*, motherfucker." He picked it up, feeling the satisfying heft of it, and aiming it at the far wall before placing the pistol down.

Gantry was a strong man, even though he was sixty-five years old. He usually felt he could handle just about anything. But this was different. This was surreal, like an evil ghost you can't see. "Hell, the guy could have walked right up to my front door," he thought as he put the key in the ignition and started the rental car.

The message and clue had really shaken Gantry; he was now reluctant to handle the envelope, and just wanted to get some distance from his apartment. He promised himself he'd wait until he got to Quantico to handle it any further.

He first swung by the *Rolling Stone* office, where he had arranged to meet early with the chief of security and pick up the digital surveillance file. He then went up to Alex's office to retrieve the McKernan envelope.

"Alex, I got a Fedex with another message. This time about Peter Ham's death," he said as he walked in.

"Jesus, you're fucking kidding me. What did it say? What's in it?"

"Don't know. I'm taking it to Melendez. He needs to dust it for prints."

"OK, let me know as soon as you find out."

The drive was tedious and took longer than before. A major accident had slowed everything down and the state police were motioning all cars into one lane on I-95. He decided to pull over and sit on the shoulder for a while. Once he'd turned off the engine, Gantry took a deep breath. It was still at least two more hours to Quantico.

Strange that he had not heard back from Melendez. He called again getting his voicemail for a second time. *Not like him,* he thought to himself. *He would want me to look at the contents,* He reasoned, trying to give himself permission.

Carefully re-opening the zip of the FedEx envelope using a tissue this time, he now saw a small piece of paper and a matchbook, along with the note he'd already seen.

Delicately pulling the paper out, Gantry recognized, to his surprise, a prescription slip. It read, "Sixty tablets, Antabuse. Take one every morning with food." There was a doctor's name and a phone number and address for the St. Albans Pharmacy in London. It was made out to Peter Ham.

Gantry knew about Antabuse, a drug that makes a person violently ill if they drink any alcohol while taking it. Rehabs used to use it all the time. One swallow of alcohol on top of Antabuse, and the drinker would vomit, experience excruciating cramps, and generally just want to die.

He laid that on his leg and took out the matchbook. Some matches with a club name on them, a logo script that read *Thingamajig Club.* No address.

The timing was impeccable. Not only did the killer know where he lived, he knew he was going to Quantico today! That's why it was sent to his home by FedEx instead of dropped at the office like the others. This guy wanted to make sure Gantry had this last clue before that meeting with the FBI.

Does that mean the son of a bitch is listening to my phone calls as well? he thought.

Gantry was nervous. *Why this one? How is this tied to the others? What the fuck is this guy doing?*

Before he started the car, he thought that he should have Ham's obituary in the Myth of 27 file. It was much different than the others, more like Jones's. The other three had supposedly died of overdoses or by suicide, but Jones and Ham were different. Jones drowned, or at least that's what the police in London said, and the papers reported that Ham had hung himself. He'd retrieve that obit.

As Gantry pulled back onto I -95, he recalled something obscure about Ham. His band, Badfinger, had been the first band produced by Apple Records, the Beatles' label. Also some kind of controversy...

At the next rest stop he decided to make two important calls, the first to Alex, the other call would be more important. Digging into his files, he found the obituary and quickly skimmed it. It confirmed his recollection about the Apple connection and how he died:

Peter Ham, founder of the group Badfinger, died on April 27, 1975. He was 27 years old.

Ham was an accomplished songwriter and gifted guitarist, best known for Badfinger's huge hits, 'No Matter What,' 'Day after Day' and 'Baby Blue.' But his most celebrated songwriting success was 'Without You,' which became a number one hit for Harry Nilsson

Badfinger's first hit song, 'Come and Get It' was penned and produced by Paul McCartney after John Lennon rejected it for the Beatles. When Apple dissolved Badfinger moved to Warner Bros. Records.

Badfinger's bouncy pop sound, left Ham little opportunity to display his guitar virtuosity. Many felt that he was being held back by his producers and management. Even his searing public cover of Jimi Hendrix's 'Purple Haze' was ridiculed as a fake.

Frustrated by his professional limits and despondent over the apparent mismanagement of the band's financial and legal affairs, he was found hanged in the garage of his Surrey home, an apparent suicide.

Gantry pulled up to the security gate at 11:45. He felt far more confident than he previously had been, armed as he was, with two security surveillance video files, the latest clues, and his freeway phone call. But overriding all that, he now he had a heightened sense of urgency and a very real personal exposure. He felt threatened. Personally threatened.

After passing through security, he parked and went directly to Melendez's office. Opening the outer door, he noticed that on the wall where the government portraits had hung, there was a new picture. A blow up of The Beatles' "White Album," their ninth, and one that John Lennon had been extremely proud of.

Gantry immediately knew the significance it must have had for Melendez. It was a time of turmoil for the band, a time when Ringo Starr had quit the group temporarily, after hearing that Paul McCartney had played the drums on two tracks. It initially received poor reviews, but eventually went platinum.

Before Gantry could knock to announce himself, Melendez came out, his big hand extended immediately.

"Like it?" he said to Gantry, seeing him eyeing the poster, "We *are* the avant-garde branch of the Bureau, you know," he said laughingly, but abruptly stopping as he saw the serious expression on Gantry's face.

"Why didn't you return my calls? I called you twice," a perturbed Gantry asked.

"I'm so sorry. I apologize. I had a little scare last night. But it turned out to be just a little acid reflux and indigestion. Back now good as new," Melendez said, downplaying the situation, not wanting to draw any attention to his deteriorating heart condition. "Do you have the surveillance files?"

"Yes. But I got another package. A FedEx package delivered to my home."

Melendez shot up straight, "Your home?"

"Yes, the son of a bitch knows where I live!" he said angrily.

Gantry fumed, then reached into his bag and pulled out the two surveillance video files, along with the two new clues. Both of the manila envelopes inside the folders were in a plastic Ziploc bag. Gantry then laid out all the objects and notes in front of Melendez.

Raphael looked up.

"At your apartment?" Melendez asked again.

"Yep. After you read these, I have more to tell you."

Gantry pulled out twenty dog-eared and slightly moldy manila files and dropped them on Raphael's desk.

"What are those?"

"My Dead Artist files going all the way back to 1969. Everything I read in the papers, wrote myself, or acquired otherwise is in there."

Melendez took a pair of latex gloves from a box in his desk, unzipped the bag, and noted Gantry's name and address on the front.

"This was the item that was delivered to your home?"

"Yes, and that's one of the things I want to talk to you about. This son of a bitch now knows where I live, and on top of that, he must be listening to my calls, because he had to have known I was coming here. You'll note that the Saturday overnight option is checked on the bill of lading. Why the urgency? He had to have listened to our conversation the night before."

Raphael rocked back in his chair. "This is starting to get interesting," he murmured, trying to calm Gantry down.

"Interesting…interesting? Hell, yes. But I don't like it that I'm one of the things that's interesting."

"Okay." Melendez said in a more assuring tone.

"Oh, thanks…that makes me feel *much* better," Gantry responded sarcastically.

"Let me read this latest for a second," Raphael said. He pushed a button on his phone for the intercom. "Hank, can you come to my office? I have a couple of surveillance files from that case I told you about. Need you to analyze them. I have Gantry Elliot here in my office. And keep this between us."

Melendez began to skim the files, then he pulled out the FedEx on Peter Ham. He glanced at the prescription, which was for sixty tablets of Antabuse.

"Do you know what Antabuse is?" Melendez said.

"Yeah. I saw that, too, but it didn't send off any signals."

"Well, according to your note here, Peter Ham hanged himself."

"What's that got to do with Antabuse?" Gantry surmised.

"According to the articles in your file and the police report, his stomach was full of alcohol. Doesn't figure that he'd be taking Antabuse and still have a stomach full of alcohol."

"You're right. Doesn't make sense. But here's something else. When I opened that and I saw Iveys and the Thingamajig Club, I remembered that Iveys was Ham's original name for the band Badfinger."

"Go on," Melendez asked.

"Well, that was before he hooked up with Apple Records. So that means this may be a club date right before they changed their name and became famous. On the way here I made a couple of calls. The first one was to Alex. I described the package, the prescription, and the reference to the Iveys. That's when he validated the Apple Records thing. I told him to Google it.

"He found an incredible version of 'Purple Haze', but it wasn't Hendrix playing, it was Peter Ham."

"Okay, so what was the connection to Hendrix?"

"Neither of us knew, but I knew someone who did," Gantry admitted.

"Who?"

"Macca."

"Who?"

"Sir Paul McCartney, to most people," Gantry replied in a half bragging voice.

"So...what happened?"

"That was my second call."

"You have Paul McCartney's phone number?"

"Yep."

Melendez couldn't help but smile. He pushed his chair back and said, "So what did he tell you?"

"It was funny because Paul is so laid back. He answered the phone, 'Hello, Paul here.'"

"Yeah, go on."

"Well, I just said, 'Hey, Paul, this is Gantry Elliot at *Rolling Stone*, and I need your help with something.'"

"'Certainly, anything for you, Gantry. Shoot,' or words to that effect."

"Jesus." Melendez said, clearly impressed.

"I asked him if he'd known Peter Ham pretty well, and he had. McCartney produced some songs for him and the group, and even wrote one of their biggest hits, 'Come and Get It.' He went on a bit, saying how the business had really killed the poor guy, metaphorically speaking. He said he'd even suggested the name 'Badfinger' to make them sound more hip.

"When I asked him if he remembered Peter playing at the Thingamajig Club in Reading in 1968, he recalled the night as if it were yesterday.

"McCartney talked about how Hendrix's label, and his management were furious that Peter had covered 'Purple Haze' and played it so well. They'd invested a ton to promote Jimi as the best rock guitarist in the world, and now this no-name kid was creating an underground buzz. Paul noted that Hendrix, in fact was flattered; but the gig created a mini shit storm as disinformation and FUD rained down on Peter Ham. The industry was ruthless back then."

"So, the upshot?" Raphael asked.

"I don't know, I'm just saying. It's clearly another piece of the puzzle that someone desperately wanted me to have. I don't know how you guys here at the Bureau do it, but when I'm doing investigative reporting, half the time I don't even know what I'm looking for. I just gather up facts and if I see connections or clues, I try to group them together. Later, when I sit down with my notes, I rearrange them and, eventually, a pattern begins to form. It almost always works out."

By now Melendez was getting the sense that he and Gantry would make a good team, but it was still too early to form that partnership. Mayflower, his boss, would go nuts if that happened. But Melendez also knew that, if this was for real, he had no one on staff with Gantry Elliot's incredible archival memory and personal knowledge of the rock stars and the Myth of 27.

I may have no choice but to use him, Melendez thought as he leaned back in his chair and crossed his hands behind his head.

To Gantry, that was a tell. Body gestures tell a reporter everything, whether someone is lying, relaxed, tense, thinking, or whatever. Raphael was thinking.

Then pointing to the overstuffed files, said, "Anything else in your magic bag?"

"Like I said, that's everything I have, more than forty years of stuff."

"Can you be more specific? What kind of *stuff*?"

"Here's one example that fits nicely with the other connections. We have here Brian Jones, Al Wilson, Jimi Hendrix, Ron McKernan, Peter Ham, and Janis Joplin. All the clues tie those six together somehow. Those are the 'who's.' I already left you the other four obituaries. This one is a retrospective article on Morrison," Gantry said. He handed the newspaper article to Melendez.

He slowly stood up and walked around the office reading out loud, parts of the article. "Nice title...Jim Morrison: Still Controversial Forty Years On," Melendez said nodding his head.

...From 1967 to 1970 the lead singer and chief lyricist for the Doors ruled the rock world as a rock & roll Alexander the Great, even styling his hair in imitation. A lifelong student of philosophy and the classics, Morrison brought a depth and imagery to the Doors songs that make them sound avant-garde even today.

"Gantry, did you know he had a genius IQ?...No wonder the songs have been enduring works of art," Melendez mused.

... closed casket and immediate burial. The lack of autopsy, conflicting accounts of how and where he died, all continue to spark controversy and contribute to Morrison's overall mystique.

"Pretty bad police work," he mumbled, as he was internalizing the mishandling.

In the beginning there was no controversy, no spin control, no management issues, no excess, just pure poetry, much of it influenced by William Blake and French writers Louis-Ferdinand Celine and Arthur Rimbaud.' Morrison was a literary. A true renaissance man.

The story of Ray Manzarek and Morrison meeting on Venice Beach, when Morrison recited his haunting 'Moonlight Drive,' is rock legend. Within 24 months of that serendipitous meeting, the Doors' 'Light My Fire' would be the number one song in the nation.

"Do you remember how huge 'Light My Fire' was in the summer of '67? Even Jose Feliciano's cover became a top hit," Melendez enthusiastically added.

...controversies only added to Morrison's legend, fueling record sales for the band...four smash albums in two years...quintessential leather-painted rock god...a role model for front men ever since.

"Couldn't handle it." Melendez said under his breath.

...Morrison's lifestyle and heavy drinking created serious issues with record and band management. Isolated, overweight, and bearded, he left with girlfriend Pamela Courson for Paris, in an attempt to simplify his life.

"He really tried to clean up his act in Paris, didn't he?" Melendez asked Gantry, who nodded in agreement.

...spent hours writing poetry and sipping coffee in the backdrop of Victor Hugo's house...unfortunately began drinking heavily again.
   ... found dead in his bathtub on the morning of July 3. His final journal entry from the day before read like a premonition: 'Last words, last words...out.'

"A poet to the end. What a loss." Melendez said, slowly shaking his head and turning back to Gantry. "Yep, I do have the others, but I didn't read them over the weekend."

"Read them," Gantry instructed," I figured they'd come in handy for something, even if the death reports might not be exactly correct, considering there were never any real investigations done, and only a few autopsies. At least we have the dates they died, where, and supposedly how.

"The thing is, no matter how they died, they all died at the same age, hence the Myth of 27, and that's the 'what' piece of the puzzle."

"And you think all of them were the work of a possible serial killer?"

"Exactly. And now, we have another problem," Gantry interjected.

"What's that?"

"He knows where I live."

"Okay, okay, so you're wondering just exactly what it's going to take to get the FBI involved."

"Right. What's it going to take—and am I going to be the next victim?"

"Okay, slow down. Let's go down the hall and look at the footage. If the mystery delivery guy is on that footage, and if we can identify him, we're on. It may not be a criminal case, maybe just a nuisance, but at least we can find out what the heck he's trying to do."

On the way to the lab, Melendez was silent. He could tell Gantry was thinking as well, hoping against all hope they would be able to identify the mystery man. Little did Gantry know that the global data sources and astounding computing capability in Raphael's lab would go deep into this information and highlight numerous other links.

As the two men walked, they were joined by a large man wearing a gray-blue suit. Gantry guessed he was a security agent, judging by his size and the bulge on the side of his jacket. They stopped at a door with signage that read, EMERGING TECHNOLOGY LAB in bright red letters.

"Thanks, Albert, we're fine from here," Melendez said as he gestured for Gantry to step in.

The inner sanctum, Gantry said to himself as the door closed behind them.

The lab was a brightly lit, two-story room with a glass-enclosed server farm at one end and a huge video wall at the other. Sectioned-off glass offices around the sides on both levels were identified with signage: VIRTUAL CRIME SCENE TECHNOLOGY, PREDICTIVE/INFERENTIAL ANALYTICS, FORENSIC DNA TECHNOLOGIES, and the like. In the center was an open bullpen-type space, "the collaboration center," as Melendez called it.

He introduced Gantry to the chief of Photo Forensics.

"Hank, this is Gantry Elliot. Hank, I know you haven't had much time, but have you come up with anything?"

"I narrowed it down to the seventy-two-hour period you gave me, but started earlier this month to document the routine. It's always the same. The postal service comes first to the room, where this kid takes their plastic trays filled with mail, and after that the private services like UPS and FedEx."

Hank pointed at the monitor.

"See, here is the door where all the mail is received. In the background is the room where it's all sorted. You can see the workers handling the mail. The building is twenty-five stories, and that means a lot of daily incoming and outgoing. Most of the deliveries are from the various mail services, but occasionally there's an individual dropping something off. But it doesn't happen often."

Hank abruptly stopped the footage with a roll of his mouse. "Here, look at this guy—look at the way he walks, and how he's dressed. See him?"

Gantry and Melendez leaned in closer. They could see a group of about eight people apparently walking to the elevators. One man extracted himself from the crowd and quickly walked over to the mailroom, dropped the package on the counter and walked away without hesitation.

"The man with the Irish walking hat and sunglasses," Hank said. "He's in several sets of frames. He's appeared three times over that time period, always wearing the same chesterfield-collared, camel hair coat along with that Sherlock Holmes-style hat. But see? Always wearing gloves. They look like expensive racing gloves, maybe English, dark leather with a cinch strap to keep them tight. So no fingerprints."

"Yeah," Melendez said, "and probably poor facial recognition. Can you do anything with it? It's our only lead right now."

"It'll take a few hours, maybe the rest of the day. We'll have to deconstruct and then reconstruct this and then match it against our data universe. I will also use the new global Internet photo-search capability that we're testing, and we'll see what surfaces."

"Fine. Call me when you get it," Melendez said. "Good work. Thanks. Gantry, it's getting close to quitting time. Why don't you and

I go to a little place down the road that's quiet? We can grab a bite to eat and talk more about this."

As they left the building, Melendez made some mental notes. The first step would be to get the Clue Management System set up so that his team and Scotland Yard could collaborate with one common data source. The U.S. Combined DNA Index System was set up to share with the UK police. Four of the deaths had happened in Europe: Hendrix, Jones, and Ham all died in or near London; Morrison died in Paris. The others died in the States.

"Let's take my car," Melendez said, "I'll drop you back here later."

The two men climbed into Melendez's old Crown Victoria, drove down Roan Street and took a hard right on Bauer. A few miles down the road Gantry spied a large body of water and stared out the passenger window at the blue expanse.

Melendez said, "Lunga Lake."

"Huh?"

"Lunga Lake. I see you are admiring our local fishing hole."

"Oh, yes, I miss living near lakes. Didn't know there was a body of water that big here on the base."

"Oh yeah. Great fishing. Do you fish?"

"Yeah, but I haven't done much lately," he answered in a wistful tone.

"Well, maybe one of these days when you're up here for a weekend, I'll take you out. Would you like that?"

"Yes, I would like that very much. What kind of fishing?"

"Largemouth bass, black crappie, bluegill, red-ear sunfish. Where are you from, anyway, I mean originally?"

"Irving, Texas. We had plenty of good fishing around there. Later I moved to Austin and UT, and then to San Francisco with Alex in the early days, and finally Manhattan."

"Interesting route. When's the last time you were home?" asked Melendez.

Gantry didn't answer right away. He wasn't sure he wanted to get into a personal conversation, one that would likely just bring up unpleasant memories. Then again, if he was going to work with

Melendez, it was inevitable, especially if he wanted to work closely.

"To be honest, it's been a long time. The last time I was there was when I met my ex-wife, Jodi. Actually, then we were just dating. I was about to graduate, and I'd just met Alex, as well. He offered me a job at the magazine, which was in San Francisco then. Jodi didn't like the idea of moving. Her family was in Austin, but she followed me there anyway."

"So, what happened? You got married...but now you're not?"

The car was quiet. The big Victorias were equipped with police pursuit engines, but the interiors were well upholstered and heavily padded. Gantry kept his silence.

"I'm sorry, guess I'm getting too personal," Melendez said. "You can see I don't have many people around me close to my age in this place anymore. All my former colleagues are either retired or making money as security consultants."

"No, no—that's alright," Gantry answered. The image of Jodi from the photo in the apartment faded as he snapped back to the present. He answered elliptically. "It's the same way at my office. The majority of the staff is under thirty."

He continued, "Things worked pretty well in San Francisco. I got my start. Jodi got a job in the forensics department at the San Francisco PD, and it all went well until Alex told us one day that we were all moving to New York. By then her job was more complicated. She was experimenting with more biotech-type work, and couldn't leave the Bay area.

"Biotech and forensics? My kind of woman," Melendez said as he smiled.

"We tried having a long-distance marriage. Eventually my involvement with the magazine and my constant traveling put a real crimp in our relationship, and we divorced. I didn't want it, but I knew it was best for her, and I just couldn't stop working. I still love it. But I guess you know what that's like."

"Yeah, I get that. We're a lot alike. But, I've never been divorced. Been married for forty-two years to the same woman, if you can believe that," Melendez said proudly.

"I'm impressed. Really, I am. You must love her very much."

"I do."

Gantry scanned the horizon as they approached a set of one-story buildings: a small gas station, a convenience store, and a farmers' supply on one side, on the other, a down-at-heel pharmacy and a bar—with a hitching post. Next to that was a post office, and next a walk-up burger joint with a dead neon sign on a rusted steel pole that read: The Busy B.

"I thought you might like this place. I stop by here on occasion," Melendez said with a grin.

"It's the closest thing to a cowboy bar around here. Actually, it's not a cowboy bar as much as it is a rancher bar, as in thoroughbred-breeding ranchers. It's quiet, but the food is decent, and we can talk. It's also reasonable—as you probably already guessed."

The men got out and walked into the cool, dim barroom.

"Hey, Raphael, how're you doin?" the bartender said to the familiar customer.

Clear with a Chance of Rain was the name of the bar, taken from the name of the owner's prized thoroughbred. A large picture of the magnificent animal was framed in gold above the bar. The room was more ornate and elegant than it deserved to be, given its location, but it did good business between the Marine officers and the FBI agents just ten miles up the road.

They took a booth in the back.

"Jacob, two Bushmills. No ice. Doubles," Melendez called out. On nearly every wall of the bar were mementos, pictures and pieces of tack. Gantry found it very comfortable.

When the two drinks arrived, Melendez told the bartender to run two tabs. Then he toasted Gantry and they got down to business.

"Okay. This is where the rubber meets the road," Melendez said. "Here's the deal. With my situation at the Bureau, I only have limited time to work on any case, and you see the kids that work with me? Wicked smart, but they don't have what you have up here," he said, pointing to his head.

"Does that mean you're taking the case?"

"Maybe, depending on what we find on the video. I can work on one cold case at a time, provided I handle my three classes of rookies each week. That's easy enough, and I can have pretty much free rein of the facilities and some personnel. However, I can't do everything. And we'll have jurisdictional issues. We may have to team with London and Paris."

Melendez didn't reveal everything that he was thinking. And he needed to ID the deliveryman before he made his next move. If the identity panned out, he'd be all in.

Melendez leaned in.

"Ever since you called me about this, I have been remembering some of the stories I'd heard agents talking about when I first joined the Bureau. They revealed that when some famous rock stars died in Europe, the investigation and autopsies were pretty suspect, and cases were closed quickly. I always had a suspicion that it was the same in the U.S., but had no reason to look into it since it wasn't relevant to my job. I had completely forgotten about all that until you called last week."

"Do you remember which musicians?" Gantry asked.

"No," replied Melendez. "I think I already told you last week, just based on my instincts, even though this is a long shot, we could be dealing with someone who isn't just flat-out crazy, but also very smart. We'll see what Hank uncovers. That will be key, okay? But that envelope and the prescription you brought in today for Peter Ham doesn't compute."

"How do you mean?" Gantry queried.

"Ham taking Antabuse, and the officials finding all that alcohol in his system, would be like finding a person who had a severe peanut allergy dead with a stomach full of peanut butter and jelly sandwiches. In my business, that would look like a 'staged' death scene.

"Staged?"

"It means it was made to look like a suicide hanging, but it wasn't. The clue you got infers that the death scene could not have happened as was officially reported. I am sure Scotland Yard would conclude the same thing. Your ex-wife Jodi probably would as well.

"What I'm saying is, based on that one hypothesis, we should at least have a conversation with Scotland Yard. If we can identify this guy in the Irish walking hat, and if we can find him, then we can see what is going on. He might just be a messenger. That one clue that he wanted you to have before you came here is very telling. He knew what we would conclude," Melendez added.

"Most serial killers have strong primal emotions like jealousy, anger, and the desire for revenge."

"Okay, that makes sense," Gantry said. "What I don't understand is why all this is just now surfacing, after forty years."

"I'm not sure either," Melendez admitted. "However, I do know we can just about rule out a woman—there are not many female serial killers. For a host of reasons, they usually don't fit the profile. It's similar to the fact that most women don't commit suicide by shooting themselves. It's too messy, too violent. They prefer other methods, like poison, that kind of thing. Men, on the other hand, will do just about anything if they're truly motivated. Whatever is quickest.

In any case, I'm going to put you up in town tonight at the Wingate. It's only a three-star, but my expense account isn't what it used to be. Tomorrow morning, we get started, provided Hank has something concrete."

Gantry grinned, raised his glass, and the two men clinked them together without a toast and finished them simultaneously.

"Thank you, Raphael."

The following morning Gantry rolled out of the rock-hard hotel bed with a shot of adrenalin. He couldn't wait to see if Hank had identified the messenger, and he was eager to start working with Raphael.

He made coffee before jumping into the shower. Drying off, he heard the phone ring.

"Ready to go?"

"Almost," Gantry said, stretching the truth considerably. "Just gotta get my boots on."

Gantry smiled when he slid into the Crown Victoria and saw Melendez's coffee cup in the cup holder. He put his own cup in his holder. As the long black four-door loped through the countryside, Gantry took a swallow of his coffee and asked Melendez, "Can you tell me more about serial killers? If this guy could be the killer…he knows where I live and what I'm doing," he said, his voice slightly quivering.

Melendez quickly pulled over onto the shoulder and stopped the car.

"Give me your cell phone," he said.

"What?"

"Your cell, man. If this guy knew you were coming here, it might be bugged."

"No, I don't think so. It rarely comes out of my pocket."

"Give me your phone."

Gantry handed Melendez the phone. Mendez promptly pulled the back off, slipped out the battery and scanned the interior.

"Good, nothing in there. Might be a bug in your apartment, though," he said, pulling back onto the highway. Gantry fumbled his phone back together.

"So…tell me about serial killers."

"The FBI defines a serial killer a little differently than other law enforcement. We say that a series of two or more murders, committed as separate events, usually, but not always by one offender acting alone, constitutes a serial killing. Some of the killings involve sexual contact, but for us, we think the motives are usually, like I said before, anger, rage, and desire for revenge. There could be a strong narcissistic component.

"The thing that stands out in this case is that the victims have something fundamentally in common—age and rock and roll. But there are probably a number of things we haven't considered yet. That's where you'll come in. You're the source for the private, little-known stuff."

"Is serial killing the same as mass murder?"

"No. However, cases of extended bouts of sequential killings over periods of months, with no apparent cooling-off period, have caused some in the Bureau to suggest that there might be a hybrid category, a spree-serial killer." Gantry silently stared at him.

Melendez continued, "Serial killers share certain characteristics generally, like having average or below-average IQs, even though they are perceived as smart and sometimes actually are. They have trouble holding jobs. They often seem normal, with families. They were often abused as children, physically or emotionally. Sometimes there are odd similarities, like bed wetting, fascination with fire, that kind of thing."

Gantry was riveted. He soaked it all up like a sponge.

The car began to slow and turn into the now familiar security gate. In a matter of minutes, they would know whether Hank had been able to identify the messenger—or maybe even the killer.

Alex Jaeger's Apartment, New York City

Alex was getting antsy. Perhaps it was the pounding headache from last night's pre-wedding dinner party.

"It's only been three days since Gantry called the FBI. You are obsessed with this." Daniel told him. The two men were having coffee, and Daniel was making his traditional omelet. Both had horrific hangovers. Alex requested hash browns, the greasier the better.

"I told him to touch base every day," Alex said, pacing.

"Alex, I know you want to get this story, but personally, I think you're letting the money side of this cloud your judgment," Daniel implored.

"Christ, you're already incredibly wealthy. How much more do you want?"

Alex sat on the purple chair. The sunlight was filtering down through a cloudy sky. He poured four Motrin out of the bottle, grabbed his coffee, and downed them all in one swallow.

"Christ, my head aches. Are we arguing already?"

Silence.

"I know. It's not really about the money, though. You know as well as I do that's just a way to keep score. But it got me thinking about starting another magazine, one for boomers only," Alex said. "You mean like AARP?"

"Shit, no! Something that nobody else has thought of. Something that really tweaks their interest, their common interest. I just keep seeing that number: eighty million people. *Stone* is one-point-three, give or take. If you multiply eighty mil by just one-quarter of one percent in subscriptions, that's two hundred thousand! That's what drives the ad revenues."

"Alex, you're way over your skis on this. Just slow all this down before it gets out and damages your reputation. That demographic has moved on. I know it and you know it. Just keep rotating your focus to Millennials not to a declining segment. If you love me, you'll stop this nonsense and just focus on our new life together."

Alex nodded as he let Daniel's personal and rational concern for him sink in.

When the phone rang, Alex said, "Maybe that's him." Daniel grabbed it before Alex could react.

"Hello, Daniel Culain," He answered abruptly.

"Daniel, it's Gantry Elliot, can I speak to Alex?"

"Gantry, he can't talk to you right now...Listen, *we* have spent just about enough time on your *hallucinations*. *We* have a business to run, not take sentimental trips to a bygone age." Daniel condescendingly explained.

Alex grabbed the phone before Daniel could hang up and without explanation. "Gantry, it's about time. Whatcha got?"

"Jesus, what's that all about?"

Alex didn't answer.

"Are you sitting down?" Gantry slyly asked.

Alex answered yes as he paced in a circle.

"Raphael and I just left the FBI computer lab."

"And?"

"They were able to identify the messenger with facial recognition software."

"Is he the killer?"

"Don't know yet. Raphael doesn't seem to think it's likely. I'm going to stay here for a couple more days. There's a ton of work to do now."

"Fine. You do that. Keep working. Who is the guy?"

"That's a little less clear at this point. We expect to find out more this morning."

"That's great. I can't wait. I just keep thinking of all those boomers—" he caught himself.

"What boomers? What are you talking about?" But Gantry instinctively knew even before he'd finished his question. *I know him. It's all about the money.*

Silence.

Daniel was staring daggers at him, obviously sensing that Gantry was drawing Alex in more and more.

"Alex, are you there?"

"Yeah, buddy. I'm here."

"What are you cooking up?"

"Nothing. You're doing a great job."

"Alex, I know you. You're planning something."

"Well, it can't hurt to be a little creative with all this."

"What do you mean, 'creative'?"

"I'm not going to go into it over the phone, Gantry," Alex snapped. "Just do your fucking job. I gave you the time you needed, the money, the opportunity. Now do something with it. Find this guy. Let's get this story."

"Oh, I'm going to get the story. You can take that to the bank — just like you always do," Gantry said. "But this is bigger than your turning a story into revenue."

Gantry was standing outside the BAU building, pacing with his cell phone, fighting his irritation and trying to be calm. He'd been excited with the discovery of the mystery messenger, and now he was really agitated. He took a deep breath.

"Alex, think about it this way. You gave me a job forty-six years ago. I was a nobody with a passion for rock and roll. You were just starting, and you were creating this incredible new magazine, a unique approach to journalism and music—"

"Yes, but—"

"Alex, don't interrupt. Give me a chance."

"Okay."

"I'm not belittling what you did back then, but you did it with the help of a lot of other people. From that beginning, and when I joined you with the same dream, you built an empire, an enormous empire. And you know what?"

"What?"

"You literally built it on the backs of these artists, these musicians, these singers and songwriters. If it hadn't been for their incredible talent, neither of us would have had the chance to live this dream. Those were the days you've forgotten—when you had a little bit of money and a whole lot of chutzpah. Same goes for me."

Gantry felt calm now, almost serene.

"I don't want to get all misty-eyed about it, but I know you're going to try to turn this into some gaudy sideshow, a TV movie or something. Just try to remember how we were in 1969, how people were creating new music forms, experimenting—and fearless. We were all in it together, you, me, *them*."

He paused to catch his breath.

"The reason we've had this great life, and this opportunity, is because *they* existed. We didn't create the music, *they* did. All we did was write about it after the fact."

After a long pause, Alex said slowly, "Well, you have a point, a good one, I guess. I never thought of it that way. But it's not like they didn't make a boatload of money, too."

"That's true. But I'm still going to dig as deep as I can," Gantry said. "To me, it's like their ghosts are reaching out from the graves to us, pleading for justice. I think these people were murdered. I know you want to know why as much as I do."

Gantry could hear Alex slurping his coffee.

"I'm just yankin' your chain, Gantry. I'm a little hung-over. You missed a hell of a party, but listen. Believe it or not, I do get it. We do owe them, but that's no reason why we can't also make the magazine bigger and better."

Gantry said, "Remember another thing about those days: we were groundbreakers. This is groundbreaking. This is one of the biggest fucking stories in the world right now, as far as I'm concerned."

Alex took a deep breath and glanced peevishly at Daniel, "You're right…keep me posted."

Alex walked out of the room without talking to Daniel.

FBI HQ, Quantico, VA

"Commonalities," Melendez said, almost to himself.

Gantry was seated across from Melendez, who was behind his desk reviewing the security file Hank had given him. Attached to the manila file with two paper clips were a black-and-white photo of the messenger dropping a package on the mail counter, and a shot Hank had pulled off the Web. It was a forty-year-old picture of a man identified as Angus Hislop, a tax accountant at Coopers & Lybrand's London office. That was the only reference to date, nothing on him since. Hank had even managed to pull up an ancient bio on the man.

"A very unlikely suspect," Melendez said. Standing behind him, Hank frowned but said nothing.

He slid the file across to Gantry.

"I don't get it, Hank. We have an old picture of a tax accountant, and nothing else since?"

"Can't find a thing. But we are just starting,"

"We'll find more," Melendez assured Gantry—and himself.

"How could someone like that be so stupid as to think he wouldn't be recognized—especially with that hat?" Gantry asked.

"He isn't stupid. Remember, most of these guys want to be caught, that's part of the profile. But I'm far from convinced that he is a killer. Maybe he just wants to guide us with these breadcrumbs."

He stood up.

"Let's go into the conference room and use the whiteboard."

Gantry followed Melendez to a large conference room with an enormous whiteboard at the head of it. Melendez told Gantry to take a seat in any of the twenty or so chairs, as he picked a black marker out of the tray.

"This is going to be what I call 'Commonalities 101.' I teach it early in the first part of my classes. If we assume—for now—that this fellow is a killer, and we further assume he is responsible for at least the seven deaths you've brought me, we first need to start with what all the deceased have in common."

As he spoke, he drew a matrix on the whiteboard with the names of the rock stars along the vertical and topics along the horizontal.

"This is where you come in, Gantry. You've interviewed them, broken bread with them, and I'm sure shared more than a little whiskey and wine? Here." He handed Gantry the marker. "Start writing."

"Gladly. Let's see. How about the most obvious first?" He said, writing *friends, enemies, recordings, concerts, acquaintances, neighbors* in a long vertical column.

He stopped to think.

"You've got a long way to go, my friend. Keep thinking. How about bankers, roadies, lovers, ex-lovers ..."

"Oh, great one. Shoulda thought of that one first."

"...managers, PR and marketing agents, club owners, studio engineers, drug dealers."

By the time Gantry had run out of ideas, there wasn't much white space in the matrix.

"Good start." Melendez said. "Now, we need to build a cross tabulation."

"What's —" Gantry interjected.

Melendez continued, "It's a way to cross-reference all of this information. Keep going. You have all afternoon. When you're done, I'll have one of the analysts take a picture of the board and then load the information into VICAP. From there we'll cross-reference all the info, and everything else we can find from our data sources, and try to boil the commonalities down to actual connections that we can use. We also have access to all the Library of Congress digital files for recordings, books, articles, posters and such, if we need it. Tomorrow we'll reach out to Scotland Yard. Lots of work to do."

"Will we need to go to London?"

"First things first."

As excited as Gantry was, his sleep that night was understandably fitful. He'd had his confrontation with Alex, and he was glad that was over. He really didn't like the idea that Daniel was trying to insert himself into this, but that was Alex's problem. For now, his mind was whirling with ideas, cross references, commonalities, links…He couldn't sleep at all.

Sitting up in the queen-size bed with its grotesque quilted cover, he wanted three things: a joint, a glass of Chianti, and some music. He couldn't remember seeing a liquor store or even a grocery store on the way back to the hotel. Melendez had dropped him off at ten o'clock. It had been one hell of a long day and the next one would start at seven sharp.

Then in the dimness he spotted something he'd overlooked in his hurry to get into bed: a small college student refrigerator, nearly hidden behind a large chair. He swung his legs out of bed, walked over and opened it to find it nicely stocked with airplane bottles of vodka and cheap chardonnay—and a Snickers bar.

Pouring both of the bottles of wine into a water glass, he returned to bed, propped himself up on a pillow and took a taste. Not terrible.

As long as his mind wasn't going to let him stop thinking, he wouldn't fight it. For some reason, Janis popped into his mind again, and he started thinking about the time they'd spent together, especially when she came to Austin. Janis had been just twenty-three that year. No one would ever have guessed how incredibly famous she would become, and how quickly.

She wasn't even pretty, not really. Wiry dark hair, a just-a-little-too-big nose, and smallish breasts. A country girl. But those eyes—deep, dark, chocolate brown, and she just exuded sex from every pore. Thing is, she was a perfect example of what he'd reminded Alex about—she was brilliant in herself. Nothing else mattered.

He took another swallow of the cheap wine and remembered something that Janis had said to him one night. "Whatever the limitations of a hippie rock star, it's better than being a provincial matron or a lonely weirdo."

Janis had metamorphosed from the ugly duckling of Port Arthur to the peacock of Haight-Ashbury, but she'd always been beautiful to him.

A beauty born of energy, a deep soul, and her invented conceit. Later, when she became famous and Gantry had only been with *Rolling Stone* for about two years, he realized that she'd single-handedly changed society's ideas about strength and independence for women all over the world. The fast-evolving culture of liberation and rebellion forever changed the equation between men and women. She definitely had a part in it. Her part. Her way.

By the time he'd finished the wine, Gantry finally felt tired. He could feel himself slipping, and he was glad. A quick glance at the clock told him he'd be getting about four hours of sleep. Unfortunately, even with the wine, he tossed and turned. Thoughts of the FBI, mingled with memories of the dead played out in vivid detail all night...

In his dream, Gantry was reliving the meeting between himself and Al Wilson when Canned Heat was in town for a performance at the Fillmore West in July of 1969. The Everly Brothers split the bill. He remembered Wilson walking through the dingy coffee shop near Union Square the morning of the concert, and seeing distress in Wilson's face. Wilson told him that there had been tension within the group and that Mike Bloomfield was filling in on guitar.

Gantry could almost taste the lukewarm, bitter coffee in his reverie. How unlikely Wilson had seemed as leader and front man for a top band with his Coke-bottle glasses and baby-blue-striped mock turtleneck that looked borrowed from the Beach Boys. Wilson definitely wasn't the Haight-Ashbury type. But what a student of the blues. He knew the styles of all the old Delta and Chicago blues masters and could imitate them perfectly.

Half-dreaming, Gantry reached for the water glass beside the bed. He saw Wilson as clearly as if he was standing next to him, when he asked, "What was your proudest moment?"

Expecting to hear, "The Grammys" or something about the group's success, he was surprised when Wilson sat erect and proclaimed, "When John Lee Hooker said I was the best harmonica player ever. Not bad for a nerdy white boy from Boston."

The words "Muir Woods" popped into his head, and he remembered that, as he was saying goodbye, Wilson asked him how far out of town Muir Woods was. He thought the giant redwoods were the most magnificent trees in the world, and said he couldn't come this far and not see them firsthand. Gantry never realized how touched Wilson was by their majesty until he heard that his family had posthumously dedicated a redwood grove in his memory...

Snap!

It was time to go to work.

The morning greetings were quick and perfunctory. Melendez had apparently put his happy face away, and Gantry could see he was all business—a good sign as far as he was concerned. He was part of the team now, and he felt the surge of energy he guessed these agents felt each time they started a challenging new case. The hunt was on. Gantry could sense it in Melendez's intensity and in the sharp orders he gave those around him.

"Are you ready?" Melendez asked, picking up an armful of files from his desk. "Follow me. It's a bit of a hike."

"Absolutely."

"We're going to the boardroom. It's quiet, and it's a great place to display commonalities for quick visual comparisons."

Melendez had another agenda, though. He needed Gantry, but he also had to hide him to a certain extent, and keep him low profile out of view of his boss, Mayflower. All he needed was word to get out to his boss that he had a reporter in the FBI's Emerging Tech Lab. That would not go over well.

Gantry had to kick it up a gear to keep up as the two men hustled down the long gray hallway, barely lit with small recessed lights casting down halos of yellow every thirty feet.

As they came to an intersection of four hallways, Melendez steered right and then turned right again. The boardroom was twenty by thirty feet and contained a long Steelcase-type conference table with ten high-back chairs, a cabinet at one end, no windows, no pictures, walls covered with whiteboards running the length of the room on both sides, and one occupant. Someone had transferred all of Gantry's work from the day before onto one of the boards in neat handwriting.

"This used to be our war room, before we built the Emerging Tech Lab facilities. If these walls could talk! I still like to use it from time to time," Melendez said, thinking to himself that it was also as far away from the lab as he could get them. Gesturing to the agent sitting at the conference table, he said, "Gantry, this is Agent Tanner. Tanner, Gantry Elliot."

Tanner nodded. He was young, neatly dressed, and he exuded confidence. He had a cup of coffee and a laptop in front of him. In the middle of the table were a stack of white legal pads and a cluster of ballpoint pens.

Introductions performed, Melendez told Gantry to pick a seat, tablet, and pen.

"As you can see, one of my students transcribed everything you came up with yesterday. But we also used it to prompt a much larger commonalities search. Now the real work begins."

Melendez pulled a small remote out of his pocket and aimed it at the far end of the room. A large movie screen descended slowly out of the ceiling, and simultaneously a projector descended from the back of the room. The lights dimmed.

"Tanner was working most of the night on your entries and all the new ones too. He is an analyst. He rarely leaves the campus except to sleep and feed his goldfish. His assignment last night was to come up with as many commonalities his advanced search applications could assemble, and to add that to your notes."

Tanner smiled.

Melendez clicked the remote again, and a graphic chart appeared. On the screen, a multicolored graphical display, detailed the total number of common hits for each of the dead stars in question, and highlighted their many cross connections in separate cells. The visual was so complex that Gantry was having trouble taking it in.

"We're just getting started," Melendez said, pulling a small laser pointer from his jacket pocket. The red beam cast a precise red dot on the screen.

"Note the categories here," Melendez said. "We have engineers, roadies, friends, managers, producers, and even drug dealers accounted for, for each of the six stars. Now, look carefully here." Melendez used the red dot to focus on another section. We even have performances listed."

"Amazing. Seriously," Gantry responded.

Tanner smiled.

"We've even isolated those performances down to formal and informal, as best we could," Melendez said.

"You'll note here next to 'Hendrix/informal/performance' there is the word 'bars,' then if I double-click on that, another tab comes out with a complete listing of all the bars he performed in, or at least the ones we know about. Switching over to this side, you can see we've even listed doctors, psychiatrists—even a podiatrist for one of them."

"You couldn't have done this with just my whiteboard notes," Gantry said. "There must be hundreds of connections here, all interlaced and in hierarchies."

"Gantry, we are in the testing stages of an advanced-search capability that allows us to access most of the digital databases in the world, a full array of data, photographs, recorded music, contracts, pre-HIPPAA medical records, even local community papers. There is nothing like it in general use anywhere," Melendez said.

"On top of that, we are using our own unique version of the Apache Hadoop platform, which allows us to crunch massive amounts of data. But the real secret sauce is the commonalities application that Tanner developed. It allows us to interpret that diverse information so people like you and me can make sense of it."

Tanner smiled.

"That said, this commonality cross tabulation is still in its infancy. Tanner still has a lot of work to do, and you're going to have to help him, because you are the key to the history of all this. You have the insider facts we cannot possibly know, even with all this sophisticated software. The technology is very smart, but it cannot 'think' without detailed input. The missing link obviously is your brain, your memory and your insight—those small details that only you could know. They are very, very important, and may hold the key inferences for us.

"So," he continued. "We'll need to beef all this up and then share it with our friends in Europe. London first."

Tanner opened his laptop. "Go, boss," he said.

"Okay, Tanner, let's start with engineers."

Tanner tapped the touch pad and instantly a pointer raced to several names which, when clicked on again, popped up names: Keith Grant, Glyn Johns, Jimmy Miller, Eddie Kramer, Owsley Stanley.

"Wow. Now that is really amazing," Gantry said, thinking, *Eddie Kramer. What a coincidence.*

"Tanner, double-click on 'friends' and then bring that up alongside 'drug dealers.' I want to see a quick match here."

A 3-D graphic that looked like a molecule with hard edges popped up in bright red, and then another came up beside it. Between the two were thin white lines interlacing the name Jean de Breteuil—a name Gantry remembered—with three of the six stars. But on the other side of the matrix was a long vertical list of what seemed to Gantry to be a random list of rock and roll names. Some of those names were not so famous, but Gantry recognized them all, and saw the little white lines immediately race from de Breteuil to ten of them as well.

Melendez loved these charts, and he loved what they could do. The next stages, which he hadn't yet discussed with Gantry, would involve evidence from the cold-case boxes yet to be retrieved: DNA analysis, hair, fingerprints—the list was long, but it all began here, simple, logical, and very visual. Even a schoolboy could see immediate patterns at a glance.

The room was silent for a moment as Gantry made notes. The depth of connections was unbelievable—*but,* he thought, *there are still missing pieces.*

"You look disappointed," Melendez said, as if reading Gantry's thoughts.

"No, absolutely not. I'm impressed, but there are a few missing names, connections.

"Tanner, can you double-click on 'friends' again," Gantry said.

"Sure."

"Do you know who Jean de Breteuil is?" Gantry wanted to know how much Melendez understood about the connections his analyst had come up with.

"No. In fact, I don't know who half these people are. That's your job. Who is he?"

"I heard he was some kind of minor royalty who hung around backstage at Stones and Hendrix concerts, always dressed to the nines. The rumor always was that he was *the* drug supplier to European rock stars."

"Do you know which ones, specifically?" Melendez asked.

"I think he was tied to the Stones and Hendrix for sure, maybe Joplin, too. And I heard through the grapevine that he hung out with Pamela Courson as well."

"Who?"

"Morrison's girlfriend, Pamela Courson."

"Double-click on 'producers,'" Melendez said to Tanner.

More options flooded the screen.

Gantry was impressed, but as he got into the details, he could see where there were lots of gaps, missing names, missing commonalities. He felt good knowing his expertise was going to be vital to piecing this puzzle together, and it was beginning to make sense to ask Alex for help as well.

"I'm going to leave you here for a while, Gantry. Tanner and I have other work to do. What you need to do is use this laptop," he said while walking over to Tanner, picking up the Dell and putting it back down in front of Gantry, "and use it like this." He used the touchpad to highlight and double-click on terms and names.

"You can double-click on any area to bring up deeper information, but you can't delete anything, so don't worry about that. Double-clicks take you to the second and third levels, and a right-click brings out the sidebars. Those will cross-reference with these white lines to any other part in the graphic where there is a connection. Simple. Got it?"

"Uh, yeah. Got it. So, I search and play with this, and you want me to fill in any gaps in my notes?"

"Precisely," Melendez said. "See there, Tanner, you're gonna lose your job. Gantry's got it covered."

Tanner smiled. Gantry may have been a writer, journalist, and rock trivia expert, but Tanner was the mastermind of analysis for the Clue Management Database, and Melendez was the veteran investigator. A good team, at least to start.

As the three men rose from their chairs, Melendez said, "By the way, when you right-click and those sidebars come up, you'll get horizontal info stacked front to back, accordion style, for peripherals on each topic or person; another Tanner idea. The front ones are the most recent."

"Raphael, can I get some coffee? And where is the bathroom? This is going to take a while," Gantry said, unzipping his now bulging tan valise and reaching into the folders inside.

"Bathroom's down the hall to your right. It's unisex, so knock. Coffee's coming right up. Two pots okay?"

"Great."

Gantry looked back at the screen and double-clicked on Les Perrin. Perrin had been hired by Hendrix's management just two weeks before Hendrix died. He also noted the Stones and possible Apple connections. Then he right-clicked on a subhead in a red box titled OBLIQUE COMMONALITIES, and out popped a horizontal bar that included pharmacies, law firms, banks and record rights.

Melendez and Tanner made their way back to the Emerging Tech Lab, stopping first in a small room with a large video conferencing screen and audio set up.

"Gantry's really going to help us with this," Melendez said. "His memory is phenomenal. Hell, Tanner, he's got records a lot older than you are. You probably don't even know what most of those names stand for or what they did. Maybe after all this is done, you'll have a new appreciation for the classics."

Tanner just smiled. He was an under-the-radar Beatles fan, but he didn't mention it.

"I'm going to conference London now. I want you to get on this again and come up with a more completed matrix. You have forty-eight hours. By that time Gantry should have pretty much filled out the existing chart and you can integrate it all, including what we get from London."

"Boss, why the rush? This stuff goes back more than forty-five years."

"A lot of moving parts have to come together very quickly, and Gantry's worried about this messenger knowing his address and possibly planting a bug on him."

Melendez also was looking at a personal deadline: mandatory retirement. In six months he would only be able to teach, and even that would have to be on a volunteer basis.

"I'm going to dial up the conference bridge and see if I can't get a hold of an old friend."

"Who's that?"

"Robert Bruce. He works for Scotland Yard. We've stay in touch usually once or twice a year. He's a senior agent and can get the ball rolling. By the time we have all the commonalities done on our side and the CODIS system is set up to share with Scotland Yard, he'll make sure we all get on the same page.

"Oh, before I forget, get Lancy up to New York to sweep Gantry's place for bugs. Leave whatever you find. I don't want anyone knowing we know they're listening. Could come in very, very handy."

CODIS is the acronym for Combined DNA Index System. Melendez, after talking with Robert Bruce, would then apply his Virtual Crime Scene technology in the lab to speed up the preliminary assessments. VCS technology wasn't in widespread use yet, but would be a huge help in instantly recreating and analyzing each crime scene. The first thing they needed to do was get hold of every crime scene box from each of the seven deaths, starting in London.

Melendez dialed into the conference bridge and turned on the eighty-two-inch Samsung video monitor. He was a few minutes early, but wanted to make sure there were no reception issues and that the collaboration software was operative.

He plugged his thumb drive containing the clues into a small PC next to the speaker box and smiled to himself. How odd, he thought, that after all the technological advances, state-of-the-art applications, advanced testing equipment, and sophisticated chemical analysis, the most important parts of any crime scene were labeled and placed in a cardboard box and put on a shelf. But Melendez knew from experience that there was almost always something in those old boxes that could help unlock the true story of a murder.

While he was waiting, he mentally cataloged the scenes. The greater London area was where Jones, Hendrix, and Ham died. Morrison's death meant contacting the FBI office in Paris and then French Police Nationale. Wilson and Joplin died in L.A., and McKernan died in San Francisco. It could ultimately be a cross-country, cross-continent investigation, a complex analysis of hundreds of commonalities.

Gantry was vitally important, but he'd need to be kept on a short leash. He was at heart a reporter, and naturally, he wanted to get his story. Melendez had to make sure his superiors were not fully aware of how deeply this "side job" was going to go. He had to keep it safely under wraps until they had built a strong case and had a bead on a killer. Then he could unveil it.

He remembered the conversation he'd had with Gantry, when Gantry mentioned that his ex-wife was with forensics in San Francisco. She might come in handy for crime scene information on McKernan; like Gantry, she would have firsthand knowledge about the city's rock culture at the time.

Eventually though, he and Bruce would need to put together a joint Homicide Evidence Assessment Team, which would consist of a physical evidence analyst, a toxicology and autopsy specialist, and maybe a corporate financial analyst to look into whatever insurance policies had been in force at the time of the deaths.

Gantry chewed on the end of his ballpoint pen. He'd made a list of the people, and pertinent information about them, that were missing from the matrix. Tanner had missed a considerable amount of detail; still, how could he know the thousand and one details one could only know if they'd been there?

As he compiled more commonalities, he kept coming back to Jean de Breteuil, the possible drug-dealer friend, Les Perrin at both the Hendrix and Jones death scenes, and record company song rights, contract, and management issues—all of them hot buttons. The corporate issues of the stars kept haunting him as he thought about a story he'd written back in 1974 about the artists and their arguments with record company management.

It all started with Peter Ham's death and the subsequent media reports. Gantry had investigated, and then wrote the article, but nothing further came of it. He dug through his valise and pulled out the article and a copy of the newspaper report of Ham's death... Reported as a suicide, he left no note, and there was little investigation beyond a summary autopsy. Rumor was that Ham was extremely distressed about management issues.

He even remembered the journalist's name, Larry Williams. Gantry wondered if he was still around.

Robert Bruce's face popped up on the monitor. It was 10:00 a.m. in Quantico and 3:00 p.m. in London. Melendez tested the Polycom. "Robert can you hear me clearly?"

Bruce appeared to be speaking, but no sound came from the speakers. Melendez pointed to his ear. Bruce nodded.

"So sorry, had it on mute, my friend," Bruce said.

Bruce was sitting at a desk next to a window. Behind him was a large architectural rendering of the new Police building. Melendez had been to Scotland Yard several times, once during a vacation with his wife, and twice on investigations, one of them a cold case in 2001. The new building was quite stunning; designed by the same architectural firm that created the new Google headquarters in King's Cross.

Robert Bruce was sixty-five, silver haired with a tinge of brown, and always sporting a healthy glow. He was known as a bit of a rogue. He'd been with the London Metropolitan Police for more than thirty years, most recently as head of the Specialist Crime Unit. He and

Melendez had become friends while working on the Lennon murder case together and had stayed in contact ever since.

"Good morning, Raphael."

"Good afternoon, Robert."

"How do I look?" Melendez said, meaning the video quality.

"You look like you've gained a few, mate."

"Naw, it's just this suit jacket bunching up."

Both men laughed.

"What brings you to London, my friend?'

"Cold case, what else?"

"Ah, of course. How is Lucia, by the way?"

"She's good. Arthritis is bad, but she never lets on. You'd never know it. She still tries to keep up with her gardening and the grandkids. And you? Still single?"

"Gawd, yes, mate. Are you kidding?"

They laughed again, then got down to business.

"Right, then. What have you got for me, mate?" Bruce asked.

"Have about half an hour?"

"Certainly, for you, always."

Melendez explained who Gantry was and how the manila envelopes were delivered to him in Manhattan. He outlined the connections between the rock stars and described what he was doing with the information, and what they hoped to find. He'd set up the call to be able to share his notes and digital photos of each of the clues using the FBI's custom Video Collaboration software. They could see each other and the documents.

The two men read the stark initial clue on their monitors:

Brian Jones was murdered. It was not an accident. There were others. Look and see.

"That was Gantry's first message from the courier, and with that note was a slip of paper that read: 'My Little One.' According to Gantry, that song was a little-known number from the sixties," Melendez explained. "Only a handful of people knew of that recording session, and another piece of paper was included, a fragment of the demo label—"

Bruce raised his hand, stopping Melendez cold. "Raphael, I only have a half hour today. I'm sorry, I don't mean to be short, but…slips of paper, forty-year-old mystery songs, demo labels? Seriously? Out of respect for our relationship, I hope this is not going to be a rock and roll history lesson."

Melendez had half expected this—in fact, his own first take on the case had been quite similar—so he forged ahead. He adopted the persona of a prosecutor, building his case systematically.

"Robert, the point is that an obscure demo label has been taken off the original demo tape box of a rare, private recording. It's very likely one of a kind and would have to have been retrieved by this person or someone else from the decedent's personal belongings.

"Bear with me," Melendez said. Bruce's impatience showed clearly in his face. "Let's call this someone 'the courier,' and let's suspend judgment for the moment and assume that he is signaling that he had rare access to Jones. You and I both know that a common trademark of most serial killers is personal souvenirs, and that is what this could be."

"Granted. Please continue."

Melendez explained that "My Little One" was an informal Hendrix and Jones collaboration, a possible signal of things to come from them. He even logically introduced the Myth of 27 as an obvious commonality. "I understood from Gantry that the two musicians had to be very secretive about this session because they didn't want their management people to find out," Melendez added.

"Gantry received another manila envelope later that evening at a New York bar—the Super Concert 70 clues, left on the table where he had just had a drink. Robert, the details of this Berlin concert and Al Wilson's unused Pan Am ticket support our premise that our 'courier' collected souvenirs he could only obtain from intimate contact either with the deceased or his personal belongings. Wilson was scheduled to fly out the day he died, suggesting this came off his person," Melendez pointed out.

"Janis Joplin was on the bill with Hendrix and Canned Heat. Her death is connected in a number of ways, but we haven't received any clues directly related to her—yet. There does, however, seem to be a common thread to the clues that connects all these stars to one another in specific situations. These five artifacts and typewritten notes from our courier seem to suggest a strong causal connection," Melendez suggested.

"That said, there is one seemingly obvious link." Melendez paused for dramatic effect and to make sure Bruce was still listening.

"Hendrix, Wilson, and Joplin were all dead within thirty days of that concert; and all were twenty-seven years old. Imagine if that happened today? We'd be on this like white on rice."

Bruce's expression didn't change. He merely tapped his index finger on his desk lightly, a telling sign that he remained unconvinced.

Melendez continued with the next clue, quickly clicking on a photo, the bar napkin and the other piece which he described, as Gantry had, as part of an obscure album cover made for a jam session at the Scene in New York. He went on to describe the handwritten note on the back of the napkin from Morrison to Hendrix suggesting that they record together.

"This napkin with its personal message was kept by either Hendrix or Morrison that night," he said.

There it was. Five stars possibly intimately connected.

Bruce appeared unmoved, so Melendez deftly moved on, still wearing his courtroom persona, to review the facts.

He began, "Jones, Wilson, and Hendrix dead, with oblique references to Joplin and Morrison. And now…Ron McKernan, with a note that read, **"Ron McKernan did not die of natural causes. He was murdered. It didn't stop."** And another artifact that read, 'Recorded at the Euphoria Ballroom, San Raphael, California, July 1970. Turn on Your Love Light.'

"Joplin had walked on for a rare duet with Mckernan to end the concert. They had been lovers," he explained. "Lastly, one final item…. What we believe is Joplin's bracelet," Melendez emphasized.

"Robert, she died shortly after this concert," he said, his voice trailing off.

"Robert, we have been at this point together before, when a set of simple facts, our common sense, and our professional intuition introduce us to a set of probable outcomes. And sometimes those outcomes may not be what previous investigations concluded. Not that the original investigations weren't handled well, but they didn't have the technology we have now. I know we need much more work to confirm my hypothesis, but if I were a betting man and calculated the odds that there was an important connection between all these deaths and our courier, I'd have to take the odds that these deaths were the work of a serial killer and that either our courier is that man, or he knows who the killer is.

"Look," he said, almost in desperation, "think of this as five ordinary people—not rock stars, not legends—with all these things in common and their personal, intimate artifacts delivered anonymously. We both know what we would do.

"Let me finish up with one very important case that took place near you. Maybe the most telling clue of all is this last one—Peter Ham."

Melendez shared the clue:

Peter Ham did not commit suicide. He was murdered.

"Was he…Badfinger?" Bruce asked.

"Right. Look at the matchbook from the Thingamajig Club in Reading."

"I actually remember that place," Bruce said. "It's been closed for years.

"I have to admit, Raphael, I don't have your level of knowledge with most of these artists, but I do remember Badfinger, and I was a fan of their music." Bruce sheepishly admitted.

"I know you'll remember that Ham reportedly hung himself," Melendez said, drawing him in.

"Yes, I do recall that. And I believe his partner did as well, some years later. There was a lot of press on that here, as there was on Hendrix and Jones. Wasn't Ham a drunk, among other things?"

"To the contrary, he apparently had stopped drinking. Here—" he clicked on the prescription slip— "is the other clue that was in the envelope. Dated March 2, 1975, St. Alban's pharmacy, London. It's for sixty tablets of Antabuse, and note the dosage for—"

Bruce cut him off abruptly and gestured to an assistant who had been standing off to the side, out of the camera's view. The man had apparently been making notations on a large whiteboard during their conversation. Bruce adjusted his screen so that the assistant's work could be seen.

Written in red were the points Melendez had been making.

"Good morning, Agent Melendez," the man said. "Hope you don't mind my eavesdropping but I took the liberty of recording your points." He turned and spotlighted the first point with a red pointer and then continued down as he narrated:

- Five deaths with implications for two others (Joplin/ Morrison)
- Clues are ALL intimate. Almost assuredly someone knew or was there in each instance. Possible souvenir collection.
- All died at age 27. Three within a span of 30 days.
- All the deceased knew each other fairly well.
- All the deaths were considered overdoses or accidents (exception Ham).
- Possible previous autopsy or crime scene investigative flaws.
- Early insights suggest numerous commonalities.
- Hypothesis and next steps:

Melendez was impressed. He complimented Bruce's assistant.

"Robert, focusing on Peter Ham for a moment. I asked myself, how could a man who is taking heavy doses of Antabuse be found hanged with a belly full of booze? Physically he would not have been able to do it. We both know how that drug works. And even if he could have mustered the strength, there would have been a big mess. I don't recall any mention, but I could be mistaken?" Melendez posed the question to Bruce.

"Yes, I believe you're right." Bruce was thinking about other evidence that could have been missed by local investigators.

"Okay. Finally, we believe that we have identified the "courier," but we haven't found him yet. Our facial recognition analyst found a forty-five-year-old photo of one Angus Hislop, who was a tax accountant at Coopers & Lybrand in London at the time. He might still be in London, but he made the deliveries in New York City."

Melendez put his pen down and waited for what felt like several minutes.

"Well, Raphael, I have to admit you've got my interest. I'd like to print all these documents out—notes, copy of the envelopes, slips of paper, et cetera. And I need to think through some jurisdictional issues as well."

Melendez felt a wave of relief.

"And I have a question," Bruce said.

"Yes?"

"How are you getting away with having a reporter work on this case?"

"Let me just say he's not officially working on the case. But he is going to be absolutely essential to it. The man is a walking encyclopedia of rock and roll."

"Right, then. Let me print these out and think about it tonight. I'll call you Monday morning—morning my time."

"Thanks. And, uh—one more thing," Melendez added, doing his best Colombo.

"Yes?"

"That last clue about Ham? It came via FedEx to Gantry's apartment right before he left New York to come down here. That means this Hislop fellow knows where Gantry lives, and might have even known his travel plans. He knew Gantry was coming here to see me, and he apparently wanted him to have those specific Peter Ham clues at that exact time. We are doing a bug search of his apartment right now. Understandably, Gantry is concerned."

"Very good. Talk to you Monday. History awaits," Bruce concluded as his image disappeared from the monitor.

Melendez smiled and closed his laptop, stood up, turned off the lights and walked back down the hall to check on Gantry.

Gantry had to go home. He'd been at the motel now for three days and was out of clean shirts, among other things. It was a four-hour drive back to New York, and he had to let the rental agency know he'd need the car again in a day or two. He was not looking forward to fighting the Friday afternoon traffic on I-95.

Melendez came in.

"Gantry, a couple updates before you leave. First, I have a follow-up call with London early on Monday. I'll need you to come back down for that. Second, and I didn't want to alarm you, but I sent a couple of agents out to your apartment after you left."

"Why did you do that?"

"To sweep for bugs. I knew you were concerned. I thought it prudent."

Gantry's first feeling was one of relief, followed quickly by anger that Raphael hadn't told him in advance, which would have relieved his men of the need, apparently, to break into his place.

"And?"

"They found a typical device in one of your electrical sockets. Good place for it, too. I mean, there's never a good place to have a listening device in your house, but by using the socket, your wiring provides a perfect power source indefinitely, and the wiring can also act as a wireless network for other things."

"What other things?" He was trying to picture how many outlets he had in his apartment.

"Cameras for one, maybe explosive devices."

"Explosives! You're shittin' me, right?"

"Calm down. The team didn't find anything. But I want you to know the bug is still there."

"Why didn't they just take it out?"

"So we can lead this guy. As long as he thinks you don't know about it, he'll take everything you say as gospel. Just remember it's there before you say anything, either on the phone or otherwise. If you need to call, use your cell phone and go outside. These devices typically have a range of thirty-five feet, with good reception. Besides, as long as he thinks he can hear you, you're safe. He'll want to keep using it.

"The two agents will remain out of sight and they'll keep an eye on things. You won't even know they're there. Go home, clean up, take care of your business, and get back here by Monday at 6:00 a.m. Check back in Sunday night if that helps. I'll call you if I hear from London before then. And thanks for the great work!"

Melendez felt for Gantry—anxiety was painted all over his face—but he wasn't worried. Gantry struck him as a fighter from the first time they'd met, during the Lennon investigation. But no one, unless he's a seasoned agent, could go home to a house bugged by a potential serial killer without feeling both worried and invaded.

"You okay?" Melendez asked.

"Fine. Just peachy…" Gantry pulled his shoulders back. "See you Monday morning."

Elliot Gantry's Apartment, New York

Five hours later, Gantry pushed the key into his door lock and turned the knob gingerly, half expecting an explosion.

He felt very worried, but he hoped he hadn't let on to Melendez. Suddenly, every word he uttered, every phone call, every remark… everything would be monitored by the man with the Irish walking hat. At this point, regardless of what the FBI thought, he'd pretty much put a label on the guy: serial killer. Was the guy really dropping all this evidence to lead them to someone else? But that was ultimately for Melendez to figure out.

He dropped his suitcase on the floor and poured himself a whiskey. He rarely drank hard stuff alone at home, but Chianti wasn't going to get it done tonight. He wanted to calm down quickly, and a double of Bookers 150 proof would do the trick.

Knowing his place was bugged, he kept quiet—even though he was alone. When he became aware that he was even keeping his breathing low, he smiled.

Okay…okay…

But still, it felt very odd, almost like being naked in a crowd of people who were all dressed in suits. At this moment, someone was listening, waiting to make another move.

Gantry walked with his drink over to the bay windows. He pulled back the heavy velour curtains and looked to the street below. There sat a Crown Victoria, two men inside it. He wished he'd been given their cell numbers. He had to laugh, remembering that Melendez said he wouldn't even know they were there.

When the phone rang, Gantry nearly jumped out of his boots. He didn't know whether to answer it and take his chances with a conversation, or to let it go to the recorder. He chose the recorder as safest; he didn't want to say something the listener could pick up. He turned the volume down as low as it would go and put his ear up close.

"Hey, mate. It's Dennis. You've been gone a while, yeah? I've called you twice. How was it in Quantico? Give me a ring and tell me how it went."

Gantry noticed the machine's red light was blinking. He wondered who else had called. No one had called his cell. He was relieved Dennis hadn't said any more than he did, and he didn't like hearing the reference to Quantico, though, and decided not to listen to any more messages for the time being.

A hot bath was in order. A hot bath and a brain massage from the Doors.

Turning on the hot water, Gantry fixated with apprehension at the room's outlets, then eased his six-foot-two frame down into the five-foot bathtub. Jim Morrison's haunting voice relaxed him... *Take the highway to....* The hot water melted him. And the Bookers was taking effect... *Take a journey to the bright midnight.*

Gantry didn't need an alarm, and felt like he never would again. He jumped out of bed at 5:30, having dreamt vividly all night of Jim Morrison still being alive and helping him solve mysteries.

With a coffee mug in his hand he checked the window. The same Crown Victoria was down there, only this time on his side of the street.

He decided to stretch his legs. It was not quite daylight, but he was comforted by the fact that the agents might have spent the night in their car, so he poured two more mugs of coffee to take to them.

Walking slowly past the red-brick facade of his building, he sauntered up to the two men sitting in the black Victoria with the coffees. The streets were dead quiet this early, and nearly devoid of human activity. Down the way half a block, the early-morning grocer was the only one out, putting fruits and vegetables in two carts on the sidewalk. There was an unusual chill in the late April air.

He tapped on the car window.

"Morning, fellas."

"Good morning Mr. Elliot." The agent rolled his window down.

"Coffee?" Gantry held out the two cups.

"Absolutely. Kind of you to think about us."

"No problem," Gantry said—and then as he straightened up he saw a man across the street, a tall man wearing an Irish walking hat. The man glanced toward him and then quickly picked up his gait.

"Jesus!" Gantry said.

"Anything wrong?" The driver leaned over, on alert.

"He's gone," Gantry said.

"Who's gone?"

"Might be just a coincidence, but I saw a man that looked like our 'courier' over there. The one who probably planted the bug in my apartment."

"We'll check it out," the agent in the passenger seat said. He quickly handed Gantry the two cups. "Better go back upstairs. We'll get back to you." The car turned in a wide U and drove off in the direction the walker had gone.

Gantry beat a hasty retreat back inside. He watched for half an hour, and when he saw the two agents return he took the stairs down to the lobby —but he took the back way out.

As he walked, he found himself breathing normally again. He liked this part of the city because it was older and not crammed with high-rises. The area had character and history and a sense of neighborhood. NYU was close by, and the streets had the vibe of a college town.

In less than fifteen minutes, he was on his old buddy, Dennis' block. He debated whether to wake him this early, but he didn't want to go back to his place. He rang the buzzer and waited. No answer. He tried calling his cell. No answer.

"Boo!" Gantry almost jumped out of his skin.

"Sorry mate, was just going for a walk," he turned to find Dennis, "you must have finally gotten my message. Come in. What the hell is going on?

Gantry took a quick look down both sides of the street before going in and walked straight to the back of the shop with Dennis.

"You wouldn't believe what's happening. I just got back last night from Quantico. I can't even remember the last time we talked, I've been so wrapped up in this," he said. "Got any coffee going?"

"Of course. Sit down. You look a little pale."

He got them both coffees and sat down.

"Okay, mate, the last time we talked was over a week ago when we did the Google thing on that song, 'My Little One,' and you lured me into your magical mystery tour of rock legends. What happened? I left you a voice mail and didn't hear back from you."

"What about?"

"I found some more information on Hendrix, personal stuff I thought you might be able to use."

"Really! Where?"

"In my girlfriend's attic."

"What girlfriend? You haven't dated anyone in five years...have you?"

Dennis laughed.

"You're right. Jesus. At any rate, I knew this bird in London a few years ago that I didn't tell you about. Seemed just another of those quick romances. She was a feisty Irish kicker. We had a go for a bit but then after I came back to NYC, we naturally drifted apart. She was fifteen years younger than me, and I adored her, but there was always a bit of tension because of my father's money. She always kept saying she was my bird from the wrong side of the tracks. I told her I didn't care which choo-choo she rode, as long as she rode me," Dennis said sarcastically.

"That would make her about forty—not exactly robbing the cradle," Gantry offered.

"Yeah. I suppose when you get over forty or so, the age difference doesn't matter anymore, but you would've thought she was a teenager, the way she acted. As I always do when I'm in London, I was hunting around for albums or memorabilia; garage sales, antique shops and the like. The old rockers and groupies always needed cash. I found a box of things that a guy claiming to be Jimi Hendrix's former landlord swore belonged to him, just some clothes and some other junk. That was about three years ago.

"But I remember this one interesting thing —a journal. It had periodic entries, sketches, poems, lyrics, things like that. It looked authentic. I thought the poetry and song lyrics could be valuable. I never did look at it carefully, though. I was just interested because it was his."

"When I left, I asked her to keep the box with some other stuff I'd picked up, and she said she'd put it in her mum's attic with some other stuff I had up there. I didn't think about it anymore until you brought up Brian Jones and Hendrix last week. I could give 'er a ring if she's still at the same number. Maybe I could ask Fraser's to pick them up and authenticate the contents."

"Fraser's?"

"Right. Fraser was a friend, artist, chemical supplier, and uber-groupie in London years ago. I think he actually lived with some of the Stones. His family now has one of the leading memorabilia stores in London."

"Might be worth a call, but first let me tell you what's been going on."

Gantry spent the next hour filling Dennis in on all the details, including the bug in his apartment. Dennis was stunned at all that had transpired in just a few days. He had a look of concern for his friend.

"This is really serious now," Dennis said. "I think I'll make that call to London, maybe see where that bird is."

In some ways, Gantry was energized about what was unfolding, but in others, he was very anxious, even scared. It was consuming him. It felt just like the old days when they made up the rules as they went along. He felt like he'd been methodically drawn into something much bigger than he'd originally imagined, something out of his control, as if an invisible hand were moving chess pieces and had already thought through all the moves and countermoves. He was just afraid that *he* might be one of the pawns.

Gantry was fixated on the "courier." How quickly would they locate this guy?

Alex Jaegar's Apartment, New York

"Gantry. What the hell is going on down there? Haven't heard from you in forever. I hope this is going to pan out to what we discussed. I don't like being left in the dark."

Alex was in another of his moods. He could swing from gregarious to overbearing in a heartbeat.

"Yeah, I just got back from Quantico and I'm packing for another trek down for our next round. Good progress so far, but I'll know more in the next few days. Melendez has come aboard. It took some work. I had to lay out all of the clues and really fight like a beggar to get him to see it all."

Alex interrupted, "Gantry, this is not feeling like its got legs under it, and getting the kind of support you need to get a serious investigation going. Are you sure he's not just being polite to you?" Alex lectured in a stern professional tone. Daniel nodded in agreement as Alex looked at him.

Polite to me? Gantry thought. That was unlike Alex to make a comment like that.

Gantry thought it best to not to share any information about the English accountant, nor did he tell Alex about Dennis's possible journal discovery. Instead, he brought Alex up to speed on the whiteboard work and the initial London involvement in general.

"Gantry, it sounds as if this is going to take much longer than we thought. Let's make a call on this thing in the next day or so. OK?"

Gantry didn't respond. Alex never questioned his judgment.

"On a separate note, I do have a bit of news for you now."

"What's that?"

"Jodi called me." Gantry's blood started rising. "She said that you had been trying to reach her."

"Why would she call you and not me?" Gantry sharply replied.

He instantly was transported back to the confrontation years ago with Alex, when he first found out about the brief affair that Jodi had with Alex. "You son of a bitch!" Gantry kept saying as he flailed away at Alex, almost knocking him unconscious. "How could you!"

Gantry abruptly quit his job at Stone and moved out of the house, having decided to go back to Texas and start his life over.

Jodi had begged him not to leave. But he wouldn't relent. This was not the first time this had occurred. It wasn't until he reluctantly met with Alex and he tearfully explained what had happened when they ran into each other that night. Alex pled with Gantry to forgive him. Eventually, Gantry agreed and went back to work.

In a perverse way, it became kind of a sick joke with Gantry, thinking that Jodi drove Alex to come out of the closet.

"She thought you didn't sound yourself and she was worried," Alex insisted. He didn't want to summon up the past either.

Quantico, VA

Gantry arrived back at the motel late Sunday night and hung up six clean shirts, his sport coat and two pairs of jeans. He stuffed his underwear in the dresser and put his mini CD player on the night table. No more scratchy country & western tunes coming out of the decrepit radio next to the bed. It was midnight, but he put in a voice mail to Raphael anyway, telling him he was here and would see him at 6:00 a.m., as they had agreed.

The following morning, Gantry, friendly by now with the Marine gate guards, showed the guard on duty his pass and parked near the BAU building. Melendez met him inside, and the two men adjourned to the conference room next to the lab. Gantry saw that Melendez had coffee set out alongside a plate of pastries.

"Go ahead, have one," Melendez said, sitting.

"What are they?"

"They're *conchas*, amigo," Melendez said. Gantry had never heard Raphael use a single Spanish word, so amigo and conchas made him laugh.

"What's in 'em?"

"Jeez, they aren't poison. Are you on a diet or something? They are just Mexican sweet breads. Lucia made them for us," Melendez said.

Gantry took a concha and dipped it in his coffee, and Melendez laughed. Then, getting down to business, he said, "Robert Bruce has all the clues, and his analyst has been corresponding with Tanner since we spoke last week. This is our go-or-no-go call. If he doesn't get on board, we're done with this."

Melendez dialed into the video bridge, and Bruce came into view immediately.

"Good morning, Raphael," Bruce said. His voice came through loud and clear, and his picture was vivid and sharp. "It's a little early for you, isn't it?"

"Yes it is," Melendez replied, smiling. Might as well get to it, he thought.

"So…what do you think?" Melendez said.

Bruce stroked his chin and said slowly, as if delaying gratification, "Raphael, I may be crazy…but…I think you're on to something here."

Melendez breathed as silent a sigh as he could muster. He glanced over at Gantry in the corner, who gave him a thumbs-up.

"That's great. I hoped that you would concur," Melendez said. "Have you thought about how we will handle the jurisdictional issues?"

"Yes. Since Hendrix, Jones, and Ham died in or near London, we will take the lead on those cases. Wilson and McKernan will be yours. We can engage the Police Nationale if we end up pursuing the Morrison case, and you can handle the Joplin case if that comes into play. For now, we start with the first five. How does that sound?"

"Great, exactly what I thought," Melendez said.

"Perfect," Bruce said, closing a file he had in front of him.

"Joint H.E.A.T. teams?" Melendez suggested. He and Bruce would need to put together a Homicide Evidence Assessment Team—a physical evidence analyst, a toxicology and autopsy specialist, and maybe a corporate financial analyst.

"Yes, I will have Maxwell contact Tanner to get that coordinated."

"Absolutely."

"Robert, how difficult will it be to get into the original files and cold-case evidence boxes? We've contacted the Los Angeles and San Francisco PDs, on a preliminary basis, of course, no official requests," Melendez said. He pictured the whereabouts of the evidence: a dimly lit, grimy warehouse outside London with rows of steel shelves holding the disintegrating cardboard boxes —for years, with lots of English damp to help things along.

Bruce smiled and turned his screen so that Melendez could see a coffee table stacked with boxes.

"Well done, Robert!"

"That's it, at least for the boxes. We may have more in our system, of course, but we haven't had time to sort through that. This will be a good start."

The boxes were labeled PETER HAM, BRIAN JONES, and JIMI HENDRIX with their death dates and the date each investigation was completed—or just back-burnered.

"Raphael, I will have my assistant, Maxwell, put these in an evidence room. We'll get our initial teams together and schedule a call for tomorrow to review Peter Ham first. He is the most recent and most complete and the one that took both of us from conjecture to, well, to something more. If we can get some momentum on the others, we can add them as well. Make sense?"

"Absolutely," Melendez answered. "We'll unpack them together and see what we have."

"Game on, mate! Of course, you're free to come over to London again and see it all at first hand. I'd love to take some more of your money. Which will it be?"

"Let's decide later. What time should we get our Ham team together? How about three-thirty, your time?"

"That works. See you then," Bruce responded. The monitor went to blue.

As Melendez and Gantry were gathering their materials, the door opened, and Senior Special Agent Weldon Mayflower, Raphael's boss and head of the Criminal, Cyber, Response and Services Division walked in.

Despite the fact that they'd worked in the same division for the last eight years, Melendez and Mayflower did not like each other. In fact, Melendez despised the man who seemed to thrive on the enforcement of minutia. Mayflower was beyond "by the book," as far as Melendez was concerned. He was the most anal—and intensely unlikeable—person Melendez had ever met.

Mayflower wore a uniform: black suit with a too-tight jacket, nondescript tie, and pants pegged a little short. He could have been a salesman at—and was at least a walking advertisement for—Sears and Roebuck, circa 1961.

Melendez never could understand their mutual animosity. At first he thought it was jealousy, but that didn't make any sense. Mayflower was his boss, was making more money, and had more power—he just couldn't figure it out.

Mayflower stood in the doorway, arms crossed defensively, shoe tapping like an aggressive fourth-grade English teacher. Melendez knew immediately what was happening. He pulled his shoulders back and stood up straight, forming an invisible Maginot Line between himself and Gantry.

"Who is that?" Mayflower hissed, pointing to Gantry.

"Sir," Melendez said through gritted teeth, "This is Gantry."

"Gantry who? Or is that a last name? What the fuck is this man doing inside this secure facility?" he demanded.

"Well, sir, Gantry Elliot, he's…my consultant."

"Of what species?"

"Music, sir."

Mayflower seemed to consider this as he looked Gantry over.

"What the hell are you talking about, Melendez? Are you seeking an even earlier retirement than the one you're facing?"

"No, sir."

Turning back to Gantry, he said, "Mr. Elliot, I'm sure you are a music expert. However, you need to turn in your ID card at the gate and be on your way. This isn't a test lab for music theory."

Mayflower turned, without another word, and left the room.

"Shit," Raphael said sitting down. "I think we're in a real jam now."

Gantry didn't answer. He didn't feel as negative as Raphael because he was used to flying under the radar, and he had something else on his mind right now: his ex-wife. What in the world would she be calling Alex for and not call him back? He assumed it was something personal. He had no way of knowing that, as part of the investigation, Raphael had already put in calls to the SFPD and the LAPD to pull them into the joint efforts.

Melendez said, "I have to get back to my office and review my curriculum for Wednesday."

Gantry was surprised. Melendez had given no further indication of where he stood on the investigation. He felt all the energy leave the room. But they'd come too far to give up now—they were on the precipice, and he didn't want to lose this opportunity.

"You better leave now," Melendez said. "I'll have to think about this."

"What am I supposed to do, go back to the motel and cool my heels until I hear from you?"

"Exactly. For now, anyway, unless you want to go back to New York."

"Christ," Gantry said angrily. "Look, I know this guy is a jerk, and he's your boss and all. I get that, but this is too big to just—"

Melendez put his hand on Gantry's shoulder.

"Just go back to the motel, and I'll call you. Sit tight. Give me a few hours."

Instead of going to his room, Gantry decided to take a drive. Once in the car, he headed go to the Hitching Post to have a drink.

The place was almost empty with only two men seated at the bar and another in a booth. Gantry ordered a Bookers neat and began to relax, and as he did, he remembered: the magazine had a state-of-the-art video conferencing center. He'd only been in it a couple of times to play reruns of the Hall of Fame induction ceremonies. It was a great room, much better equipped than the one they'd just used in the BAU building. There were four 120-inch hi-def screens, an HD sound system, and all the collaborative technology any investigator could want. It was not secure, but maybe Tanner could connect London and New York through the FBI's secure network.

His mind started to race. He decided to call Alex now and get him back in the loop.

Gantry walked out to his car and opened his phone.

"Are you here or there?" Alex asked.

"I'm here at Quantico. We've had a little snag."

"About what? Is this thing unraveling?"

"No, nothing like that. But I need to borrow our conferencing facility tomorrow."

"Huh? What for? Don't those guys have all that shit?"

"Yes, of course they do, but there's been a conflict with another case they're investigating, something very big, and we got bumped."

"So, what do you want me to do? Any breakthroughs yet?"

"Yes, a breakthrough, that's a good way of putting it. Raphael and I just had a long video conference with his counterpart in London. We're going international, and that's a good thing."

"Why international?"

"Because Ham, Hendrix, Morrison, and Jones were killed in Europe," Gantry said. "That makes it their jurisdiction. You know all these law enforcement types are like dogs pissing on trees—gotta define their territories."

"So now we know for sure they were killed? That's incredible!"

"No, I just meant that is where they died. Raphael had a conversation with the go-to guy in London and laid it all out to him. The guy is right on the edge of firing the starter's pistol, but they need to have another conference tomorrow morning early to wrap it up and lay out a plan."

"So what's the hold-up?"

"We can't use the room here in Quantico tomorrow, and also Raphael's getting a little heat from his superiors about the time he's spending on this, so I need to commandeer our facility in New York. You told me to have at it when we started, so I need you to help me on this."

"Okay, but with one caveat."

I knew it.

"What is that?"

"I get to sit in on the conference."

Shit!

"Okay," Gantry replied. *Too many goddamn cooks!*

As soon as he hung up, he called Melendez and told him his plan.

Melendez expressed reservations. If he were caught, there would be hell to pay.

After a pause, he said, "Okay. Let's do it. Fuck it. This case is far too important. If Mayflower causes me problems, I'll deal with it. Once we get this moving, it will have too much momentum for anyone to stop, especially now that Alex and *Rolling Stone* are involved. Mayflower is scared of the press. A reporter at the *Times* crucified him years ago for botching a case by trying to garner publicity for himself instead of following leads a reporter had confidentially given him. He's been nursing a grudge against the media for eight years."

At 5:30 the following morning, four men climbed into Melendez's Crown Victoria. They would have over four hours to discuss the conference call and then, assuming it was a go, they would plan the next stages of their work.

Melendez was driving, Gantry riding shotgun, and Tanner in the back with another analyst who was introduced to Gantry as Moxie. Tanner and Moxie asked question after question, what if after what if: Had he ever heard of any crazed fans or death threats on any of these stars? Would any of the remaining band members be able to help? The more they brainstormed, the more detailed the discussion got.

A bored Gantry finally closed his eyes and feigned he was napping.

Rolling Stone Offices, New York.

When the men finally walked into the *Rolling Stone* conferencing facility on the twenty-third floor, Tanner and Moxie, both twenty-eight, tech wizards, and huge rock and roll fans, were clearly impressed. Tanner was star struck as he shook hands with Alex Jaeger.

"Mr. Jaeger, this is an honor," he said.

Alex was as excited as the young agent, but more reserved about it.

"Gentleman, *mi casa es su casa*," he said with a flamboyant gesture.

The conference had been set up for a10:30 call from the East Coast. Tanner had sent a tech in earlier to remotely link to the FBI's secure network. Bruce would be in his office at 3:30, London time.

Ordinarily the camera would follow the speaker, but in this case, the camera would be narrowly fixed on only the four men and part of the conference table. Melendez did not want Bruce knowing that Alex Jaeger was now included. Melendez would sit at the head of the table and Jaeger off to the side, off camera.

The team settled into place and the London image came up. Bruce looked surprised to see so many men sitting in on the conference.

"Already assembled your analysis team, I see," he said.

"Yes, Robert, I thought it prudent. This will be my core team, and I see you have yours. We might as well get organized right from the start."

"Agreed, mate. Inspector Prevot is coming online now," Bruce said as the video screen split into two pictures. "He's with the Police Nationale, as you may recall."

As Inspector Prevot came into view sitting behind a desk, Bruce continued, "And your old friend, Inspector MacAlistair from Scotland

128

Yard, is here."

MacAlistair's image now split the screen into three sections, with Gantry and the three FBI agents' images in the corner of the screen.

"Are we all here?" Bruce asked. "Good, let's begin. Raphael, I've briefed MacAlistair and Prevot," Bruce said. His not using their titles clued Melendez that Bruce was all in and this was a team.

Bruce and Melendez reviewed the history of what had prompted their engagement and this call: the anonymous packages; the apparent personal effects of the deceased; the unusual sets of commonalities, including the age of the dead stars; the condensed period of deaths; the serial killer-like patterns that had emerged; and the probable autopsy and crime scene deficiencies—too numerous to dismiss.

Alex sat enthralled on the sidelines. Gantry knew he was itching to get involved and prayed he wouldn't say a word.

Bruce said, "I thought we'd get a jump on this as well, Raphael. We've pulled all the digital files we have from London and Paris. We've also retrieved all the cold-case boxes we could find in addition to the ones I showed you before. Prevot and MacAlistair have theirs, as well. There isn't that much, amigo; pulling these out reminded us of how antiquated our techniques were in sixties and early seventies.

"Even though this is out of the order that Mr. Elliot received the clues, I suggest we begin with the Peter Ham case, as that is the most recent and seems to have some inconsistencies," he continued without hesitating. "Let's first look at the crime scene photos, then we can go into the autopsy, the evidence boxes and the investigator's files.

"As you can see from the image here, Peter Ham was found hung. He died on April 27, 1975, at the age of twenty-seven."

Bruce pulled on a pair of latex gloves. He then delicately lifted the top of the Ham case evidence box as if he was opening an ancient Egyptian sarcophagus.

"I am now removing the police and autopsy report on this case and emptying the contents of the cold-case box," Bruce said.

He pulled out a file folder, two spiral notebooks, and a crocodile wallet along with what looked like a bag of prescription bottles and another bag filled with brushes and combs.

"According to the police report, Ham was found hanging by a rope from a cross beam in his garage. There was a wide purplish bruise around his entire neck. Here are three more pictures of the crime scene that we will scan and send right now. Looks like a tipped-over drummer's throne and a pool of liquid below the body—urine released as he expired," Bruce narrated.

"The coroner's report describes the cause of death as a combination of cerebral edema leading to a lack of drainage from the brain."

He directed the participants to a picture of Ham's swollen face and neck. "Cerebral hypoxia, or a lack of oxygen, is a typical cause of death in hangings. Additionally, the coroner found a fracture of the hyoid bone."

Melendez interjected, "Cerebral edema and cerebral hypoxia are typical in hangings, but a fracture of the hyoid bone is not. As you all know, the hyoid bone is mid-neck and is seen more typically in strangulations, not hangings. It can happen, but is not typical of a suicide hanging."

"According to the coroner," Bruce responded, "Ham's belly was full of alcohol. The crime scene investigators found two empty one-liter vodka bottles in the waste bins in the garage. They apparently were not retained or dusted for prints."

Bruce then picked up the bag with the prescription bottles. "Here we have some allergy medicine, some pain reliever, sleeping pills…and Antabuse," he said. "The prescription is drawn on the St. Albans Pharmacy, London. Dated March 2, 1975, for sixty pills, 500 mg dosage. 'Take daily in the morning.' There are twelve tablets left in this bottle. Antabuse, as most of you are aware, is used to treat alcoholism by creating a severe aversion to the ingestion of alcohol."

Bruce paused for a moment.

"Hmmm…It appears that Mr. Ham may have been taking the prescription up to the morning of his death, by my count," he said.

"Raphael, can you share the artifact that was recently delivered to Mr. Elliot by an anonymous courier?" Bruce asked.

On half of the monitor, the team read the typewritten clue: "Peter Ham did not commit suicide. He was murdered." The matches from the Thingamajig Club were in the picture, as well. On the other half was the written prescription for Antabuse, the one Bruce had just shared in the cold-case file.

All three rooms were silent as the men stared at the evidence on the screen.

"The courier's clue directed us to Peter Ham and this specific non sequitur related to Antabuse. Can we all agree that it is highly improbable that Ham could have ingested a large volume of alcohol and then taken his own life while under this medication?" Bruce asked. Everyone either nodded or voiced a yes.

"And in my opinion, Robert, it is unlikely that the broken hyoid bone could have come from a self-administered hanging," Melendez added.

"Agreed," Bruce acknowledged. "All of this would suggest that we possibly had a staged death scene, and the original determination was erroneous. Gentlemen, I am going to recommend that London Metro reopen the Peter Ham case as a murder investigation, and recommend we revisit the evidence, analysis, and interviews. This is now a live murder case."

The energy level immediately spiked. Gantry and Alex stared at each other in disbelief. What had been originally written off as some wacko wasting their time was now the catalyst for the opening of a cold-case investigation.

Bruce then laid out the procedure for how they would use the Emerging Tech Lab in Quantico to quickly re-analyze the physical evidence using chemical isotope analysis, reconstruct the crime scene using the lab's virtual crime scene application, and begin to harden up the commonalities in an effort to identify possible persons of interest. Melendez added that the virtual crime scene technology could prove extremely valuable in re-creating full-scale holographic images of the entire crime scene.

"Allow me to turn back to the first message that Mr. Elliot received," Bruce said. "We've summarily reviewed the Ham case and agree on the way forward. Now let's look at Brian Jones, the founder of the Rolling Stones."

On the monitor appeared the words: "Brian Jones was murdered. It was not an accident. There were others. Look and See." The image of the "My Little One" demo label also appeared and Bruce explained its significance.

Then, in an alarming departure from what they'd just seen, a full-frame image filled the screen: Brian Jones's body lying on the concrete pool deck, his lips dark, his clothing still wet, a fifth of whiskey next to him, an empty pint vodka bottle, drinking glasses, a pack of cigarettes, a towel, and an inhaler, the kind asthmatics use.

"This death was heavily publicized in 1969, with lots of media attention and speculation. However, the coroner's report here states succinctly that the cause of death was 'misadventure.' Agent Melendez has suggested they may have meant that he'd had too much to drink." The group snickered.

Alex rolled his eyes and whispered to Gantry, "You have to be shitting me!"

Bruce continued.

"These files also hold interviews with a number of people who were at the residence at the time of his death, most prominently Anna Wohlin, his girlfriend, who found him in the pool and tried to revive him; his housekeeper, who originally saw Jones motionless in the pool; and Frank Thorogood, a contractor who was living in the guesthouse and also present at the time. Thorogood was a subject of speculation at the time, and again more recently in 2009 as a murder suspect, but nothing was ever proven. There was another anonymous eyewitness who claimed to see Jones being held underwater by three men. But that was not considered a reliable source, and it was dismissed as conjecture."

Bruce opened the cold-case files and removed Jones's autopsy report and the detective's notes, along with a number of personal effects, including cigarettes, two glasses, prescription bottles, an inhaler, brushes, a coin purse, an address book, and some loose papers.

Bruce read from the autopsy report: "The results of the thin layer chromatography analysis revealed no amphetamine, methadrine, morphine, methadrone, or isoprenaline in his system."

Bruce paused.

"Looks like Jones was possibly drug-free at the time of his death. However, they did find a modest amount of alcohol in his blood. Apparently he did have some brandy that evening, the report notes.

"Now this is very interesting. An amphetamine-like chemical was found in his system, approximately 1720 mgs, but apparently not a true amphetamine. The chemist could not recognize this substance. The analyst must have only performed a chemical screening and did not continue to confirmation testing. Essentially this means they only confirmed what was not in his system, not what was. The analysis also noted two spots, one yellow and the other purple, probably due to staining during the chemical analysis."

"Nothing further?" asked a surprised Melendez.

"Nothing."

"But the apparent dosage level is huge!"

"I know, I know," Bruce said.

As the review of the materials continued, Bruce moved to the evidence box and methodically read out its contents.

"Valium, an allergy medicine, a medi-inhaler, Andrax, and a pain medication. All these prescriptions—" he slowly spread his hands to frame the confluence of prescription medicines — "all these prescriptions are drawn on the St. Albans Pharmacy in London. The same one we saw in the Peter Ham evidence box. An unlikely coincidence for such a relatively obscure pharmacy."

He turned to one of his men. "Hammond, check out St. Albans Pharmacy pronto and see if it is still in existence."

Melendez said, "Robert, how has the evidence and the organic samples and test results been stored?"

"Normally, we would seal them individually in nitrogen cases. But back then they were most probably placed in jars and frozen. But the chances of this stuff still being around is low.

"Let me pause for a minute. How are we doing on time? I'd like to go through the Jimi Hendrix and Al Wilson material, agree on a way forward, and then adjourn for the day," Bruce said. Everyone nodded in the affirmative.

"Raphael, can you take us through the clues involving Hendrix and Wilson that were delivered to Mr. Elliot as I set up the Hendrix files?"

A quick scan of the faces around the conference table revealed an intensely inquisitive group. Alex was out of the picture, but leaning forward, about to slide off his chair. Tanner and Moxie, both relatively new to this process, were nearly as focused. Gantry wasn't even looking at Bruce; he was writing as fast as he could capture the enormous body of information. Until this point, he'd been relegated to working on commonalities and hadn't really looked at the clues the way these veterans were.

Finally, Melendez answered Bruce's question.

"Gentlemen, I am going to display two clues. Remember that Hendrix is already associated with the Jones clue."

On the monitor were the words, "It didn't stop." Next to that was the *High Live and Dirty* artifact and the cocktail napkin with the note from Morrison to Hendrix.

"This clue refers to a jam session at the Scene Club in New York City that Hendrix and Morrison participated in. The cocktail napkin is a personal message to Hendrix from Morrison inviting him to record with him.

"Here's another clue that Gantry received," he said as the next image appeared on the monitor. "Not drug overdoses. Murder. There were others. Look and see. You will know. It didn't stop."

"Next to that, the Super Concert 70 artifact. This clue refers to a concert in September of 1970, headlined by Hendrix, Canned Heat—Al Wilson's group—and Janis Joplin. As you all are now aware, Hendrix, Wilson, and Joplin all died within thirty days of that concert at the same age as Jones, twenty-seven. I have one other artifact that was also in this last package." Melendez displayed Wilson's unused Pan Am plane ticket to Berlin.

"Wilson was found dead the day he was scheduled to fly to Berlin for the concert."

"Thank you, Raphael," Bruce said and took the floor again.

"James Marshall Hendrix died on Sept 18, 1970, in Notting Hill, a residential community in London. The police report states that they received a call about a possible fatality at about 11:18 a.m. Police and an ambulance arrived at 11:30 to an open apartment door. There was no one inside, and Hendrix was dead. He had apparently been dead for hours.

"The autopsy report suggests the cause of death was asphyxiation from aspirated vomit, with large amounts of wine in his stomach and esophagus. A high dosage of barbiturate was found in his bloodstream. No injection marks on the body. It is interesting to note that there was only an average alcohol level in the blood. There was no further analysis or findings beyond the obvious one of asphyxiation," Bruce concluded.

Two crime scene photos flashed on the monitor showing Hendrix's body on a sofa, the head tilted back, hair and clothing apparently saturated with liquid.

"His head is tilted back?" asked Melendez. "I assume CPR was done, and this photo was taken after that?"

"No CPR is indicated in the report. He was cold when they arrived."

"But that is not the position of someone who has been vomiting," Melendez said. "And he looks saturated with liquid. Can you enlarge his face?"

The monitor filled with Hendrix's face.

"Are those scratches or cuts on his nostrils?" Melendez asked.

"Let's review the contents of the evidence box," Bruce continued. "A notepad, cigarettes, a lighter, over-the-counter headache medication, asthma inhaler, Vesparax sleeping pills, Vitamin C, Valium and Librium," Bruce methodically listed. He then stopped abruptly.

"Gentlemen, these prescription bottles are all drawn on the St. Albans Pharmacy, London."

There was silence in the group. This was beyond coincidence or serendipitous commonality.

Violating their agreed ground rules, Gantry suddenly leaned into his microphone. "Gentleman, I wanted to say something sooner, but I didn't think it was relevant."

All eyes were now on him.

"There was a dirty little secret in the rock and roll industry at the time that was never openly discussed. Some stars, friendlies, and record companies owned pharmacies during this era in order to supply pharmaceutical-grade drugs so they could avoid the law, contamination or blackmail. You never read about it or heard it discussed, but it occurred."

"Mr. Elliot, is that true or just speculation on your part?" Bruce asked.

And then Alex jumped in: "Of course it's true!"

The men from Europe were stunned. Who was this man? Why did he have an opinion? That question went unanswered as they all immediately refocused on the bigger picture. This case was rapidly becoming much more real and complex.

Bruce quickly addressed the pharmacy issue.

"Hammond, get back on this and run down who worked at—and who owned—the St. Albans Pharmacy!"

"Al Wilson," Melendez said loudly, anxious to refocus the team and withdraw attention from Jaeger's outburst. "Al Wilson, the founder of Canned Heat, was found dead in Topanga Canyon, a suburb of Los Angeles, on September 3, 1970. The autopsy revealed death by extreme barbiturate intoxication that led to cardiac arrest. No detailed investigation or autopsy was conducted. Wilson had no history of drug abuse. We have only been given an initial file from Los Angeles and are in the process of getting their people involved. There was only one crime scene photo in the file, I am displaying it now."

"Quite a bit of ground churned around the body for a suicide. Is there any mention of a struggle?" Bruce asked.

"No."

"Any mention of the unused plane ticket?"

"No. Apparently, it was not found on him when the police arrived. The barbiturate bottle found at the crime scene was drawn on the Carlton Pharmacy in Los Angeles. It appeared to be an open-and-shut case of suicide. No additional follow-up work done," he added.

"Thank you, Raphael. Gentlemen, I suggest we review where we are and then call it a day. Agent Melendez can you please summarize for us? After which, we can adjourn and give our teams time to assemble and conduct their forensic analyses and prepare recommendations. We'll regroup on Thursday."

All nodded in agreement.

"Raphael, would you wrap up, please?"

Melendez nodded and began his summary of the discussion in a precise fashion.

"Peter Ham. London Metro SCU is reopening the case as an active murder. Quantico will re-create the crime scene to test the hypothesis and send an analyst to London to help test available DNA and perform chemical isotope and signature analysis, if required. SCU will perform re-interviews of persons of interest and original investigators, possible surveillance tape analysis and investigate St. Albans Pharmacy.

"Brian Jones. SCU will re-examine the case and re-analyze the chromatography and chemical isotope analysis, physical evidence and DNA analysis. Inconclusive crime analysis to date.

"Jimi Hendrix. Our discussion suggests a possible staged scene. SCU and Quantico will re-create the crime scene, test DNA and perform micro-photo analytics and chemical signature analysis of drugs in system and source. SCU will perform re-interviews.

"Al Wilson. Possibly a staged suicide. Quantico will re-create the crime scene, test DNA and perform chemical analysis."

"Thank you, Raphael." Bruce smiled at him. "Let me suggest that on Thursday we also review an initial analysis and recommendation on the other rock stars that Mr. Elliot received messages about: Jim Morrison, Ron McKernan, and Janis Joplin.

"We will distribute later today a summary construct for each of us to succinctly present our conclusions on each case as well as our initial profiling of the possible perpetrator," Bruce instructed. "I recommend we make a go, no-go call on all of them at that time?"

The attendees all nodded in agreement.

"Gentlemen," Bruce continued, "what prompted this call today was the inference that we may still, even at this late date, have a serial killer on our hands. The messages anonymously delivered to Mr. Elliot have guided us to at least one cold-case re-examination. It appears likely that we may have more."

Turning to look at Gantry, he said, "Mr. Elliot, can you make yourself available to work over the next forty-eight hours with a joint commonalities team that Tanner will compose, and also with Hammond on the pharmacy ties? It will help us focus our investigation in those areas. Your insights can be of great assistance. I am hoping that our analyses will help us to triangulate a suspect or set of possible suspects."

Gantry nodded his acceptance.

"Robert, I'll call you back in a few minutes to discuss what we have just uncovered about the courier," Melendez said.

"We reconvene on Thursday," Bruce said.

Within minutes, Melendez called Bruce back from a private room. He'd just received some information from the lab about Hislop.

"Robert, I have news for you. As you recall, Angus Hislop seemed to disappear after he left Coopers & Lybrand forty years ago. His last known address was in London. The team at London Metro could find nothing more, and our fingerprint analysis of the packages to Gantry proved negative."

"I heard," Bruce replied.

"One of our interns had the brilliant idea to try to find a match for his clothing utilizing our new global-photo data base. We had been testing digitally matching clothing with some success recently. We did just that and found an exact match. The chesterfield coat he was wearing was apparently made by an Italian manufacturer and was sold exclusively at Barney's in New York City for the past five years."

"Really? I could have sworn it was British," Bruce chuckled.

"No—and we had no trouble gaining access to the store's sales records and video surveillance footage in the men's department for the last five years. There were only twenty-two men's coats of that size, style and color sold during that time. We investigated each name over the last twenty-four hours and tried to match each purchase to a video image. I just sent you what we found."

Bruce opened the video file in which a distinguished gentleman was trying on a coat.

"This is our guy Hislop. He changed his name to Simon Jennings. He lives in Westport, Connecticut, a waterfront town a little over an hour north of New York. He matches the *Rolling Stone* courier photos exactly," Melendez exclaimed enthusiastically. "We have already dispatched a field agent to set up surveillance on him until we determine how and when to approach him. He could be the killer, not just a 'courier.'"

"I will have to ask for your indulgence that we reconvene on Friday instead of Thursday. I think it may be a good idea for me to pay a visit to Mr. Hislop as soon as possible. Don't you think?"

"Yes, I agree. Friday it is. Let me know what you find."

Melendez came back to the conference room where Tanner, Moxie and Gantry were still talking.

"Gantry, you and I are taking a ride to Westport, Connecticut. Tanner, you and Moxie get back to Quantico now. Take one of the NY Learjets out of Teterboro," Melendez ordered.

Tanner and Moxie quickly packed up and left.

"What's in Westport and why are we going there?" Gantry asked.

"Angus Hislop. I will explain on the way up."

Gantry was wired. As they were pulling out of the parking lot, Melendez's phone rang. It was Robert Bruce.

"Raphael, glad I caught you. Good news! Someone up there is rooting for us. We did preserve the original Brian Jones test material, including nail samples and hair clippings, possibly some glasses and urine samples. Not sure how much is usable, but we seem to have enough to work with. We're scouring to see if anything from the others was maintained as well."

"Excellent, Robert, thank you."

Merrit Parkway near Westport, Conn.

As they were navigating out of New York, Melendez explained to Gantry what had been uncovered about Hislop: his name change, his move to Westport, and the surveillance that had been set up.

"Gantry, I am taking you with me because Hislop chose to communicate with you for reasons known only to him. I am banking on him opening up to you when you are in front of him."

"Do you want me to meet him without you?" Gantry asked.

"No. I can't let you do that. We don't know if he is just a messenger or if he is in fact a killer. I have to go with you, but we will have backup in case of a confrontation," Melendez explained, keeping his eyes on the road.

The afternoon traffic on the Merritt Parkway was going to make this a much longer drive than Melendez had originally thought. This could end up being a three-hour excursion.

Melendez was deep in thought and not very communicative for most of the ride. Because Hislop lived in Westport, both men assumed that he must be wealthy, which made his name change even more perplexing. What would drive a person like him to create a new identity? Fear? Failure? He'd been a prominent accountant with a large firm in London and been very visible. Then apparently he disappeared, changed his name, and reappeared in a wealthy Connecticut suburb. Obviously, it had something to do with this case, even though records showed Jennings had owned his home for more than twenty years. Why did he wait so long to surface?

It was all conjecture, but Gantry was relieved that he wasn't being stalked anymore. The roles were reversed; the hunter was now the hunted.

Finally, the Crown Victoria turned onto Burnham Hill Road and into a neighborhood of multi-million dollar homes within walking distance of Mill Pond and the beaches of Long Island Sound. The Nantucket-style two-story house was set back about fifty yards from the road, with a long brick driveway leading to a *porte cochere* to the left of the house.

"Well, Gantry, welcome to the NFL. This is where it gets real interesting."

Turning off the ignition, Melendez turned to Gantry. "Remember, this guy had a good reason to feed you those clues. We're here to find out what that reason was. We can't assume anything. He might be the killer, but we have absolutely no proof of that. At the very least, he must know who did this or at least have some very incriminating information. Either way, let me do the talking. I'll let you know when you can engage him. Don't let him bait you. Don't give away anything. We want *him* to talk. Got it?"

"Yes, boss," Gantry said. He hadn't any intention of jumping into the conversation. That said, he was an accomplished investigative reporter and would make his own observations, but as the car pulled forward the reality of the situation began to sink in. What would he do if it suddenly became apparent that Hislop was the killer? Raphael would have to take him into custody. Where was the backup?

Melendez stopped the car beside the house and turned off the ignition. In the sudden silence, he and Gantry looked up at the house. The curtains all were drawn, but there was light behind them.

Before he got out of the car, Melendez instinctively checked his gun, a 9mm Beretta with fifteen rounds in the clip. He pushed off the safety and holstered it again under his left arm beneath his suit jacket. He also positively tested his monitoring device. Backup would engage if the FBI code word was spoken or if they sensed a problem. Melendez had to be prepared for any possibility.

Gantry could feel his temperature rise. His heart began to beat faster.

Melendez's knock was answered by a Hispanic woman in a

housekeeper's uniform.

"*Buenos tardes. Es Simon Jennings en casa?*" Melendez said.

"*Si. Uno momento, por favor,*" the woman answered as she closed the heavy door.

In a moment, Jennings appeared in the doorway looking exactly as Gantry pictured: natty, Burberry suit sans jacket, and a buttoned-up vest.

"Good afternoon, gentlemen," he said. "How can I help you?" He was self-assured and polite—to a point. He looked at them with a condescending expression that also expressed curiosity and, Gantry thought, a touch of apprehension.

Melendez reached into his suit jacket, withdrew a leather wallet and flicked it open with two fingers, displaying his gold FBI badge.

"FBI, Mr. Hislop?" Melendez said. "May we come in?"

"By all means, gentlemen. Please come in. I don't think I've ever met an FBI agent," he said with a light British accent, not showing the least hint of surprise that the agent knew his real name.

"Well, I guess that's history now, isn't it?" Melendez said sternly. Gantry was a little surprised. He'd never seen Melendez in an aggressive stance. But of course, he'd been involved in hundreds of murder cases—and was a trained agent.

"Please follow me," Hislop said, leading them into a large room filled with art and furnished with two heavy brocaded sofas and overstuffed antique chairs. A window displayed the large backyard framed by wooded areas on both sides of an unobstructed view of Mill Pond. Gantry walked closer to the floor-to-ceiling window and surveyed the bucolic setting that centered an ancient Irish stone cross.

"Please, sit down. Can I get you some tea or coffee?"

"No thanks," Melendez said.

Their first impression was that Hislop was one cool customer. He had the perfect physique for a James Bond role, about six-feet-two and around a hundred ninety pounds. He walked ramrod straight with great bearing. And he smelled like money.

But then, if he were a serial killer, Gantry thought, *he would probably be stoic and prepared. He must have known we'd come eventually, and wasn't that the point of all the clues anyway?*

Hislop had been a classmate of Prince Charles, and ran in fast, lofty circles in swinging London during the 1960s. At night, he wore Carnaby Street—the hippest of the hip. Now, almost seventy, he came across as refined, almost regal. He had been a creative tax accountant for Coopers & Lybrand and on the fast track to making partner, a very prestigious position in London at the time. But his real expertise was his uncanny ability to creatively and legally move money around and hide it in every corner of the globe. And he was a born salesman.

Hislop took a large chair next to the window and waved Melendez and Gantry toward a sofa. "Well, gentlemen, I see you've done your research. You know who I am."

"Yes, Mr. Hislop. My name is Raphael Melendez. This is my associate, Gantry Elliot. Allow me to explain why we are here."

"That won't be necessary, Agent Melendez. I know who both of you are and why you're here, and you obviously know who I really am."

"Okay, then, let's cut to the chase, shall we?"

"Be my guest," Hislop said extending his arm.

"Clearly, we originally identified you as Angus Hislop, then we discovered your identity change. Further, we have video surveillance of you delivering packages for Mr. Elliot. Why did you want him to have those messages?"

"How much time do you have, Agent Melendez?" Hislop quipped.

"As much time as you need," Melendez brusquely answered.

Hislop appeared to collect his thoughts. "Well, there is a little history involved, but I'm sure you expected that," he explained and continued.

"My job in the old days was to handle complex tax issues. I was young, but smart, and I landed a great job at Coopers after I got my degree from Cambridge. It was my responsibility to come up with tax minimization strategies—you know, the kind where our clients could forego the formality of paying taxes. In those days, the income taxes in England were astronomical, in the seventy-five percent range. I was the one who perfected offshore accounts and special purpose companies as a way to transfer funds to enable our clients to, shall we say, legally lower their tax obligations. Not much in those days was generally known about offshore shelters, but I had studied them thoroughly, and I became quite accomplished in their use. To my way of thinking, a seventy-five percent tax was, and still is, immoral and obscene."

Hislop described how he could layer corporations on top of trusts twisted within other sub-corporations and partnerships so deep and complex that even Her Majesty's Revenuers and the IRS could not piece it together—and of course, that was the point.

"I was invited to lunch one day by one of our potential clients, a record producer and his attorney, at the Savoy Hotel. They explained that their business was expanding exponentially as the British and American rock scene was exploding, and that UK taxes were killing them. They needed an effective tax-minimization strategy, and I was the man they were told could help them. But they didn't want Coopers. They only wanted me.

"They offered me a job on the spot at almost three times what I was making at Coopers. I was single and without real responsibilities. And it was rock and roll, considerably more exciting and much more money. So I accepted the job the next day."

Gantry and Melendez listened intently.

"We had a small office in London, one in Los Angeles, and one in New York City," Hislop explained. "My boss had become incredibly successful and very powerful. He had his hands in most of the major music groups and rock stars at that time but, surprisingly, he rarely met any of them. He approached the business like how a stock-and-bond investor would manage his assets."

"Who was he?" Melendez asked.

Hislop ignored the question.

"We set up an elaborate set of companies and partnerships and maintained bank accounts in more than thirty different countries. Only the three of us knew where everything was. The elaborate construct made it virtually impossible to see the whole picture, and equally as impossible to see who was pulling the strings.

"One evening, I was at my boss's home office outside London

reviewing a rather large monetary transfer. He'd received a phone call and dismissed himself to an adjacent room for a moment. I could not help but overhear the heated conversation, at least from my boss's perspective."

"What was it about?" Melendez asked.

"I'm getting there. He was physically a very powerful fellow, stern, quick Irish temper, and prone to outbursts about business, religion, or money especially when things deviated from his expectations. I could hear him getting very angry with a partner about someone in a band—someone I took to be Brian Jones of the Rolling Stones."

"Are you certain?" Melendez asked.

"As I said, I made an assumption. From what I heard of the conversation, it sounded like they had kicked Jones out of the Stones. I remember it vividly, in spite of it being more than forty years ago.

"Then I heard my boss scream that 'This Jones, this ungrateful Judas—' that's what he said—was out of control. His partner apparently told my boss that he thought Jones was trying to take the Rolling Stones' name and start a new band. The last thing I heard him say was, 'His bandmates can't control him. You know what to do.'

"Brian Jones was found dead a week later," Hislop said.

Gantry and Melendez saw Hislop's confident veneer fade, and they could sense the fear he had felt—the fear he still felt.

"Mr. Hislop, who was your boss?" Melendez fired at him. "Is he still alive? Why did you leave those messages for Mr. Elliot and why did you bug his apartment? Who else is involved? Why didn't you just come to the authorities?"

Hislop slumped in his chair and looked off into space.

"Come on, make it easy on yourself. We don't think you killed Jones or anyone else. We just want the same as you…the truth," Melendez sympathetically offered.

Hislop, regained his composure, sat up straight, and said, "I can't give you his name. I gave you all I have. That was deep in the past when he was my boss. I have moved on since then. I don't know where he is right now, but with his power and money, he could easily reach out from anywhere in the world and squash me like an insect under his shoe."

"So you know that he is still alive?"

Hislop answered in a low voice. "Yes. He's alive."

"Mr. Hislop, I know this scares you. Nevertheless, you did come to us. You started this cat-and-mouse game and got our attention and now we need to move forward. It appears possible that Brian Jones was killed for business reasons, but what we have is only hearsay. We need something more to go on. You chose to stir up this pot by engaging Gantry. Why? And where did you get the objects you delivered?"

"Look, I'm trying to right a wrong, a very big wrong," Hislop said. "I was the one who put the pieces together for you. I'm the one who got the ball rolling. I never intended to get engaged beyond what I provided you. Now, it's up to you two very bright fellows to figure out the rest. It's all there."

"But why choose Mr. Elliot?" Melendez asked. He wanted to keep the pressure on.

"Because he was the only one who could've seen the connections."

He turned to Gantry.

"Mr. Elliot, you lived with and wrote about all these rock stars. You knew them like no other person, outside their families. With your encyclopedic knowledge of the era you would see what had happened—with my help. And you did. You brought it to the point where the authorities are now engaged."

"You must have known that we would find you," Melendez interrupted.

"Yes, eventually. But, I thought it would be after it was safe for me," Hislop said.

He stood up.

"Gentlemen, please. I can't get involved any further on this. This was a long time ago, and I have a new life. I have probably gone too far as it is. You don't know what you are dealing with, but I do. And I am afraid that your coming here today may have placed me in real danger."

Melendez stood up and walked to the windows. Then he turned and looked again at Hislop with an intense expression Gantry had not seen before.

"Mr. Hislop, based on how you describe your former boss, I think you may be right, but if you are in danger, you're much better off letting us place you in protective custody until all this is behind us. But I can't help you if you don't cooperate."

"Oh yes, that's a great idea. Can you see me going from my beautiful home to some obscure flat on a street somewhere near Hobart, Indiana, hiding for the rest of my life? He would find me in no time. You don't know what kind of people you're dealing with? "

"You started this for a reason. Perhaps it was your conscience, maybe you just want to see justice done. We certainly do. I don't know what your motives are, but you took this train out of the station and got it up to speed, and one way or another it's going to keep barreling along with or without you." Melendez made a sweeping gesture with his hands.

"You know it's highly probable that you are an accomplice. Tax avoidance, mail fraud, maybe even murder?" Melendez slowly articulated each possible offense.

Hislop stared at Melendez. His eyebrows furrowed down slightly, though his body language gave no other clues.

"I'll tell you what. Give me a couple of days to think about all this. I have your card, and I will call you. I promise I'll do that."

"All right," Melendez said. "Twenty-four hours. If I were you, I would stay put and not venture out. Do you understand me? You will have no protection."

"Yes, of course."

Melendez and Gantry didn't speak until they were a few blocks from Hislop's home.

Melendez immediately dialed up Tanner. "Get New York to set round-the-clock on Hislop. Don't let him out of our sight."

"Gantry, I'm going to drop you off and head back to Quantico tonight. I think I can make it back before midnight," Melendez said.

Gantry thought for a moment.

"Raphael, why don't you just stay at my place, then leave early tomorrow and beat the traffic? I have some fifteen-year-old Bookers in the cabinet. We can order some Thai."

Melendez smiled.

"Now, that's not a bad idea. Less wear and tear. I think I'll take you up on that offer. One problem, though—you still have that bug in your place," Melendez pointed out. "I'll disable it when we get there."

"So what's your take on this guy?" Gantry asked as they cruised down the Merritt.

"Well, he's been in Westport quite a while, is well-established, and has ties to the community. I can't think he's going anywhere anytime soon. But he's unpredictable right now. I can't arrest him because he's right—everything we have is circumstantial.

"He clearly knows a lot more than he let on, but he's scared, that's for sure, which makes it even more important to figure it all out as quickly as possible.

We still have to talk to San Francisco and the LAPD. There's a lot of work to do. But I'm going to call in to Quantico and have a unit maintain an eye on him. I'm not completely convinced he won't run."

As he finished what he was saying, his cell phone rang.

"Yes, Tanner what now?"

Melendez listened intently as his ace analyst described what had just been uncovered in the Brian Jones investigation.

"No shit. That's unbelievable! I will send a text to Bruce and have him set up a call first thing. Send me the synopsis. Good work," he said, disconnecting.

He pulled off to the shoulder of the expressway and told Gantry what Tanner had said. He then sent a text to Bruce suggesting they have a call with the entire team first thing in the morning to talk about Jones. The information on Hislop would have to wait; he wanted to share that with Bruce privately before bringing it to the team. Unfortunately, he wasn't going to get as much sleep as he thought.

Elliot Gantry's Apartment, New York

Once in Manhattan, Gantry navigated Melendez through the narrow SoHo streets to his favorite Thai restaurant, where they picked up dinner. Upon arriving at Gantry's apartment, Melendez went directly to the electrical outlet and quickly disabled the bug.

"There, now we can talk freely," he said. "Where's that Bookers?"

Pointing to Gantry's massive record collection, Melendez added, "Have any Grateful Dead?"

Gantry laughed. "As my good friend Dennis would say, 'Is the Pope Catholic?'"

"Who's Dennis?"

Gantry explained as he put *American Beauty* on the turntable. The sweet melody of "Box of Rain" filled the room. "Dennis is one of my best friends, originally from London, he owns a collectibles record store not far from here. He's almost as much a rock and roll nut as me."

Gantry held his glass up and toasted Melendez.

"Here's to solving the case of the century!"

"Amen!"

Gantry laid out their take-out to the table and they began to eat.

"So…are you a Redskins fan?" Gantry asked trying to make some small talk.

"Of course," Melendez laughed. "There weren't any NFL teams in Mexico, and it's the only team in the DC area. And you? I suppose you're a Giants fan?"

"Hell, no. Are you kidding? Born and raised on America's team, the Cowboys," Gantry responded. "Thank god they're a decent team again."

"Amen, brother. The Skins…"

"Don't get me started…"

After finishing dinner, Melendez excused himself to go take a shower. Gantry saw that there was a message on his answering machine and walked over to the desk and pushed the play button, recognizing Dennis' voice immediately. He called him back.

"Hey, mate. Where the hell have you been?" Dennis asked, somewhat impatiently.

"Been wrapped up in this case, man. You wouldn't believe what's going on. It's a real morass. I wouldn't even know where to begin. We need to catch up, but I can't today. Long, long story. What's up with you? Is all okay?"

"Not really…It's pretty damned ominous."

"Dennis? What is it?"

"Remember me telling you about that little dolly I dated in London?"

"Yep. I remember. Something come up with her?"

"Something came up all right. It was *me*, and now baby makes three."

"What? Are you fucking kidding me?" Gantry said.

"Would I joke about a thing like that? Come on, mate, she's had a child."

"When? Are you sure it's yours? I mean, you haven't seen her in what—two, three years?" Gantry asked.

"Well, I can't be absolutely sure, but that's what she claims. Shit, man, I can't be having a kid at my age. I should be having grandkids!"

"Okay, wait a second. Settle down. What did you tell her? What does she want?" Gantry asked.

"I was speechless, and I didn't know what to say, it was all so out of left field. She called me a few days ago and woke me up. Basically, she wants me to come back to London and meet the little lass. That was about it."

"How old is this woman?"

"Thirty-two."

"Jesus, Dennis."

"I know, I know. I have a proclivity, as you would say, for the young ones."

"So what did she say? Does she want to get married, want money, what?"

"She didn't say. She just said, come back home and meet little Mindy. She's two years old."

"So…why has she kept all this from you this long? Why now?"

"Goddamn it, mate, if I knew that, I wouldn't be callin' you. I have to go through and sort this out. There's no getting out of it. I know you're all wrapped up that case and all, but I need you to come with me. I can't do it alone."

"Shit, Dennis. Let me think."

"Well? Can you come?"

"When?"

"As soon as we can do it—couple of days? I won't be able to sleep until I figure this out. I'll pay for the tickets. I'll pay for everything. I just need your support."

Gantry thought for a few seconds. Maybe this trip could fit in with the case. He needed to check with Melendez, who'd mentioned earlier that they would probably have to go to London at some point. The Hendrix case was sure to heat up, and Dennis had all those boxes with Hendrix's belongings in them.

"Yeah, I think I can go, but I can't do it in a couple of days. Let me see how this all unfolds, and I'll get back to you. She's waited this long, she can wait a little longer."

"You're right. Sounds like you have a full plate. Give me a teaser. Where are you with it all?"

"Okay, here's the ten-second synopsis. We know the guy who sent all those clues. He's a former accountant for the record companies. Can't tell you any more than that on him for now. Melendez, the agent, put together an entire team of guys in London and Paris to work on the case, and they've reopened the Peter Ham case as a live murder investigation."

"Jesus, this is for real, then?"

"Yep. There's a lot more, but I have to go. Talk to you soon."

As Gantry hung up, Melendez came walking into the living room in a borrowed bathrobe. Gantry was trying to get his mind around Dennis's call and wondering how a trip to London might work into the investigation.

After complaining about how bored and irrelevant he had become, now he had things exploding all around him. *I'll never complain again. Never.* He said to himself.

Quantico, VA

Bruce had scheduled the urgent team call at Melendez's request for 5:30 a.m. EST. Melendez had been up since four forty-five, been briefed by Tanner, and was ready to drive back to Quantico as soon as the call ended. He sat on Gantry's oversize leather chair with a large cup of coffee and dialed into the conference number.

"Gentlemen," Melendez began, "I apologize for the short notice, but I wanted to pass on these surprising early findings on Brian Jones immediately, because we think it might have implications for how each of us approaches the other cases.

"The unidentified amphetamine-like substance in the original report has proven to be PMMA, an ingredient now found in the drug Ecstasy, a compound rarely heard of or used at that time. In high doses it spikes the body temperature acutely and can cause cardiac arrest. The forensic techniques in 1969 would not have been able to identify this chemical, ergo the inconclusive original analysis.

"There was no evidence to suggest that the drug was injected. We believed that a massive instant dosage would have to have been taken in liquid form. However, our testing of the glasses and alcohol residue from the crime scene proved negative on that.

"We then tested the two inhalers as possible vehicles. The one from Jones's bedroom tested normal as an asthma medication. The one at poolside was filled with a liquid form of PMMA in an extremely lethal concentration. If inhaled, it would have immediately entered the bloodstream, causing his body temperature to rise quickly and shortly thereafter cause cardiac arrest.

"It is improbable that Jones would have done this on purpose, and there was no evidence or history of PMMA elsewhere. His allergies and asthma had been acting up in the days leading to his death. The inhaler from his bedroom was almost two months old and nearly empty. The one found poolside was brand new and dated July third, the day he died.

"Gentlemen, our analysis suggests that Brian Jones did not die from 'misadventure' as originally concluded, but from a lethal dose of PMMA administered via his asthma inhaler. The contents had apparently been substituted—transformed into a sophisticated and undetectable murder weapon," Melendez concluded.

For a moment, there was no response from the team. They all knew what this meant and realized that they were dealing with an extremely cunning and sophisticated killer. One who used the eagerness of the authorities to quickly close these cases and cite the most obvious causes of death, and in doing so created the perfect cover—time would do the rest.

Somewhat anticlimactically, Bruce announced, "Based on this startling new insight, I am now compelled to also reopen the Brian Jones case as a homicide."

The whole team's adrenaline rose. As experienced as these assembled experts were, this was unlike anything any of them had seen before. Each knew that he would need to bring their best to these cases.

Melendez dreaded it, but he would now need to sit down with Mayflower, and possibly the Director, to lay out the full extent of what seemed to be unfolding. This had implications for the Agency and would instantly go high-profile when word leaked. He also thought it would be prudent to ask Bruce to arrange another conference call with London to emphasize their mutual interest. They would need the full profiling and analytical expertise of the BAU and Scotland Yard to find this serial killer. No more back-channeling and improvising.

There was more at stake than just solving the case and looking ahead to possible new ones: Morrison, Joplin, and McKernan. It was early spring, and his "use by" date was December 30. He and Lucia had already put a down payment on a home in Palm Desert, California.

He'd miss the bureau, but not the weather.

And Melendez was getting tired. He never let Gantry know, but while his heart, not in the best of shape, still raced at the thought of a hot cold case, even the best of careers can lose their luster and intrigue after too many years of redundancy. He didn't want to start a new career, but he had always hoped to write his memoirs. That is where he would set the record straight and share some of the most intriguing cases he'd ever solved.

Melendez saw this case as the *coup de grace*, a fitting and proper way for him to go out with a bang and a story so unbelievable that there would be no way he could top it. He would smile at his retirement party, raise a glass and say "Fuck you" to Mayflower in front of the entire room. His exact words would be, "Fuck you and the Mayflower you claim your family sailed in on." He laughed thinking about it.

Gantry was just getting up as the call finished. Melendez filled him in on the latest news, and then hastily said goodbye and thanks.

"I will let you know the next steps, including London," he said.

He stopped short of the front door, just as he was about to leave. He slowly walked back up to the poster and squinted at the longhorn charm bracelet on Joplin's ankle. "Gantry, look at this. Isn't this the same bracelet that came in the package?" Gantry didn't turn to look.

"That's the symbol of the University of Texas, isn't it?" Gantry nodded his head.

"You knew that…didn't you?" Melendez asked. Gantry nodded.

"Did you give her this bracelet?" Gantry nodded again.

"Jesus fuck, Gantry, why didn't you say something. What else aren't you telling me?" Melendez yelled at him.

Gantry's heart was almost busting out of his chest as his adrenaline pumped in overdrive…his head spinning.

It had been almost fifty years, but Gantry had recognized it immediately on the call. Janis had kept the bracelet and had reached out to Gantry over the years. The summer she died, she had been in constant communication with him about her health, her career, and her future. For her, Gantry was one of the only people she felt she could trust. He had been the only one who could settle her down after

Jimi died, when she became paranoid.

"What else aren't you telling me, Gantry? Goddamn it, what for Christsakes?" he yelled again.

"Raphael, she and I didn't just have a fling. We kept seeing each other right up until she died," Gantry explained in a calm voice. Melendez stared at him still angry.

"Do you know anything about her death?" a more settled Melendez asked.

"I know she was scared for her life after Hendrix died. She thought she might be next."

"Why was she scared?"

Gantry shook his head. "I don't know. I always found it so hard to believe that she overdosed. She had been trying to clean up her act for the past year. Didn't make any sense. I never believed it."

Melendez put his arm around Gantry.

"Raphael, this wasn't a clue like the others. Hislop knew I gave it to her. We have to get this guy!"

Gantry poured himself a cup a coffee and was getting ready to get in the shower when his cell phone rang. He didn't recognize the number.

"Hello, this is Gantry Elliot."

"Gantry, it's Angus Hislop."

Gantry was surprised, but before he could respond, Hislop began talking a mile a minute.

"I'm not ready yet to talk; I need to think this through. I'm going to take a short trip to tend to some business. I know Agent Melendez told me not to leave, but it's too dangerous and I'm too vulnerable remaining here and—"

"Mr. Hislop, I understand how you feel, but that's why he offered to put you into protective custody," Gantry patiently explained.

Hislop snapped back, "I don't need to hear any of that right now! There is something very important that I need to share with you. You and Melendez can handle it however you want, but you need to know about a particular woman. A D.C. lawyer. You need to talk to her. Her name is Br—"

Gantry abruptly cut him off, as all his anger and emotion finally erupted, "Listen you son of a bitch. You bugged my home, deluged me with messages about murders, sent me Janis's bracelet. Her *fucking* bracelet! Fuck you and you 'not wanting to hear any of that right now.' Fuck you!" yelling into the phone.

"Gantry, I did not mean this to be so personal, but you were the only one I knew would care enough and was smart enough to figure this out. But if I don't get out of here now, I won't be able to help you with anything. I'm sorry."

The line went dead.

"Hislop...Hislop? Gantry asked, "Oh fuck, what did I do?"

He tried to call Hislop back, but of course it was an unknown number.

Gantry sat down and closed his flip phone, then reopened it and called Quantico.

"This is Melendez."

"Raphael, Hislop just called me."

"What? What did he say?"

Gantry recounted the short conversation he'd had with Hislop and how it ended.

"You what? Why the hell did you do that for?" an irritated Melendez blurted.

"I was pissed and it just happened," Gantry said apologizing. "I'm sorry."

"Did you get a number?"

"I tried calling it but it was an unknown number," Gantry responded.

"So all you got is a D.C. attorney that starts with a B?" a pissed off Melendez asked.

"Yeah, that's all," Gantry answered

"Alright then, call me if he calls you again?" and he hung up.

Melendez called Tanner. "Get the New York agent assigned to Hislop on the line. Gantry got a call from Hislop. He may make a move. And have a search done on any D.C. attorneys whose first or last name begins with B. I'll explain later. Call me back."

Within five minutes Tanner called back with rookie agent Stratton on the line.

"Yes sir, his Mercedes has not left the home since we arrived. It's still parked in the garage."

"And the housekeeper's Camry as well?" Melendez asked.

"Sir, only one car is at the home," Stratton answered.

"There were two when we were there. Go check on Hislop. NOW!" Melendez shouted.

Just then the garage door went up and the silver Mercedes sped off.

"The Mercedes just took off. I'm going to pursue." Stratton excitedly exclaimed.

He took off in pursuit, following the car for about a quarter mile before pulling it over. As he approached the car, he recognized it was not Hislop driving, but a Hispanic woman. Hislop's housekeeper.

He jumped back in his car and called Melendez immediately.

"Agent Melendez, the driver of the Mercedes was Hislop's housekeeper. I am going back to the home now, but if there was a Camry… then Hislop?"

"Goddamn it." shouted Melendez, "Put out an APB for the Camry. Hislop has a jump on us!"

PART THREE

Elliot Gantry's Apartment, W23rd Street

Morning

Gantry pulled himself out of bed and stretched his arms over his head to try to relax his tense muscles. He felt like he was coming down with something. But then he felt like that a lot these days. *Getting old sucks.*

He'd been having vivid dreams again. This time it wasn't about rock stars, but about Jodi. In his dream he had called Jodi. But when she picked up the phone, she was in London, standing in front of Scotland Yard with her arm around Dennis. She didn't even like Dennis.

Too many floating loose odds and ends is making me crazy.

Turning on the morning news, he got dressed and sat down to have a coffee.

Raphael told him that he'd already contacted the Los Angeles and San Francisco PDs and initiated similar investigative procedures, as they had with London and Paris. It seemed incredible to Gantry that with all that had transpired, he and Raphael had only been fully engaged in the case for such a brief period of time.

The blinking message light on his recorder caught his eye, so he walked over and pressed PLAY.

"Hello, Gantry. It's Jodi," the message began.

The sound of her mellow voice was like a tuning fork that vibrated inside him, and summoned up all the pain he'd felt when she left him.

"I'm pretty sure Alex relayed that I got your call. I couldn't call you directly at that time. But you'll understand, darling. By the way, I did find your stinky old knapsack and will get it to you soon," she ended with a slight giggle.

Gantry closed his eyes and smiled. *She must be involved in the case in some way,* he mused.

Gantry took another sip of coffee and felt the April morning sun cracking through the buildings across the street as the next message came up.

"Hey, mate. I just bought us two tickets, first class, to London. I left the departure open for now. I'll tell you all about it when you call me. She remembers the boxes I told you about and thinks she stored them in her father's garage. Can't wait to see what's in there."

Gantry was irritated that Dennis seemed to be pressing him to leave after he'd said he needed time to think. There was a lot of work to do before he could realistically consider that. He also needed Raphael's go ahead.

He spent the morning working up his notes. His cell rang around 11:00 a.m.

"Gantry, this is Tanner. Agent Melendez asked me to get you down to Quantico this afternoon to continue your commonalities effort."

"Okay, but I need to rent a car. I can't get there until six o'clock at the earliest, this time of day."

"No time. Hislop is on the run. We need you here now. Do you know where the South Street Heliport is? South and Broad? Be there by noon. An agent will meet you. You're taking a chopper."

Gantry threw some clothes in a bag, grabbed a sport coat, ran out the door, and hailed a cab. The traffic was light, and they made it down to the heliport just outside Wall Street in less than ten minutes. An agent intercepted him at the door, escorted him to a waiting helicopter, and they were airborne in minutes.

Gantry took out his notebook to capture some additional thoughts he had about the Morrison connections. He felt like a young research student at UT again, poring over data for a journalism assignment. He remembered how exhilarating it was to work and brainstorm in tandem with other journalists—digging, corroborating, debating, and verifying everything before putting down a single word.

As the helicopter lifted off, Tanner's words rang in his ears, "Hislop is on the run. We need you here now."

The momentum was gathering and he was at the center of it.

FBI, HQ, Quantico, VA

Afternoon

Melendez had Tanner take point in creating the virtual crime scenes for each of the dead rock stars. This new technology was in advanced testing at the Emerging Tech Lab, and even though it was not yet in general application, it was considered a major advance in investigative science. Using it, they could digitally convert crime scene photos and photo forensic insights to three-dimensional life-sized holographic images of the entire crime scene. Investigators could step into the virtual crime scene, walk around it, test optional positions, outcomes, etc. It was the only one of its kind in the world.

"Sir, we have been working over the last twenty-four hours to digitize all available crime scene photos for each of the dead rock stars," Tanner said. "Ham, Hendrix, and Joplin have been completed, and we should have the others done shortly. The Scotland Yard and Police Nationale investigators left last night for Quantico and should be here soon. Two top investigators from the west coast have also flown in to assist with the California-based cases.

"Detective Randolph with SF forensics is leading her team. She's already sent us the pictures and is bringing all the rest with her, including three original crime scene boxes on McKernan. She can't ship them, has to carry them, something about their arcane rules out there. Davis, the agent from L.A., is delivering four full boxes from the Wilson and Joplin investigations. That ought to be a gold mine."

"That's great, Tanner. Is that Jodi Randolph? " Melendez asked. "By the way, I haven't heard from Gantry. How is he making out with the commonalities team?"

"I had to fly him down. He's been holed up and heads-down for hours on it. Everything is moving along well."

For the previous four hours, Gantry had been absorbed with the commonalities charts. He was impressed with the additional amount of information, and was feeling very satisfied about his own contributions to it. The application was now populated with far more detail on Morrison, Joplin, McKernan, and Wilson: common friends, doctors, roadies, and engineers were filling in the gaps. The teams in London and Paris, plus the FBI and the West Coast detectives, had added considerable new data and insights. The one thing that really impressed him was the numerous record company, marketing, and management interconnections now fully enhanced. The FBI search engine had been constantly learning, adding and deleting information automatically, as it refined the data.

The two to three most common links in each category were immediately enlarged in each cell as he scrolled down the categories:

Engineers:	Glyn Johns, Owsley Stanley, Bruce Botnick
Managers:	Alan Klein, Mike Jeffrey, Bill Siddons
Marketing/PR:	Les Perrin, Paul Rothschild, Ed Chaplin
Drug Friends:	Jean de Breteuil, Robert Fraser
Accountants:	Coopers & Lybrand
Pharmacies:	St. Albans and Carlton
Travel agencies:	Nevermore and Panarama
Producers:	Paul Rothschild, Jimmy Miller, Ed Chaplin
Session musicians:	Tommy Tedesco, Earl Palmer, Rick Kemp, Bobby Graham

The comprehensive list continued for more than a dozen other categories.

Gantry stared intensely at the names on the screen. He remembered these great rock patriots, renaissance men leading a revolution. Armed with exhilarating music, different than any music he'd heard before. It was magic.

Bobby Graham was probably the best rock, pop, and fusion drummer in the world at the time. Gantry could almost hear his snake-like rhythms twisting through the music of the dozens of artists he recorded with. Glyn Johns was a genius engineer way before anyone knew what digital was; when music was truly an art form, not a science project. Viewing all these names was like going through a long-lost family photo album.

He suddenly had an epiphany: he had been a witness to history, an intimate observer of an art form that neither he nor anyone else would ever experience again. That was why *Rolling Stone* valued him so much—and why he'd hung in there for so long. What he'd done for years, and what he wanted to keep on doing, had become a fundamental part of who he was.

The thought gave him a smooth, warm, delicious feeling inside that also hurt in an odd way.

Sliding his chair back, he slowly pulled himself out of his reverie to refocus on the task at hand.

"Cold cases almost always break on the most insignificant detail," Tanner had explained. "Every suspect, every lead, is equal. You never know where that small, vital clue will turn up. We'll need to re-interview each person, talk to the families, speak with each of the remaining band members and backup musicians."

Now, he looked at Gantry and said, "Can you get the information we need for all that, Mr. Elliot?"

Gantry smiled.

"Yes, and it's Gantry, not Mr. Elliot."

Tanner nodded.

Gantry looked down and thought for a minute, "Say, Tanner, what's your first name? You know, we've been working together now for a little while. Don't you think we can be a little less formal?"

Tanner looked a little surprised. "It's Elmer." He smiled crookedly. "That's why everyone here refers to me as just Tanner."

Gantry nodded.

"You know, Mr. Elliot—I mean Gantry. Ordinarily we do not allow non-agents to assist in our interviews. But in this case, Agent Melendez and Mr. Bruce believe that your knowledge is invaluable. You have the connections we need to speak to all these people. We don't. And sometimes that lack of intimacy can make the discovery process in cold cases very difficult."

"I'd be more than happy to help with any interviews. Just tell me who, where, and when, and I'll saddle up."

"Thanks, Gantry, but it's not quite that easy. There are a few things we'll have to do before we can have you engage at that level."

"Okay."

"Right. First, I need to arrange a crash course on field investigations, so you learn the do's and don'ts."

Gantry stared at him. Did Elmer have any idea what a real journalist did?

As if reading his mind, Tanner said, "Believe me, I do know what you guys do, it's just that here, we do it our way. We'll get you set up with a field monitoring device so we can record what you uncover."

"Whoa, partner. No way I'm going to wear a wire! You know what can happen if you're caught wearing one of those?"

"Gantry, calm down, it's not a wire. For God's sake, this is 2016. It's a remote audio and video device. You won't even know you're wearing it. If you're going to be interviewing people on your own, we need to ensure that we are able to document everything. I know you're a good investigative reporter, but this is different. Trust me."

"Well, if that's what it takes, that's what it takes. Not keen on it, but I get it."

"Last thing, Agent Melendez is considering temporarily deputizing you. I didn't want this to be a surprise," Tanner said.

Gantry was stunned, "What? What's this all about?"

"Well, there are two very practical reasons. The first is that it will allow you unescorted access to our facilities and systems. That will make working on this program much easier. It will also allow you to request info and data, not just provide it. You'll also have remote access.

"The second reason is that you'll need to maintain the cover of a reporter so as not to draw attention to the investigation. You won't be interviewing under our authority."

"You mean I'll be undercover?" Gantry asked.

"Yes."

"Will I carry a gun?"

Tanner shook his head no.

"I probably need to clear this with Alex Jaeger?"

Tanner nodded.

Gantry thought for a moment, then slammed his hand down on the table. "Fuck it. Let's do this. By God, my grandfather was a Texas Ranger!"

Tanner smiled, "You ready to get a glimpse of our Virtual Crime Scene Facility, deputy?"

What Tanner hadn't told Gantry was that he and almost everyone he knew, would all be discreetly investigated. They also did not want it known that they were investigating the pharmacy, travel agent, and record company connections, as well as employees, ownership, tax records, and flow of funds.

The door had no identifying signage, but there were two warning lights above it, one red, the other green, as in a recording studio. The green light was on, so Tanner ushered Gantry inside.

The room was unlike any other in the building. A handful of the most advanced image technologists in the world had worked for the last three years to get it to the point of practical application. The room was circular, the upper part built in the shape of a dome, and covered with recessed digital projectors all aimed inward to the center of the room. The walls were over twenty feet high.

"Mademoiselle Laurent, Mr. Jenkins, and officers Jackson and Randolph," Melendez said, "this is Agent Tanner and Mr. Elliot. Mr. Elliot is consulting with us on the case. Mr. Jenkins and Mademoiselle Laurent arrived late last night, and I understand that Detective Randolph and Mr. Elliot already know one another. And Detective Jackson from LAPD. We thank you all for joining us here today on short notice."

Gantry heard nothing beyond "Detective Randolph" as his eyes adjusted to the room's soft lighting and he found himself looking at his ex-wife. She was smiling, and gave him a small wave from across the floor. She looked good. He could feel a slight pounding and wondered if machinery was operating somewhere in the building. He realized it was his heart.

The old tapes played in his head. Gantry had been a go-getter, a nonparticipant in the relationship, immersing himself in his work, and eventually Jodi looked elsewhere for comfort and companionship. And found it. Nevertheless, he thought they'd sorted it out—until she had another affair, this time with a cop, and before he could even get angry, she was gone.

And yet, he still missed her.

"To reiterate our purpose, we will be collectively analyzing a set of virtual crime scenes utilizing our test lab holographic technology," Melendez explained.

The group exchanged handshakes and smiles, but Gantry stood aside.

Then Tanner briefly described the technology. He had set up real-time transmissions back to their country teams so their colleagues could participate remotely, if they wished. All the photos and data that had been provided had been digitized, loaded and interpreted, and all optional scenarios had been simulated.

"Let's start with Peter Ham," Tanner said.

The lights dimmed and the room was instantly transformed into a garage with a lifelike holograph of Ham hanging from a crossbeam. The investigators, tech-savvy as they were, still were stunned at the realism. Jenkins instinctively put his hand out to touch the body, and just as in a movie special effect, his hand went through the image. He jerked it back, a little unsettled.

"I cannot believe how real this appears," Laurent remarked, walking closer. "Absolutely amazing, how do you do it?"

"It would take half the day to explain it all, but essentially all of what you are seeing is derived from photographs from the original investigation," Melendez said. "The photos were digitized, then a set of algorithms was used to create and fill in the dimensionality, only in this case, the output is a holographic image."

The investigators walked around and through the lifelike scene, noting the low cross beam height of seven and a half feet, the crude noose that gripped Ham's neck under his chin, and the placement of the drummer's throne. Jenkins took a measurement of the length of the overturned throne.

"May we simulate the hanging now?" Jenkins asked.

Ham's image appeared, standing on the drummer's throne, about two feet from the ground. With a single movement, the seat fell backwards, and Ham dropped down and dangled. The noose slid under his chin and pulled his head back.

"Do you see that?" Jenkins commented. "Run it again. See, he only dropped about a foot, no snap. That could have suffocated him, but that fall would not have broken the hyoid bone." Pointing at the lower neck, he continued, "Look closely here at the two bruises and cuts. They are fingernail indentations, typical of strangulation."

"Your conclusion?" Melendez said.

"This man died from strangulation that broke the hyoid bone. I believe the crude hanging was staged after the strangulation."

"What about the alcohol in his stomach?"

"Very unlikely it would have been self-ingested, because of the Antabuse. Even if attempted, there would have been a huge mess, as in vomit, maybe even some blood. It must have been forced, as part of the staging."

"Okay, let's move to Janis Joplin."

Instantly they were in her room at the Landmark Hotel. Her body was wedged between the twin beds, and her head was lying back against the bedside table, badly cut. Her feet were splayed. Bruises covered her legs, arms and the side of her mouth, and she had multiple needle marks on her arms. The room was disheveled, as if a struggle had taken place in it.

The image made Gantry sick to his stomach. He quickly walked out of the facility and into the men's room. After putting some cold water on his face, he made his way back to the conference room he had been working out of and back to the commonalities program.

So much for wanting to see the technology so badly, he thought.

In the virtual crime scene room Jackson was talking.

"Look at the location of her body," he explained. "Seems an unnatural position for a fall. Let's test alternative falls and positioning."

With that, Joplin's holograph fell from one bed, then the other, and then fell from the front and also backwards, with no outcomes close to what the crime scene photos indicated.

"Now let's test the scenarios of her being pushed and held down," he said.

The hologram simulated this, and the resulting image was similar to the crime scene photos.

Jackson said, "The autopsy originally concluded that Joplin died from acute heroin intoxication. Our re-examination of the test results and hair analysis last night discovered a lethal dosage well beyond that of usual overdose victims. The fourteen needle marks you can see on her arms suggest multiple injections. It's extremely unlikely they were self-administered, and their presence is inconsistent with the original investigator's notes, which stated that she was trying to get off drugs prior to her death."

He turned to Melendez just as Raphael was reflecting on what Gantry had also told him about Joplin.

"Agent Melendez, my conclusion, based on these simulations and the re-examination of the original test results, is that Joplin had been restrained against her will and administered multiple injections of heroin, causing cardiac arrest. Because of her history, the previous conclusion was that she had simply overdosed."

The team methodically went through the rest of the cases over the course of the day, re-creating the crime scenes and testing alternative outcomes. The lead detectives went over and over the scenarios, captivated by this newfound capability. Some requested 3-D printer copies of key body parts to surgically examine minute details. It was as if they had the actual, untouched crime scene bodies to examine, even though the crimes had occurred more than forty years earlier.

The global forensic teams were well into their chemical analyses and were passing along their observations throughout the day to the lead investigators at the virtual crime scene facility.

The go/no-go conference call was in twenty-four hours, and each team was heads-down coming to their conclusions and preliminary perpetrator profile. The new technology was dramatically speeding up what normally would have been an excruciating process.

Gantry spent the rest of his day refining connections and commonalities. Tanner had asked him to prioritize his top three interviews so they could get him out into the field without delay. He also promised Tanner he would review the field investigator guidelines and case study videos to savvy himself up.

Checking his phone, Gantry saw that he had three messages. Dennis had called him twice, asking if he was cleared to fly to London, and Jodi had left a message asking if he wanted to get a drink later that night. In spite of the tremendous swirl of activity in was in the middle of, it was all he could think about the rest of the day.

Later that night he met Jodi at the roadside bar. It was the first time they had been alone since she left him. He was visibly anxious and stumbled with his words until she reached over and stroked his hair back behind his ear as she used to do.

"Gantry, this is as difficult for me as it is for you. You don't have to talk," she sweetly offered.

He nodded and suddenly felt calm.

She leaned in towards him. "Isn't it insane that we reconnect over a possible murder case after all these years? And a case that we both bring our unique insights and experience to help solve." Gantry just smiled.

"Gantry, when I first heard about the possible re-opening of these cases, something drew me in like a magnet," she explained.

"Me too," he answered.

"And then I heard how it all started with you, and it seemed almost cosmic. Like *they* needed you and needed me to solve this.

I wanted to call you, but protocol demanded that I couldn't.

"That's why I called Alex. I got really worried for you as this began escalating into something sinister." Joni reached over and wrapped her hands around his.

"Gantry, this is not a random kook. This is a sophisticated killer. I know. Promise me that you insist on having protection." He smiled again. He wasn't scared. He actually felt at peace with her.

They walked out to her car.

"I have something for you." She popped the trunk and pulled out his old knapsack.

"I opened it to look inside to see what was so valuable, but it smelled like a cesspool and had roaches crawling all in it!" She laughed, "Happy hunting." She gave him a long hug that Gantry didn't want to end. "See you tomorrow," she added.

When he got back to the motel, he emptied the bag on the floor and sifted through his old journals, pictures, a roach clip, a paisley bandana, twenty-year-old chewing gum, and a pair of pink tinted horned rim glasses, and what he was hoping to find...the letter from Janis.

The forensic and chemical-analysis teams had agreed on three areas of coordinated focus. The first was to retest the available DNA of each rock star for any inconsistencies with the autopsy reports, and to test for third-party DNA. The second was to perform a chemical signature analysis on all the drugs to determine if they came from a common source. The third was to re-examine all evidence for fingerprints, re-interview original persons of interest (and interview any new ones that were warranted), and probe for new evidence or surveillance videos. Finally, the team would retrace the original investigation and analyze all notes and reports for any insights they might provide.

The teams had been working separately for the last twenty-four hours and had scheduled an update session well in advance of the scheduled go/no-go call. Melendez had told Tanner that this was a closed call, meaning no Elliot or Jaeger.

All team members in Virginia, including Laurent, Jenkins, and Randolph, were assembled in a conference room at Quantico. Remote team members in Europe had dialed in.

Tanner was hosting the call. "Have we all had enough time to come to preliminary conclusions?"

His question was answered by a Greek chorus of low grumbling.

"Perfect," he said with a smile. "Mademoiselle Laurent, please do us the honors. What has your team uncovered on Jim Morrison?"

"Something very unexpected," she replied. "As you know, Morrison was found dead in his bathtub of an apparent heart attack, even though an autopsy confirming that was never performed. There was no evidence of drugs noted at the crime scene, but the testing of a hair sample saved in a jar as a souvenir by an investigator did prove positive for high levels of heroin. We found that inconsistent with his history. His bodyguard, Tony Funches, had previously confirmed that Morrison did not take heroin and had an aversion to needles.

"Based on the insight from the Brian Jones call, we tested another hypothesis," Laurent continued. "We went back and re-examined the contents of Morrison's evidence box. There were two shocking findings. First, all the prescription bottles were drawn on the St. Albans Pharmacy in London. Second, like Jones, an asthma inhaler was found at the crime scene in the living room, but it was not originally analyzed. Upon analysis, it proved to be filled with a deadly concentration of heroin.

"Morrison died of cardiac arrest, but it was most probably induced by a high dosage of heroin administered via the altered inhaler. It would be inconsistent with his history and habits for him to have knowingly administered the drug to himself. The massive dosage would have instantly incapacitated him and made it impossible for him to have walked into the bathroom and draw a bath. We will simulate that this evening, but I am certain of the results."

Tanner and the team were silent.

"Any questions or observations on Morrison?" Tanner asked. "No? All right, continuing on. What did the Hendrix team find, Mr. Jenkins?"

"Also something unexpected, I'm afraid. We performed a DNA hair analysis and found no history of the kind of barbiturate found in Hendrix's bloodstream at the time of his death. We then performed a chemical signature analysis on that barbiturate, and compared that to the prescription drugs found at the crime scene. There were no matches. Our conclusion is that the large volume of barbiturates found in his bloodstream were not from any of the evidence bottles. But surprisingly, most had a common imperfection, including the barbiturate in his bloodstream, meaning they come from the same source.

"We found no mention of injection marks in the original report, and we re-examined his blood-alcohol results, which proved to be surprisingly moderate, not excessive. When we combine that insight with the results of the virtual crime scene analysis, we conclude that Hendrix was forcibly drugged with a lethal dosage of barbiturate and then later 'water-boarded' with red wine to the point of suffocation. The vomiting would have been a reflexive action."

Tanner was about to move on, when Jenkins interrupted him.

"There is one more thing we found in the evidence box that seems interesting."

"What's that?"

"There is a dated journal in the box."

"And..."

"It covers January 1970 through September 1970, up until the time of his death. There is a number '2' handwritten on the cover. Inside are various entries, lots of poetry and song lyrics, lists, doodles, et cetera, nothing in any particular order. But there are some entries that we may want to look into. They describe visits to his psychiatrist about his recording legal issues. It reads as if this was going on for some time and keeps referring to an incident the previous year that, quote, 'scared the shit' out of him."

"Noted, thank you," Tanner responded. "Detective Randolph, Let's talk about the death of Ron McKernan."

"Certainly. McKernan died from massive intestinal bleeding and was dead for two days, before he was found by his landlord. A non-extensive autopsy was performed. An interesting fact is that McKernan did not use drugs other than some over-the-counter medications and prescriptions. That said, the prescriptions found in the evidence box were drawn on the Carlton Pharmacy, the same as for Joplin and

Wilson. We tested all the medicine bottles and his asthma inhaler, and conducted a hair and organic material DNA test. What was completely unexpected were the traces of arsenic found in his inhaler," Randolph said.

"Are you certain the inhaler had not been contaminated?" Laurent asked.

"We were not sure, which prompted us to perform a Marsh test, a chemical analytic procedure to detect the presence of arsenic using the recovered hair samples. The test confirmed lethal levels in McKernan's system, potent enough to cause gastrointestinal bleeding and heart failure."

The room was silent.

"Our conclusion is that Ron McKernan died from arsenicosis, or arsenic poisoning, delivered via his asthma inhaler. In short, we believe he was murdered."

"Allow me to sum up," Tanner said. "Ham, Jones, Hendrix, and Morrison all had prescriptions drawn on the St. Albans Pharmacy in London, while Joplin, Wilson, and McKernan all had prescriptions drawn on the Carlton Pharmacy in Los Angeles. We found common imperfections potentially leading to a common source for the drugs in London and in L.A.

"Three of the dead stars appear to have ingested lethal drugs via an inhaler, and two appear to have been orally forced. One was strangled and one overdosed from multiple injections of heroin. Is that correct?" Tanner asked.

"Correct," each team member answered.

The St. Albans Pharmacy had been located near Piccadilly Circus, on St. Albans Street, in the heart of London. It had been closed for years and the space was now an Indian fast-food restaurant. The Carlton Pharmacy in L.A., originally a block off the Sunset Strip, was also long gone. A Red Wing shoe store stood in its place.

The London and U.S. corporate forensic teams focusing on the pharmacies had been working independently and were now having their first joint call to compare notes.

Hammond kicked it off. "St. Albans Pharmacy was only in existence for about five years. The original municipal filing shows that it was incorporated by three individuals: Thomas S. Marland, Kenny L. Roberts, and Joseph M. Clark. We have secured their bank records and—"

"What was that last name?" said Tanner.

"Joseph M. Clark."

"We have the same name on the Carlton incorporating documents, with a listed address in Los Angeles," Tanner confirmed.

"Yes—Clark's address on the London filing is a Los Angeles address."

That night, Melendez called Robert Bruce.

"I guess you heard the teams are finding 'misadventure' with all of the dead rock stars. The murder allegations look like they might be real."

"Yes, I heard," Bruce answered.

"I wanted to run something by you. You recall the unused Al Wilson plane ticket?" Melendez asked. "It was issued by Nevermore Travel Agency out of Los Angeles."

"Yes."

"Well, the Hendrix team found a reference to the same travel agency on a list found in the evidence box. We also found in our commonality effort that many of these stars used this same travel agency. It must have been a popular one with rock and rollers at that time. And remember, travel agencies were frequently used to launder and move money around the globe."

"We used to track travel agency bank records back then," Bruce responded.

"We did, as well," Melendez agreed. "I had one of our top financial forensic analysts dig into the ownership of Nevermore and into their bank records. In the original incorporating documents, we discovered a founding principal named Joseph M. Clark. The same Joseph Clark that our teams found in the St. Albans and Carlton Pharmacy filings."

"Are the teams aware of this?"

"Not yet. I want to check bank records first. We can review what we find on our call tomorrow," Melendez answered.

"This could be a break for us. Talk to you tomorrow."

Bruce and Melendez welcomed the teams to the call. There was an unmistakable buzz as the teams were now deep into the details surrounding each dead rock star. They all knew this would be the determining call.

"Thank you all for completing the summary forms," Bruce said as a findings-and-conclusion chart was shared on the monitor. He gave them time to absorb what was in front of them.

Melendez said, "As you can all see, the forensic analyses and the crime scene re-creations for each of your cases have confirmed what Mr. Elliot's messages suggested. Each of you believes these individuals were murdered, and in most cases, the crime scenes were staged to make the deaths look like accidents or suicides. Let's devote this call to our initial profiling, and compare it to the results of our commonalities analysis.

"Staged crime scenes have usually suggested someone intimate with the deceased. And the souvenirs sent as clues would seem to confirm that."

Bruce added, "The creative delivery of the drugs suggests sophisticated chemical knowledge and access to the drug sources or pharmacies."

"Their bodies were not disfigured, molested, or bloodied," Prevot pointed out, "which means they were not killed in an angry rage."

Melendez added, "The crime scenes were purposely staged to lead the authorities to a fast, straightforward and lifestyle-consistent conclusion. The perpetrator knew how these deaths would be perceived and analyzed."

Gantry took the opportunity to add something.

"If I may, that seems to rule out a deranged fan. Jean de Breteuil or Les Perrin were at the scene of some of these murders, but not all of them, and don't seem to have a real motive. To me, the engineers and roadies don't fit the pattern either."

The conversation was now moving quickly, with voices overlapping.

Bruce asked, "Does this fall into any serial killer patterns that any of you are familiar with?"

Tanner spoke up. "We tested for a number of profiles through our VICAP database. Hammond did the same in London, but nothing hit. These murders had all the superficial attributes of a serial killer, but not the historic motives. That, combined with the sophistication and access, did not fit."

Melendez said, "Based on my experience, these have the appearance of serial killings, but don't look like the work of a serial killer." Melendez went further. "The facts seem to suggest a variety of killers carrying out a hit. To me, it looks just like the work of a mob."

The call erupted in a cacophony of voices.

"Why these people?"

"Who would do this?"

"What was the motive?"

"Why wasn't that ever a consideration?"

"It can't be."

As the voices quieted, Gantry asked to speak.

"Years ago, I wrote an article about record company management and the control they had over their rock 'assets,' as they were called. Back then, the industry was dominated by a few powerful and reclusive individuals who controlled and protected every aspect of their assets, milking profits through one-sided contracts and routinely replacing anyone who opposed them. This was strictly business for them, and they were ruthless. Many groups were afraid of them, but that was the price for access and stardom at the time."

"Gantry, I think you may be on to something!" exclaimed Melendez. "As some of you know, we found a common name in the original filings for the St. Albans and Carlton pharmacies: Joseph M. Clark of Los Angeles. Yesterday we also discovered a Joseph M. Clark in the filings for Nevermore Travel, the agency that issued the Al Wilson ticket. We have been unable to locate him. The address in L.A. was an abandoned warehouse."

Tanner chimed in. "Agent Melendez, on a hunch, I had the

property records for that address researched to see who owned it in the sixties. The owner was a small record company called Lexington Records. We have been unable to get anything on that company, but have reached out to the International Record Association for assistance. Perhaps Clark may have been associated with that record company."

"The messages I received were precisely worded," Gantry said, "and have helped us discover that these individuals may have been murdered. But I believe there was more to the messages. Aside from their age, they had another common element that we are overlooking: most were related to either recordings or performances that were done outside the norm of the musicians' contracts in some way, on the sly, so to speak. In fact, many of these stars were trying to get out of their contracts."

Gantry nodded to Raphael and then looked at Jodi.

"Let me read from a letter from Janis Joplin that I received three months before she died, "… they threatened me…that if I didn't live up to my contract that I could end up like Jimi. I don't know if they're just shittin' me or serious, but I am scared. Really scared. These Irish guys don't give a shit about anyone. It's all money to them…"

"Gantry, you may be right," Tanner said. "Some of the old papers and interview notes in the evidence boxes mentioned that Jones owned the rights to the Rolling Stones' name and wanted to start a new group with Hendrix. Ham had quit his group to break his contract three days before his death. Hendrix was speaking to an attorney about not renewing his contract. Wilson wanted out. Morrison wanted out. We see that Joplin wanted out. McKernan wanted out."

Bruce was astonished. "Could this be the commonality we need?"

"I'm not sure, Robert," Melendez said, "but let's do a formal motive analysis as soon as possible on record company motivations for these stars, and also dig into company ownership. Robert, can you, Inspector Prevot, and MacAlistair call me back on my secure line? We will reconvene this group call later today."

Within minutes, all three called back.

Melendez said, "Gentlemen, I had one of our financial forensic analysts look into the bank records of Nevermore Travel. I just sent you a graphic of the outflows over a five-year period that shows a steady flow of money, with periodic spikes. Compare that to the same chart, but this time highlighted for the dates of each star's death. Notice the pronounced spike in outflows during the preceding week: $25,000 a pop. A precise correlation between the death and the spike. The copies of the outflows we could find were all checks made out to cash."

"This is unbelievable!" Bruce gasped. "Especially now that we know that one individual was common to the pharmacies and the travel agency. Has he shown up elsewhere in the commonalities analysis?"

"Not yet. At this stage, we don't even know if Clark was a real person."

They all agreed.

The offbeat clues that began with Gantry and a plain manila envelope now appeared to support neither a myth nor a serial killer, but a concerted, well-planned series of murders. The questions that needed to be answered now were *why?* and *by whom?* And why twenty-seven? It was beginning to look like everything pointed back to the money trail.

Angus Hislop's house Westport, CT

Hislop had told the maid that he had some business to attend to and would be back shortly. He didn't say where he was going, but she thought she saw him loading a cardboard box and assumed he was going to drop or send them off somewhere. He borrowed her car because he said that his gold clubs were in the trunk of his Mercedes.

The TSA and Canadian Border Control had been alerted, and the agency put Hislop on the no-fly list. There would be no way he could fly out of the country, but it was possible that he could drive the back routes into Canada—and at any rate, he had a head start, so anything was possible.

"Agent Melendez, Agent Stratton here. No sign of Hislop at his home. Forensics is going through it top to bottom and will extract all the hard drives," Stratton explained, "but it's pretty clean thus far. Except, I did find…"

"What?" Melendez immediately blurted.

"I did find an unopened letter on his desk addressed to Gantry Elliot."

"Can you open it please?" Melendez asked.

The agent snapped on his forensic gloves, opened the envelope and began reading the enclosed handwritten letter.

"Looks like it was written in a hurry," he commented.

"Read it please," Melendez ordered.

He began:

Dear Mr. Elliot,
I have gone into seclusion to protect my life and that of my family's. This

is not going the way I had planned. I am certain that they now know that we have been in contact.

I have in my possession information that will help you bring justice to those artists that were killed. This goes much deeper than you can imagine. That is why I had to get out years ago. Having this evidence has kept me safe all these years.

Brigid Greeley is a lawyer for the recording industry and also general counsel for the International Record Association in Washington, D.C.

Go see her. Make it a surprise. Tell her your investigating some possible murders in the rock and roll industry. Cold cases. And you need access to old industry corporate records.

Can't tell you anymore, but she is a piece of the puzzle that you need.

DO NOT USE MY NAME.

She is sharp, conniving, and a fit bird, by the way.

Stay one step ahead of her.

I will make contact with you once I am safe. One favor. Please have the authorities protect my daughter and granddaughter in London. They believe I died years ago. Below are their addresses.

Sincerely,

A.H.

PS: To answer your question. The artifacts that I sent you were actually confirmations that actions had been taken.

"Agent Stratton, send a picture to me. Thank you." Melendez hung up and buzzed Tanner.

"Tanner, grab Gantry and get in here. We have fresh correspondence from Hislop and I need an investigation on a D.C. attorney named Brigid Greely immediately!" Melendez ordered.

Washington, D.C.

Late Morning

Greely and Associates and was located in the high-rent district at 2200 Pennsylvania Avenue, just blocks from the White House. The team had already done a thorough background search on Greely and, as Hislop had told Gantry, she was the general counsel for the International Record Association in Washington.

But that was just the tip of the iceberg. She also represented several large record companies, with a client roster straight out of the Rock and Roll Hall of Fame. One that interested Melendez especially was a company called 1969 Platters, based in London and a subsidiary of Sony-BMG. It was formed in 2006 and founded by Jim Wainscott. Wainscott, the team discovered, was much older than one would expect a working record executive to be; he was seventy-five. They didn't have much information on the label other than that it featured indie-rock and pop groups.

Melendez was provided an article from the London *Times* about this label's top star, a twenty-seven-year-old phenomenon with a brilliant career ahead of him, found dead of a heart attack the year before. The spokeswoman in the article was the label's attorney, Ms. Brigid Greely, who was quoted on the tragedy, along with the rest of the sentiments said at such events, "Too young for a heart attack."

Gantry didn't know what a "fit bird" was until he and Melendez were escorted into Brigid Greely's offices on Pennsylvania Avenue.

Greely was stunning. She stood to greet them from behind a massive glass-and-chrome desk. Her view from the eighteenth floor was incomparable, with glimpses of the White House, the Capitol building, and the top of the Washington Monument.

Gantry tried not to stare, but took in the landscape quickly nonetheless. She had long auburn hair and iridescent round green eyes. He guessed her age at forty-something. She was about five-foot-seven and had a stunning row of brilliant white teeth. Oddly, she wore no jewelry, with the exception of two small diamond studs in her ears. Not even a watch. The surprise, though, was her outfit. She had on a black Armani skirt, a tight knit top and, Gantry noticed as she came around the desk, a pair of red cowboy boots.

"Hello, gentlemen. Please have a seat," Greely said, gesturing to two leather chairs. "I'll take the couch," she said with a smile.

Melendez appeared to peruse the accolades, degrees, and pictures on the walls.

"Who's this in the picture with you and Bill Wyman?" he asked. Gantry leaned down to look closer at the picture of the three arm-in-arm, something familiar catching his eye.

"No one you'd know," Greely replied. There was an edge to her voice. "He's only somewhat involved in the record industry. Now, to what do I owe the pleasure of a meeting with an FBI agent and..." Greely hesitated. "I'm sorry—what is it that you do, Mr. Elliot?" Her tone sounded almost flirtatious.

"I'm an editor with *Rolling Stone* magazine," answered Gantry

"That so? Now that's one for the books, *Rolling Stone* and the FBI working together."

"Ms. Greely, Mr. Elliot is consulting with the Bureau, helping me sort through some things," Melendez explained.

"Oh, that is interesting! A kind of music historian? What, C&W or some other genre?" Greely asked.

"Classic," Gantry answered.

"Classical?" she said

Gantry corrected the misconception. "No, not classical. Rock and roll classics."

Brigid Greely could always smell a bad deal coming her way, and this one was a real stinker.

"Well, then," she said. "What can I do for the FBI today?"

"We are investigating a series of murders, Ms. Greely."

Melendez let it lie there.

Equally cool, Greely smiled again. "And?"

"And they involve several rock stars. Since you are, well, who you are, we thought you might help us."

"And who do you think I am?"

"The representative of quite a few record labels and general counsel for the International Record Association."

"That is correct, Agent Melendez," she responded. "And you do quite a bit of work involving ownership rights and copyright cases and also have access to legacy international company information."

"Also correct. So what has all that to do with your case? Really, gentlemen, I'm very busy. What do you need from me? I'd be glad to help a bona fide music historian and a special agent if you'll just tell me what this is all about."

"You're right Ms. Greely," Melendez said. "Unfortunately, I can't tell you much about the investigation, it's still ongoing. However, I can tell you that what we are looking for is some record industry account information."

"What kind of account? I'd be glad to help you."

Gantry saw her eyes flick to the window and back. *Like hell you would.*

"Right now, we're interested in information from the late sixties and early seventies for Elektra Records, a company called 1969 Platters, and Purple Haze Records."

"That's quite an order."

"I know it's an unusual request, but let's start with Purple Haze."

"It's fascinating that you should mention that particular label, Mr. Melendez. Purple Haze is an interesting story. Maybe Mr. Elliot knows this as well. The chain of rights to Hendrix's music from 1966 on was owned by Yameta, a Bahamaian company, ninety percent of which belonged to a man named John Hillman. Hendrix was simply a Yameta employee. In 1976, Yameta was dissolved, and all assets, as well as publishing rights to the music, were retained by Hillman, who had no experience in the music industry and apparently had no clue as to the marketing potential of what he'd inherited.

"There's more, but as I said, I'm very busy today. Why don't you put in a request for whatever you need and e-mail it to my assistant, Ms. Quincy. She'll give you the particulars."

Greely stood up and shook hands with Gantry and then with Melendez.

"Thank you for your time, Ms. Greely. I will connect with your assistant," Melendez said.

As the two men walked out the office, Melendez asked the receptionist for Ms. Quincy's number and e-mail, and then they continued down the long marble hallway to the elevators.

"She's a tough cookie," Melendez said. "Notice how she rattled all that Purple Haze stuff off the top of her head? She would be a good one for you to play rock and roll Scrabble with, Gantry."

The elevator seemed to stop at every floor on the way down, and it took forever for the garage valet to bring up the car, but soon the two men were out in the clamor and anger of late-afternoon Pennsylvania Avenue traffic.

Melendez was already on his phone dialing Ms. Quincy. As he pulled out into traffic she answered and he introduced himself, explaining what he needed from the record company files.

"Certainly, Agent Melendez. Give me your number and e-mail and a few days to see if I can help."

"Thank you."

Melendez knew a runaround when he saw one. He'd give Greely a little room, but not much.

Suddenly, Gantry smacked himself on the forehead with the palm of his hand.

"What's the matter?" Melendez said.

"Shit! Turn around. Now!"

"What? What for?"

"I left my valise in her office next to my chair."

"Does it have what I think it has in it?"

"Yep."

"Why the hell did you bring that with you? I thought Tanner put you through a crash course!" Melendez yelled, furious. He pulled the red light up from the back seat floor and put in on the roof.

Back at 2200 Pennsylvania Avenue, Melendez and Gantry ran to the elevators. The receptionist was on the phone when they approached her desk.

Gantry was out of breath. "Is Ms. Greely still in her office?"

The receptionist, recognizing the two men, said, "No, I'm sorry. She's left for the day and won't return until tomorrow. Can I be of any assistance?"

"Yes, I'm sure you remember us. We were just here meeting with her. I left my valise in her office. I wonder if you could get it for me? It's very important."

"I'm sorry. I can't. Ms. Greely locks her office whenever she leaves. No one is allowed in there."

Melendez pulled out his badge.

"Ma'am, I am FBI Special Agent Melendez. That valise is official government property. Now please, open the office."

"I wish I could help you, but no one has a key and I don't think Ms. Greely would be very happy if you broke in."

"Call Security, we need to get in her office!" Melendez ordered. The receptionist immediately called Security, explained the situation, and handed the phone to him. Their answer was short and sweet. Without an emergency or court order, they would not break into her office.

While Melendez tried to figure his next move. Gantry walked over to the glass wall separating the reception area from Greely's office. He could see the valise sitting next to the chair he'd sat in.

Gantry turned, "Ma'am, are you sure Ms. Greely isn't returning until tomorrow?"

"I'm certain."

"Could you call her and see if there isn't some way we can get into her office?"

"I'm afraid not. She left strict orders not to be disturbed. I'm afraid you'll have to come back tomorrow."

Gantry turned to the glass again. He considered banging his head against it.

Then he saw it.

The zipper of the valise was halfway closed. He always zipped his valise completely for fear of something dropping out of it.

"What time does Miss Greely arrive in the morning?" Gantry asked.

"She is usually in by nine o'clock."

"I'll be here."

Brigid Greely sat in her Mercedes holding a burner cell phone she'd purchased at the 7-Eleven. The phone was loaded with three hours of time. Her mentor had taught her years ago how valuable they could be when one wanted to converse discreetly about business issues—or private ones.

"These days, you never know who's listening," he said.

The car was parked at the far end of the lot near a nondescript office building about ten blocks from the Capitol building.

The late afternoon sun was bright as she waited impatiently for him to pick up the phone. After five rings, he answered.

"We have problems, big problems," she said.

A manila-tabbed file folder sat on the seat next to her, and in it were copies of some of Gantry's papers. After the two men left, she had quickly gone through the valise.

She'd been very disturbed by the visit—and by what she found afterward.

"This could create the biggest shit storm you can imagine," Greely said.

"Calm down. What are you talking about?"

"I'm talking about the FBI agent who was in my office today, along with a reporter from fucking *Rolling Stone* magazine."

"What?"

"You heard me. An agent from Quantico. He works on cold cases, apparently. He was looking for information about record companies from the sixties and seventies."

"Jesus, get a grip. You know this shit comes up every couple years. It's just time again. I've seen it a dozen times. No one's ever going to figure it out. You're good. We're good. It's old news. Nobody cares—and almost nobody is left."

"This guy is the chief of the Behavioral Analysis Unit, not some Columbo-type gumshoe. The FBI has never gotten involved in this shit, never. Hell, the police never even got deeply involved. Now it looks like it's not just the FBI, but also Scotland Yard and Paris."

"Okay, okay. What did he ask for?"

"He wants record company accounting files from the late sixties and early seventies. He specifically wanted records from 1968 through 1971 from Elektra Records, the 1969 Platters, and Purple Haze Records. He was also very nosy, asking who was in that photo with Bill Wyman. The reporter kept staring at it!"

The phone was silent. She waited, staring at the concrete pillar that blocked her view out of the parking garage. Finally, she spoke?

"Well, what the fuck am I going to do? This is just as much your problem as mine."

"Those records are long gone anyway. Give him something to appease him. We'll figure out a way to stall him. Remind him that was more than forty years ago and that it will take time. Mostly what remains is stuff for the IRS, and you only need to keep them for ten years, technically—"

"For your information, if there is a criminal audit with the IRS, there's not a statute of limitations!"

"You are on your burner, aren't you?"

"Yes, of course!"

"Look, the only incriminating files that existed were destroyed a long time ago. There's just nothing there. Calm down. I will talk to Alex and get this deflated."

"What about Hislop?" Greely asked. "He's still out there somewhere."

Silence.

Greely continued. "Listen, we better be right and be together on this, because even if I manage to deflect this guy temporarily, it may only delay him. These kind of guys don't work on a timetable. We can't afford any connection from the past to today, if you know what I mean."

"Of course."

"We have far too much invested in this. Far too much. Not just money, but everything we have and have built —"

"You're getting too worked up about this. There's just nothing there. The only guy who knew anything disappeared more than fifteen years ago. We made sure of that," he said.

"We shoulda gotten rid of him years ago. I told you. Why did we let him 'retire,' if that's what you call it? That was a real fuck-up, and now look."

"We paid him plenty. He can't hurt us. We scared the living shit out of him. You forget, he had the records that could have buried us. We agreed to take care of his daughter and granddaughter for the rest of their lives. He secured the merchandise as his collateral."

Greely detected a slight quiver in his voice.

"I wish I had your confidence about this. All I can say is, with what I'm looking at from the files, they've already formed a team with London, Paris, L.A., and San Francisco. This is not some hippie blogger stirring up ghosts."

The daily government employee exodus had begun, and they had to fight the thick D.C. rush-hour traffic all the way back to Quantico. Gantry, knowing he would have to return by 9:00 a.m. the next day to retrieve his valise, offered to stay over in town, but Melendez said they had too much to do back in Quantico. He would get him a car to drive back up in the morning.

Melendez hadn't received an update from the Hislop field agent or the TSA monitor and was getting a little anxious. "I knew I should have locked him down immediately," he mused aloud. "But we just can't operate like that anymore."

The teams also had to complete the motive analysis matrix and map out the "persons of interest" plan. That would be enough to get sign-off from the director and to mobilize their full collective resources both here and in Europe. And most important, it would provide the rationale for a judge to issue the search warrants and detainment options. It was time to get in the field. Melendez had heard and seen enough.

Now, in the car, was the perfect time to tell Gantry that he was going to be deputized. Melendez was doing something few people in the Bureau had ever done—maybe never. He was going to deputize a reporter. A rock & roll reporter. As a senior agent, he had the full authority to do this. Of course, there was the chance that it could open up a real hornet's nest, but he'd cross that bridge when it was time to blow it up. And according to regulations, Gantry was a prime candidate. New York was in the Quantico jurisdiction, Gantry was a recognized business leader—of a sort—and he was over twenty-one.

"Gantry, I want to speak to you about something important."

"You want to deputize me. Tanner spoke to me. I'm on board," replied a smiling Gantry.

Melendez returned the smile. Gantry as an undercover agent, working silently under him, would be relatively untouchable by Mayflower. Perfect.

When they got to Quantico, Gantry had his picture and fingerprints taken and within fifteen minutes, with all the prior paperwork complete, he was sworn in and deputized. He was given a shiny silver badge and an ID card.

Gantry loved it. The fold-over wallet contained his picture ID, and on the other half, the badge was embedded into the leather. He quickly slipped it into his sport coat.

Back in the office, Melendez put out his hand. "Partner, I want to thank you. Without your inquisitiveness and without your tenacity these cases—this story—would not have had a chance to come to light. It would have died in your mail room."

Gantry reddened, but the praise felt great. *It's a great day in the Bureau*, he thought. One of those "string of pearls" days, as Jodi used to say.

Early the next morning, Gantry was supplied a pool car and began his trek back to D.C. The Friday morning traffic, even at this early hour, was bumper-to-bumper.

He arrived at Brigid Greely's office at 9:00. As he approached Reception, he saw Greely sitting at her desk behind the glass wall. She was facing the panoramic floor-to-ceiling windows with her feet propped up on the credenza behind her. No boots this time, just black heels and an airtight black dress. She was wearing a headset, chopping her arm in the air, obviously engrossed in a conversation.

"Can you please tell Ms. Greely that Mr. Elliot is here to see her," Gantry said to the now-familiar receptionist behind the counter.

"Sorry, but I can't disturb her. She's on a conference call. You'll have to wait."

Gantry glared at the woman, then took a seat on one of the red leather benches that formed an L shape around a coffee table, well within clear view of Ms. Greely's office.

After half an hour, she was still talking, and Gantry stood up and approached the receptionist again. "Miss, I don't have all day. I'm afraid you're going to have to interrupt Ms. Greely. I have come to retrieve my valise. Can't you just go in and get it so I can be on my way?"

"I am sorry, Mr. Elliot. But you wouldn't want me to lose my job now, would you? I have strict orders not to disturb Ms. Greely." She smiled.

The agent in Gantry woke up.

"Sweetheart, I don't really care if you lose your goddamn job or not. I want that valise, and I'm tired of waiting."

He walked up to the large, heavy glass door, pushed it open and walked into Greely's office. The valise was still sitting next to the chair, its zipper now completely closed.

Greely pulled her feet off the credenza and whirled around in her high-back executive chair.

"Mr. Elliot! I'm sorry, my receptionist didn't announce you." She glared through the glass at the unhappy receptionist. "I'll be right with you. Have a seat." Gantry stared at the Bill Wyman photo again as he sat down.

With that, she replaced the receiver and pulled off her headset.

"You are here for your valise, I assume?"

"That's right."

"It's right over here, just as you left it."

Not quite just, Gantry thought.

Greely stood up and seductively walked over to the leather chair, slowly bent over and reached across to the far side, picked up the case and handed it to Gantry.

"Is there anything *else* I can help you with?"

"No, thank you. My plane tickets are in there. Couldn't lose those," Gantry said.

"No, of course not. Where are you going, if I might ask?"

"Oh, just a quick trip to London with a friend."

"Really?" she said, putting her pen in her mouth nervously.

"By the way, Agent Melendez asked me to check on how long it will take for your assistant, Ms. Quincy, to come up with those records we asked for."

"I'm not sure, but I will check with her later today. It was over forty years ago, and I'm not optimistic...I can't be sure how far back our database goes or whether all paper records are retrievable. We will do our best."

She wasn't going to give them shit, and he could see it in her eyes.

In the car, he called Melendez.

"Raphael, I just picked up my valise. Everything is in there, nothing missing. But she must have gone through it," he said. "The files smell of her perfume."

"Gantry, don't touch anything. Hold on...Tanner? When Gantry gets back, have his satchel checked for Brigid Greeley's fingerprints."

"Sure, no problem," Tanner said.

"And I need her office phone tapped, also her cell and home phones. Get a court order for the records. This lady is not going to give us shit, that much is clear. Let's roll it, Tanner."

Tanner hesitated.

"But what reason do we give the judge? You know how hard it is under this administration to do this without—"

"Person of vital interest. And tell him we need it yesterday."

"You got it, boss. And while I have you on the line, I've uncovered something that may be very useful."

"What's that?"

"It's regarding the Ham case. Of course, we'll know a lot more Monday, but I did some of my own research. Ham's former girlfriend, Anne Herriot, is still alive. I got her name from a Badfinger blog that Scotland Yard sent to me. I have her number and address. As luck would have it, she married an American and now lives in New York, moved there a number of years ago. She lives alone in Brooklyn."

"Give me her info, I'll go talk to her," Gantry said.

"Not a bad idea," Melendez said. "Tanner, work with Gantry on this. Gantry, position it as an interview for a *Rolling Stone* story and see if you can get her talking."

"No problem," Gantry said.

"Oh, by the way, when you get back we need to get Alex on the line with us and populate our Motive Analysis Matrix. We'll show you what to do."

Gantry made good time on the drive back to Quantico and wheeled in by 11:00 a.m. Maneuvering up to the guard house, he nonchalantly flashed his ID and badge and smiled. The guard gave him a thumbs up and smiled back.

Gantry parked his car and strutted into the office.

With Gantry and Alex's help, the Bureau team had designed a simple Motive Analysis Matrix, not unlike the ones used years ago for organized-crime assessments.

"Along the vertical are the names of each star," Melendez explained. "On the horizontal are possible motives that could be a threat to a controlling record company owner."

"You mean things like legacy song or naming rights?" Gantry asked.

"Exactly. Examples could include song or naming rights, eliminating competition, protecting investment, losing control of the talent, 'immortalizing,' and contract issues."

Melendez explained that each possible motive was given a score of one to five. A high score in a single category for all stars would indicate a likely motive. The process would be subjective, but consistency of judgment among the investigative teams would either highlight a consensus motive or de-emphasize the motive.

Melendez asked Tanner, Gantry, and Alex to collectively complete a matrix. Tanner volunteered to be the scribe.

"Let's start with 'losing control of talent,'" Tanner suggested. "How would you score Brian Jones?"

"A five," Gantry said. "He was out of the group and about to do his own thing. That probably did not play well with the 'Don.'"

Alex agreed.

"Hendrix?"

"Five," Alex said quickly. "We know he was letting his contract expire and wanted to move on."

"Ham?"

"Five again. He'd quit the group," Gantry said.

"Morrison?"

"Another five," Tanner said. "He wanted a new life without the Doors."

As the discussion continued, Joplin, Wilson, and McKernan all scored fours.

Tanner noted all of the numbers.

"Let's go on to 'eliminate the competition/protect investment.' This could either be to eliminate a franchise threat or protect what investment had been made in the franchise," he said.

As Tanner went down the list, Alex or Gantry scored each star with a five. Jones threatened the investor's investments by wanting to pull the name and start a new group. Hendrix was considering joining Jones or moving in a new direction. Ham would have been a musical threat to Hendrix and Clapton if he had launched a hard-rock group.

One by one, Tanner went through the motive matrix, with similar results. Each star scored a four or five on each motive.

"This is an interesting one," Tanner said, using the chart and a laser pointer. "Immortalize?'" he asked.

Alex quickly answered, "What we know in hindsight is that quite a few of the rock stars—or, rather, their estates—have made more money since they died than they did alive. We know Elvis has, but Jimi Hendrix? The Joplin estate, yes, and Morrison, yes, but I'm not sure about Ham, McKernan, Wilson, or Jones. Jones has certainly been immortalized, but I'm not sure his estate has made anything since his death."

Tanner added, "We also found that all of these stars had large life insurance policies, not an unusual practice; it's a form of Key Man insurance. The only peculiarity that we uncovered was that some of these policies were substantial and the beneficiary did not appear to be the family or the record company, but apparently a third party. We are running that down as fast as we can."

Insurance forensics is a tedious and mind numbing archeological process, especially when the policies and documentation are not digitized. The odds of finding an old policy and payment history are extremely low. Most old records were not alphabetized, but kept by account number and typically purged every five years, unless there was a large payout.

That is what they were banking on. By cross referencing large bank drafts from insurance companies back to the policies, they could stitch together policy and beneficiary.

As expected, the insurance team found a few Key Man Insurance policies written on Lloyd's of London for amounts ranging from $500,000-$1,000,000. What was unexpected were substantial policies for specific stars written to little known companies for amounts ranging from $3-5,000,000 to the benefit of third parties like: Ascot Livery Service and Sunset Strip Traders; all apparently written within the year of their deaths.

Later, as the matrices came back to Melendez, he was surprised by the consistency for most of the stars. There were some wider variations in the lesser-known ones like McKernan, Wilson, and Ham. But he surmised it was because of lack of local knowledge. He sent the summary results to Bruce and Prevot so they could review before the team call.

As promised, Melendez reconvened the international team that evening and shared the results, highlighting the consistencies and deviations. He projected his findings using the Webex, a summary matrix that tabulated all scores and averages.

"Ladies and gentlemen, can we concur that we have very strong motives within a fairly tight band?" Bruce asked the team.

The team acknowledged affirmatively.

Melendez took control.

"I would like to share with you a scatter diagram that charts similar control type/ homicide motives for mob-type hits over a sixty-year period since 1950 that Quantico has previously analyzed.

"Notice the tight common patterns. When the stakes are high enough and you have a strong controlling personality involved, we see very high and consistent scores. By the way, we have also found a high probability for repeat homicides in those cases. I will now super-impose our results on top of those."

The results mapped almost identically to the mob-hit patterns.

"Because we have not been able to establish any realistic serial killer pattern, and since our consensus motive analysis clearly supports mob-hit-type serial killings consistent with previous analyses, our conclusion is *that* is what we have here.

"Gantry, I now have to agree with what you said to me on our very first call." Melendez turned to look at Gantry. "The Myth of 27 may not be a myth."

Gantry felt a surge of adrenaline. He felt vindicated, even though he could not have possibly imagined how far-reaching this would become. He was not only going to help finally bring justice to his heroes, but when this was over, he was going to sit back and write the story of his career. Not because Alex might make more money, and not because he needed the spotlight, but because he would be rewriting history.

He now wanted more than ever to find out *who* and *why*.

Gantry walked back to the conference room. He now considered it his office—and left a message for Anne Herriot.

"Anne, my name is Gantry Elliot, I am a writer with *Rolling Stone* magazine. I was hoping to interview you for a story that I'm doing..."

She called back within the hour.

"Mr. Elliot, Anne Herriot here. I got your message."

"Thank you for calling me back. I was wondering if I could meet you for coffee in the next few days and chat about Peter Ham. I can come to you, if you'd like."

"Sure. I'm in Cobble Hill. Why don't we meet at the Café Pedlar tomorrow? Do you know it?"

"Best coffee in Brooklyn. Ten thirty?"

"See you then."

Brooklyn, New York

Morning

The following morning, Gantry took the subway to Cobble Hill, a tree-lined section of Brooklyn that was home to a number of celebrities, top restaurants, and intimate cafés. It had a vibe that reminded him of Austin.

Anne Herriot was a clear-eyed woman with a firm handshake. Once they'd met and exchanged some pleasantries, they found a free table and ordered coffee.

"Peter and I had found a lovely cottage in Surrey, where he wanted to build his own studio to write and record songs. He was a gifted songwriter and he was such a sweet, loving man. I miss him every day," she said.

"Was he depressed at the time of his death?"

"No, quite the opposite. He'd left Badfinger, as you know, and was pretty jazzed about the prospect of a solo career. Warner Brothers really wanted him. We had a child on the way. We were happy."

"Do you think he took his own life?" Gantry said.

"I've never thought that." She leaned over the table and gave him a direct look. "He had so much music in him—so much *life*. He would have been one of the greats."

"He was one of the greats, Anne," Gantry responded. On an impulse, he put his hand over hers.

Anne reached into her purse and pulled out a notebook and handed it to Gantry.

"Mr. Elliot, I want you to have this. It was Peter's journal. There's no reason for me to keep it any longer. He was always working on his music, and you may find a few nuggets here for your story."

She handed him the small leather notebook with a faded red ribbon hanging from the bottom.

"Thank you, Anne. I will return it, though, after I read it. Thank you so much for your time this morning."

Out on the sidewalk, they shook hands and said goodbye.

On the subway back to the city, Gantry began leafing through Ham's journal. There were lyrics to seven or eight songs with what appeared to be summary music notation above the words. One touching one was called "Grace," to his and Anne's unborn baby. There were random thoughts, a few lists, and a sketch of what he wanted his recording studio to look like with the specific equipment noted, and its placement. All the kinds of things you would expect to find in a journal.

Toward the end was the only entry in capital letters, a diatribe about someone (or something?) that had stolen his money and his powerlessness against the person. Apparently he had been threatened when he said he was going to go to the authorities. *Maybe he should ask Herriot what she knows,* he thought.

Later that evening he called Anne Herriot.

"Anne, Gantry Elliot, thanks again for taking the time with me this morning and thank you for the journal. It's a wonderful glimpse into Peter's world. But there is one entry that seems disturbing. It is about his money being stolen and threats against him. Do you know anything about this?"

"Yes, of course I do. Peter and I were starting a new life together. He saw virtually nothing—almost no money—with Badfinger and left because of it," she explained.

"What happened?"

"They stole everything from him, and when he quit the group, they tried to force him to honor his contract, which he refused. Then he threatened to go to the police. Shortly after that, one day while I was at work, some 'thug,' as Peter described him, paid a visit and roughed him up a bit. He came by a few more times after that, threatening him."

"Did you tell the police all this after Peter died?"

"Yes, but they insisted it was a clear-cut suicide and that it sounded like a civil issue. I told them that I thought Peter died by someone else's hand, but they didn't listen."

"Do you know who it was?" Gantry asked, realizing instantly that was a stupid question. Of course she wouldn't.

"No...but I remember him like yesterday."

Gantry made a mental note to pass this on to Tanner.

"May I ask you a personal question about Peter?"

Gantry took the ensuing silence as acceptance.

"Was Peter drinking heavily at the time of his death?"

"No, Mr. Elliot, he had given up drinking," she said emphatically. "I was worried that he would be around alcohol so much that he wouldn't be able to resist, but he did."

After he hung up, Gantry shot off a note to Tanner, copying Melendez, describing what he had uncovered. "Maybe Scotland Yard could help us probe into this more," he suggested.

Gantry's reading light burned late that night, as he began to experience a feeling he hadn't felt for many years. He was in a zone, oblivious to everything around him, laser-focused on the possible story evolving before him, the characters, the amazing investigative techniques he'd been learning about, and Melendez's incredible mind. He could feel the data, insights, and clues coming together, inexorably moving toward a conclusion.

He loved being a writer again.

At 2:00 a.m. he turned off the light and went to bed. He knew he'd fly out of bed in the morning despite the fact he'd only get a few hours' sleep. It had been a long time since he had flown first class. This would be a treat.

Gantry took a cab to Dusty Records the next morning. Dennis was standing out front with a leather courier bag slung over his shoulder and two large suitcases at his feet.

As the driver helped him pile the two cases in the trunk, Gantry got out.

"Hey, mate. God, I almost forgot what you looked like, it's been so long."

"I know. It's been nothing but phones. Man, you wouldn't believe what's been going on. Just incredible," he said.

"Well, I've been getting the Cliff's Notes version, but you'll have to fill me in during the flight. It'll be a long one, but in first class, who gives a shit? Champagne, caviar, gorgeous babes; no one does it like Branson," he said with an enormous grin as he slammed the trunk and got into the cab.

He turned to the driver, "JFK, Virgin."

"First class. Christ, it must have cost you a fortune," Gantry said as the cab squeezed out into the rush-hour traffic.

"Nothing but the best for my friend the investigator. Besides, it's all a write-off. I really will be conducting business, mate. Can't wait to see what's in those boxes."

"Okay," Gantry said. "So now...what's up with the baby? What's this woman's name, anyway, and what are you going to do? Forget about the boxes for a minute."

"It's Chloe. And yeah, well, I suppose a good bloke would take care of her and the baby, but to be honest, I can't be sure it's mine. I guess I'll have to sort it all out when I see her. Chloe's great, and feisty like you wouldn't believe. But, I want to hear what's been going on with you. Start at the beginning."

Gantry didn't start quite at the beginning, but outlined the story, filling in what Dennis didn't know, and talking about the atmosphere at Quantico and the technology he'd seen. He described the holographic facility in detail.

"Wow," Dennis said. "Interesting. Very interesting...I guess anything is possible with today's technology, social media—all that. Nothing is private anymore."

Gantry sensed his friend had lost interest in his story. Without saying a word, he took out his badge and held it up to Dennis.

The visual aid caught his attention.

"Geez, mate, where in the hell did you get that? Is that for real?" He grabbed the shiny silver shield and examined it closely.

"Deputy? Really? You really are into this, aren't you? So what can you do with that? Did they give you a gun, too?"

Gantry smiled and put the wallet back in his jacket.

"No, I didn't get a gun. Mostly I'm supposed to interview and gather information, and I certainly can't arrest anyone—at least, I don't think I can."

Having regained Dennis's attention, Gantry gave him more of the story, how he and Melendez had visited Hislop and how the accountant had subsequently vanished.

"And I'm working with the San Francisco and L.A. police departments. They've brought in the crime scene boxes on Joplin, Wilson, and McKernan. And—I'm working with Jodi."

"No way! She's still with the police department there?"

"Yep."

"Wow. How's that working for you?"

"Let's just say, I'm sittin' here a talkin' to you, ain't I?"

The two men laughed at the old-movie reference.

As they walked through the terminal to the Virgin Airways desk, Gantry reviewed Melendez's instructions.

"Your mission is those boxes. Find everything you can, particularly the journal. Get in and get out."

Gantry worried. Had he shared too much with Dennis? The boxes they were all so eager to get their hands on were Dennis's property, after all. Did he have the authority to requisition them? All at once his role as agent didn't feel so cool.

Hendrix might have talked to his shrink about his management problems, he thought. *Les Perrin had just been hired two weeks before Hendrix's death. There are connections to both the travel agencies and the pharmacies and the discovery of Hendrix's journal referencing a visit with a psychiatrist. Look for it.*

In Quantico, Melendez was also hoping that the Hendrix boxes would turn up something valuable. He could imagine Gantry opening them in some dusty old English attic, and inside find an old journal would be the key to the case, all in Jimi Hendrix's own handwriting. Wishful thinking?

He had a sixth sense about some cases. They only needed one good connection, one thought, one name, place, or incident that would pull everything together and set the tumblers in place. That's how it often was in cold cases: a ton of obtuse clues, seemingly unrelated, then, voila! One thing would turn up that would ignite the case and turn all the individual snippets into a full-blown picture.

The oldest ones were the most difficult: unreliable witnesses, stale evidence, and the antiquated technology of the past, all combined to make re-investigation a nightmare. So why did he love it anyway? A need to solve the unsolvable?

In Melendez's mind, whether these murders were carried out by a godfather-type figure or were a conspiracy of management or record company executives, one thing was clear: in the rock and roll renaissance era, as Gantry often called it, the big-money artists were all expendable.

Jones, Wilson, Hendrix, Joplin, McKernan, Ham, and Morrison were assets at one point. But as they became more and more involved in drugs and alcohol, they began to lose their edge, their voices, their judgment, and their reliability. They became liabilities, and liabilities don't look good on a balance sheet.

Financial liability. That's a motive.

Insurance money. That's a motive.

Melendez looked at the pieces of this puzzle.

Greely was involved, had to be. She was the link to the management and record companies. She was key, but she wasn't where the chain of command started. He knew in his gut that there were others, or maybe a single individual, pulling the strings.

He began to draw small boxes connected by lines spreading out in several directions. At the top, he drew a large box and in it he wrote, "Mr. X." It was the one completely unknown factor. Mr. X also represented a group in Melendez's mind, and so he simply wrote under that, "Group X." From there, he drew a straight line down to another box labeled "Greely."

The drawing began to look like a tree, and at the very bottom he drew boxes with each of the artists' names in them—the roots. From their ability to generate millions of dollars of revenue, the money stream flowed upward. He needed to follow the money up from its roots to the management companies. Off to the side he depicted the facilitating travel companies, the pharmacies, the record companies, the insurance proceeds, and the banks.

Where was Hislop in all this? How vital was he, and what did he know?

The pieces were there, but the picture remained opaque. Staged suicides. Murder. Notes. Fragments. What about Anne Herriot? What more did she know? Hendrix's boxes in London? The pharmacies and the links between them and the travel agencies—the Joseph Clark connection. Greely, and what she was holding back.

They needed that one break. *Look for it. It's there somewhere.*

It was time to give Ms. Greely a call. He still hadn't received anything he'd asked her for. She was stonewalling. He was about to pick up his phone and call her when he saw an e-mail in his inbox from Greely's secretary, Ms. Quincy, stating she had the information he'd requested. He could have a courier pick it anytime.

But when the courier came in later that day, instead of boxes of old files, corporate minutes, and registrations, there was an oversized manila envelope containing three plastic file folders. Each folder contained a brief history of each record company Greely had dealings with. It all looked like it had been copied from Wikipedia.

"Is this all?" Melendez asked the courier.

"Yes, sir."

Melendez punched in Greeley's cell number.

"Ms. Greeley, I am looking at what you sent back in response to our request. I assume this is just to get us started and that more substantial information is on its way?"

"Agent Melendez, I'm not sure I understand. Our records staff did the best they could."

"Is that a joke? Ms. Greeley, let's not play any chicken-shit games. We know what you have and don't have in your archives," Melendez said, raising his voice.

"Agent Melendez, as I said, we did our best. We can't make chicken salad out of chicken shit, now can we?" she snarled.

"Very funny, Ms. Greeley. Send me the information I've requested or I'll get a court order and seize everything you've got, right down to the magazines in your waiting room. You have forty-eight hours; max. Am I clear?"

"I understand, Agent Melendez," was her only response.

"Good."

Melendez called Tanner in.

"Did they ever send us any info on Lexington Records? How about the insurance beneficiaries?" Melendez asked.

"Not yet," Tanner said. "By the way, the wiretaps are telling us nothing. She goes to and from work, some social life, mostly business. Are you going to get a court order?"

"Let's see what she does."

Greely left her office and walked down the street to Lafayette Park, directly across from the White House. She pulled the burner phone from her purse and hit the redial. It was answered on the first ring.

"I just got a call from the FBI. I tried to appease them on the information request, but it didn't work. He says he is preparing a larger request and that he'll get a court order if we don't comply. God knows what is in those archives."

"I'll take care of it," he said.

The next night, there was a massive explosion in an old business records warehouse in southeast Washington that set off a four-alarm fire. It quickly spread to adjoining buildings and took until early morning for the fire department to get under control. The news reports called it a furnace malfunction. The investigator interviewed explained that age and poor maintenance, and possibly a fuel leak, were probably the cause. The warehouse burned to the ground, and its contents were reduced to ashes.

As promised, two days later Melendez stood in Greely's office with a subpoena in his hand.

Brigid Greely looked concerned.

"Didn't you see the news, Agent Melendez? The storage facility that burned housed all our records. All of our old records were destroyed."

Melendez tried to restrain his expression.

"I was not aware, Ms. Greely. Looks like you are conveniently off the hook for the time being."

"I'm sorry, it looks like I can no longer help you."

In his car a few minutes later Melendez said, "Did you guys get all that?"

"Yes, sir. Got shots of all the pictures in her office. Sending to Photo Forensics right now," the agent responded. "We should have all identified by the morning."

"I successfully attached the micro-monitoring device," Melendez added.

"Yes, we've activated it."

"Good, let's see what happens now."

As part of the routine background check on all the persons of interest, Tanner was finding that a number of those people were no longer living. While he noted specific family members who could be interesting to speak to for their perspectives, they were not eyewitnesses, nor did they have firsthand knowledge of events; their value was limited.

They had arranged for an FBI forensic artist to meet with Anne Herriot to do a composite sketch from her recollection of the man she'd said had threatened Peter. They hoped to do an age-progression analysis to determine what the man could look like today. It was a long shot.

Early in the investigation, Tanner had vetted *Rolling Stone*, its staff, the visitor list, and surveillance videos, etc and had not been surprised at what he'd found: minor infractions of the law, drug-related and protest arrests, and DWIs. Par for the course.

One item, though, caught his eye because of its rarity. It was a "restricted" notation next to one of the names. Tanner had called the analyst and inquired about it, and was told that "restricted means hands off."

Tanner reported the anomaly to Melendez.

"One of the people in the *Rolling Stone* visitor surveillance videos was labeled 'restricted' and we were denied access."

"I've seen it before. Contact the inter-bureau liaison at the CIA and ask them to run it down for you."

Tanner sent the information across to the CIA. Their response was that the restriction was not domestic, but originated in the UK.

Tanner called Hammond in London.

"Right, then, let's pull it up," Hammond said, typing the name into SCU's secure search engine. Tanner listened to the long-distance tapping.

"Okay, I get a restriction banner across the screen. This designates an intelligence community restriction."

"Really? Can you get past that?"

"Yes, I just need a different access code," he said, and typed in a fourteen-digit code.

"In," he announced.

"Well, boy oh boy, we have a wild one here: British Special Forces. Highly skilled. A real bad one."

London, UK

Early Morning

When Gantry and Dennis arrived in London early the next morning, a driver met them at baggage claim, escorted them to a large black Range Rover, and drove them to the Four Seasons near Hyde Park.

"Nothing but the best for my friend and me," Dennis said, as he and Gantry stepped out of the car. "I got us rooms overlooking the park. I hope it meets with your approval."

Gantry stared at him like he was crazy.

"Are you kidding? This is great. How the hell can you afford—"

"Forget it, mate! Now, after we check in, let's freshen up a bit and meet down here in about an hour for breakfast. Sound okay?" Dennis asked.

"Sure, I'm starving," Gantry replied, laughing. "This is too much, man."

"In the meantime, I'll call Chloe and get this party started," Dennis said.

The bellboy took Gantry to his room. Bemused, Gantry went to the windows and took in the panoramic view of Hyde Park, Buckingham Palace, and downtown London. He could have put his entire apartment in this room.

I could get used to this quickly.

After showering and changing, Gantry made his way to the restaurant, where Dennis was waiting for him.

"Couldn't wait to eat, so I got started. Go get yourself something."

Gantry returned with a plate piled high with eggs, pastries, French toast, sausage, and one strawberry.

"Need my fruit every day," he laughed.

"I spoke to Chloe," Dennis said, "and she asked that I come by at eleven. She doesn't know yet that you're with me."

"You're just going to surprise her?"

"Yep, just like she surprised me!" Dennis said. "Harder for her to lie if I have a witness, don't you think?"

Back in his room, Gantry took the surveillance device from the bottom of his travel bag, turned it on, and clipped it to the inside of the lapel of his sport coat, just as they had shown him. The device and its micro camera activated.

In Quantico, an analyst called Melendez.

"Agent Melendez, Mr. Elliot has activated his monitor. He is in downtown London."

"Please make our London office aware. Thank you."

Gantry met Dennis in the lobby and they took a cab to Notting Hill, a residential area in West London. Dennis explained that when he was growing up, Notting Hill had been a poor neighborhood populated chiefly by Caribbean immigrants, which gave it a kind of carnival atmosphere. In fact, the largest street party in Europe, the Notting Hill Carnival, took place here every year, he explained.

"My mum used to bring me here to Portobello Road on Saturdays to shop at the street market. Now, it's a very posh neighborhood and property values have skyrocketed."

"And this is where Jimi Hendrix died?" Gantry asked.

"The very place."

The cab pulled up to a colorfully painted townhouse on a tree-lined street.

"Chloe's father owns this place. She has the bottom floor flat. He lives above, and rents out the rest."

They walked down a few steps to the front door, Dennis knocked, glanced at Gantry, and they waited.

The door was opened by a gorgeous strawberry blonde, wearing a tight Chelsea soccer jersey, jeans, and high-heeled boots.

"Dennis!" she shouted as she flung her arms around him.

"Chloe! How great to see you…Chloe, this is my friend Gantry Elliot."

"Well, come on in. We have a lot to catch up on."

Dennis turned and quickly rolled his eyes at Gantry, as if to say, "Yeah, that's what I'm afraid of."

Dennis and Chloe reminisced for at least an hour. Chloe didn't mention the little girl they presumably shared until they heard a cry coming from another room.

"Mindy is awake," Chloe said, and went out to get her. A minute or two later she returned, holding a dark-haired little girl about two or three years old.

"Mindy, say hello to Mr. Briganty and Mr. Elliot."

The little girl buried her face in her mother's neck.

"She's a little shy with people she doesn't know." She put Mindy in a chair and made her comfortable. "Dennis, can I speak to you privately?"

Without waiting for an answer, she escorted Dennis to another room. Gantry heard their voices, then louder raised voices, then silence. The child sat across from Gantry, staring at him. He made a face at her, and she laughed. He made another, and she laughed even more. She made a face at him, and he laughed.

"Looks like you made a friend, Mindy!" Chloe said as she walked back into the room. "Let me show you boys where the boxes are. I can't guarantee that they are the ones you are looking for, though." Chloe's face was flushed. Dennis wore no expression.

As the three of them walked to the garage, she explained that after her mother died she had moved most of her things to her father's and had used the garage as storage.

Dennis opened the garage door to a film still from an episode of Storage Wars: furniture, boxes, mirrors, rugs and all manner of junk jammed floor to ceiling in the small one-car garage. A single low-wattage light bulb spattered a bit of light over it all.

"If it's still around, it's in here," she said. "Have at it, but put it all back when you finish."

Put it back? Gantry thought.

Dennis and Gantry moved the furniture out along with lamps, pictures, and the rest, finally uncovering three cardboard boxes stacked in the back. They pulled them out into a better light and opened one. Inside were plates, cups and saucers.

The next box was filled with shirts, pants, nothing special. But then they uncovered a tie-dyed jacket and some scarves at the bottom of the box. They looked at each other and quickly pulled the last box out.

This one contained books, records, bank statements, loose papers, and what appeared to be contracts—and a weathered red leather journal. Gantry quickly grabbed it and began leafing through it. Dennis began examining the loose papers and pictures.

"Jackpot!" Dennis exclaimed. "This is the box. I remember the black-and-white photos." He was so engrossed in the find that he didn't see the expression on Gantry's face.

"Come on, mate, let's take this treasure back to the hotel. We'll get a bottle of Bushmills sent up, light up a couple of Cubans, and rummage through it all carefully."

Gantry didn't answer immediately. He cleared his throat and said, "Great idea. Let's put her stuff back and get out of here."

The two men were startled as Chloe came up behind them.

"Did you get what you came for?" she asked.

"Yes," Dennis said. "We're kind of pushed for time, so we'll be off. I'll call you tonight to discuss the other matter. Okay?"

"That will be fine," she said, smiling. "Just don't forget me and disappear like you did last time."

Dennis smiled faintly.

On the way to the hotel, Gantry tried talk with Dennis, but his mind was elsewhere.

"C'mon, man. What did you decide? Going to marry her?" Gantry asked.

"Are you shitting me? No way. I am giving her a check to take care of the two of them," he said in an unequivocal tone.

"And that's it? Just give her a check and that's the end of it?" Gantry said, with an edge in his voice.

"Fuck yes, mate. What else am I supposed to do? I'm not father material, and besides, I'm not movin' back here, and she would never leave London. End of story. That's best for both of us, though the amount of the check is certainly still up for discussion."

When the taxi pulled up to the hotel, Dennis grabbed the boxes and climbed out. Looking over the roof to Gantry, he said, "Let's take a break for an hour and meet up in my room. I have a couple of calls to make. Need to call my lawyer about Chloe." He looked worried.

"Fine. See you in an hour," Gantry said.

In his hotel room, Dennis went through the boxes, sorting the files, papers, and photos into separate piles. But where was the journal? Had they left it behind?

In his room down the hall, Gantry sat thinking about what he'd quickly read in Hendrix's journal. Then it dawned on him that the camera on his lapel had been on the entire time. He needed to call Melendez and get some advice.

He grabbed two small bottles of whiskey from the room bar, unscrewed the caps, and poured himself a drink, then punched Melendez's number into his cell. All he heard, though, was an irritating noise. The call would not go through. He tried again, with the same result.

He picked up the hotel phone and connected with the international operator

"Sir, I cannot get a connection. Are you positive this is the correct number?"

"Yes, I am."

"Let me try one other thing for you…Please wait…Yes, I thought so. Sir, this is a restricted number and I am not able to connect you. So sorry."

Gantry needed to think this through quickly.

Upstate New York

Two miles from Canadian Border

On a brisk early May morning just off a quiet stretch of Interstate 90 running through Buffalo to Toronto, a vehicle was spotted on a dirt road leading into dense forest.

The border was in sight to the New York state troopers, who caught a glimmer of reflection between the trees. They pulled over, thinking they might nab an out-of-season deer hunter. Their patrol car crawled back along the muddy path.

A silver Toyota Camry. So much for deer hunters.

But what was a Camry doing sitting in axle-deep mud off a state highway? Stolen, most likely, the troopers surmised.

As they approached the car, they saw the head slumped against the window.

"Agent Melendez?"

"Yes."

"This is Lieutenant John DiMarco, New York State Police. I'm calling from Buffalo."

"Yes, lieutenant. What can I do for you?"

"We've had an incident here near the border, about a half mile out on I-90."

"Yes..?"

"We found a Camry in the woods a short while ago. There was a gunshot victim inside. He'd been shot through the back of the head."

"We found your card. Not much else, not even a wallet, no ID. Oh, and there was a hundred grand in cash in a case in the trunk. Know

214

anything about this?"

"No other luggage? Nothing else in the trunk?"

"No, sir."

"Have you made a preliminary ID?"

"No, but the DMV has the car registered to a Maria Salazar of Westport, Connecticut. The address is a property owned by a Simon Jennings."

"Describe the victim," Melendez asked.

"Caucasian, faded reddish hair, about six-two, nice Burberry suit. Appears to be have been dead for a while. Looks like a professional hit to me. Whoever did this used a .22 caliber pistol, and *those* guys like the .22s. They don't make a big mess, no exit wounds, nothing. I'm sending you a picture right now."

"Where was my card found?" Melendez asked, thinking if the killer had stolen the man's wallet, he certainly should have had the card. The killer would have known they would ID the man within minutes.

"That was an odd thing. He didn't have it in his pocket. It was tucked into the spare-tire well. We found it there with the cash. Anything I need to know here, Agent Melendez?"

"Just got your picture. This appears to be Simon Jennings. He was working with us in an ongoing investigation. We last spoke to him a few days ago."

"What kind of case?"

"Murder."

"Not the usual thing for the FBI,"

"This one is."

"Well, I guess we're involved now. I'll have to talk to you soon. Is this where you can usually be reached?"

"Yes. I'll send a couple of agents up there immediately. Send us the crime scene photos, so we can make a positive match."

Melendez pressed the speed-dial number for Gantry; it rang twice, then went to voice mail.

"Gantry, it's Raphael. Very bad news. Just got a call from a New York state trooper. They believe they found Hislop dead in a car near the Canadian border. Be careful. Don't take any chances."

Melendez disconnected.

Not a cold case anymore. There's someone out there protecting himself in a big way.

Obviously Hislop wasn't just being paranoid. He knew. That's why he ran. At least they'd gotten a line on Greely, but with the archives torched, they had nothing there for the time being. He desperately needed to get their hands on whatever Hislop had taken with him, or this would go nowhere.

Melendez picked up his phone again and dialed Tanner.

"The New York staties just called me. They found someone believed to be Hislop dead in the housekeeper's car on I-90 near the Canadian border, shot in the back of the head."

"Execution style."

"Exactly."

"As in Special Forces?"

"Yes, why?"

"Didn't you get that file?"

"What file?"

"The one I left on your desk yesterday about that restricted-access guy that Agent Davis and I found in the background and commonality checks."

"What the hell? I wasn't in my office yesterday. Why didn't you call me immediately? God damn it, Tanner!"

"Boss, I'm sorry. You said you were coming back after lunch. I got on the pharmacy thing you wanted last night. I forgot to check back with you."

"What did it say?"

"I was able to get into it with Hammond's help. He's one bad dude. British Special Forces, biochemical specialist, assassin, the full Monty. And get this—affiliated with the Rolling Stones in the commonalities matrix. The name popped up a couple of times with St. Albans Pharmacy as well. I'm still waiting for the CIA liaison to get back to me."

"What's the name?

"Dullahan—an alias. No record."

216

"Any prints, last knowns? Anything?"

"Not yet. Our liaison may have more."

"What are you waiting for?" Melendez shouted. "And get someone to look at highway surveillance videos out of Westport to Buffalo on I-90."

British Special Forces operative? Assassin? Proficient in bio chemical ops? Jesus, this just keeps getting more bizarre. Melendez's mind was internalizing his thoughts as fast as a computer.

As Melendez sat trying to digest the news of a suddenly dead Hislop, his phone rang again.

"Melendez."

"Hello, Agent Melendez. This is Alex Jaeger."

"Yes, hello, Mr. Jaeger. I didn't recognize the number. What can I help you with?"

"I don't think you can, but I think I can help you."

"Really? With what?"

"The mail boy just dropped off all of Gantry's mail. Mostly stuff he never reads anyway, but I told him to bring it to me until Gantry gets back."

"Okay."

"Well, there is a box marked personal to Gantry, handwritten with a Sharpie, a lot like those manila envelopes. It's heavy. Should I open it?"

"No. Absolutely not. Leave it in your office and don't touch it. I'll have one of our agents from the Manhattan office pick it up immediately."

"Can I know what's in it when you get it?"

"With all due respect, Mr. Jaeger, let us do our job."

In less than an hour, an agent picked up the box, took it to the South Street Heliport and put it on a chopper. It was in Melendez's office before five o'clock. He, Tanner, and Moxie examined it closely before Melendez took out his penknife.

Slowly he cut through the tape and folded back the cardboard flaps. "Nothing but files," Moxie said.

"What did you expect, a bomb?" Melendez said.

He put on surgical gloves and carefully removed each tabbed file. The contents seemed to be well organized. Each was clearly labeled, and as he put each one on his desk, he noted the tabs: Record companies, bank records, offshore accounts, onshore accounts, and one simply labeled, Joseph Clark. Melendez took a few minutes to spread the files out, open each one, and skim the basic information contained.

"Pretty comprehensive," Moxie said. "From Hislop?"

"Yes, I'd say it was our recently deceased friend, Angus Hislop, but let's be sure. Get on the phone and call Mr. Jaeger in New York. Find out when this box came into his mailroom and get any visuals they have. The trooper said he thought Hislop had been dead for a while."

"I'm on it, boss."

"Tanner, take this to the clean room and lock it up. Then meet me there in an hour. Get Jackson from financial forensics there and patch in Robert Bruce and Scotland Yard. We need to go over every word. This could be what we've been looking for. And get Gantry on the phone. I left him a message, but he hasn't called back. I want to know what the fuck is going on over there."

"Oh—I almost forgot to tell you."

"Yes, what? Another surprise?"

"Not a surprise, but remember Gantry activated his monitoring device? We got some footage of him rummaging through what looks like a garage. It's got an interesting close-up of what looks like a journal with some handwriting. It's silent for about five seconds, then I can hear what I think is his buddy talking."

"And?"

"He's shouting, 'This is the jackpot! This is the box. I remember the black-and-white photos.' The camera never leaves the pages. Then Gantry quickly slams it shut and then the camera goes off in another direction."

"Send me the file as soon as you get back."

Melendez asked that Bruce, Hammond, and their top financial-forensics analyst join him, Tanner and Jackson on a video call from the FBI clean room as soon as possible.

"I believe our best chance of establishing a prosecutable case is to

218

directly tie the flow of funds from business activities through offshore accounts for the purpose of avoiding U.S. and U.K. taxes," Melendez explained. "If we find a flow back out, we can possibly triangulate to the perpetrator."

Melendez and Bruce knew from experience that attempting to tie a sophisticated mob-type personality to the murders would be extremely difficult unless there was direct evidence or implications.

"These guys are too smart to have their fingerprints on anything and too well insulated. The actual killers are far removed from the brains," Melendez said. "But tax fraud has been a successful route in the past, and could be here, if we can piece together the money trail."

Melendez thought the files from Hislop might be a missing link to the flow-of-funds analysis that SCU and the FBI had been conducting on Nevermore Travel. The team had uncovered the human link from the pharmacies and travel agency to the record industry through Lexington Records to the insurance beneficiaries. It was Joseph Clark. The Hislop files confirmed that. But the Hislop files also inferred that Clark was an alias, used to provide no traceable link. He was a cover for someone or someone's. They needed to find out who.

They had successfully identified spikes in cash outflows from Nevermore that corresponded to each rock star's death. In addition, they'd pieced together record contracts, concert accounts, management contracts, and endorsements that amounted to a lot of bad deals and one-sided transactions, but nothing that suggested tax avoidance. Nothing that would stick.

"These files mysteriously showed up at the *Rolling Stone* offices in New York," Melendez explained as he held up the first file. "This folder contains corporate records for a handful of relatively unknown record companies. The next file contains registers of offshore accounts, and the next, onshore accounts. We believe they were sent from Angus Hislop before he was killed.

"We are going to scan the files and send them to you immediately, and Robert, I've assigned Agent Jackson to work with your forensic lead to develop a flow-of-funds analysis to see what we can find. Let's confer tomorrow and see what progress we've made. This may be it."

The FBI and SCU forensic leads had put together a joint team of thirty analysts, some of the best forensic accounting minds in the world. The analysts pored over the files and began to patch together the flow-of-funds analysis in an attempt to isolate cash inflows and outflows—a methodical and tedious process. They first reviewed every contract for each of the groups or stars. These included recording contracts, songwriting royalties, licensing, concerts, and endorsements. Then they mapped each of these, as best they could, to the cash receipts and bank deposits.

It was like panning for gold. Most of the information proved worthless. Eventually, though, they began to uncover a few nuggets that proved illuminating.

Back in his office, Melendez opened the file of Gantry's surveillance footage and skimmed through it. The hotel room, a ride in a taxi, a little girl sticking her tongue, an attractive woman, and then the garage scene Moxie had told him about. He only had an hour of transmission.

"Lousy battery life," he muttered. He called Moxie and asked him to come by.

"Moxie, what do you make of this?" Melendez asked.

"Well, it looks like Gantry was in a hurry. We see him flipping through pages. The wide-angle lens on his camera unfortunately has to be enhanced to read the handwriting. Hendrix's writing was very sloppy. We'll have that shortly, but I can see that Gantry stops thumbing through it and focuses on one page that is particularly hard to read. Looks like some liquid and ink stains, but we'll get it."

"I couldn't make it out, either. I was hoping it was something about Hendrix's psychiatrist. When do you think we will have this cleaned up?" Melendez asked.

"I'm hoping within the next couple hours."

"Okay. Let me know as soon as—"

"Got it, boss. Ditto on the record company files, the artist's sketch from Ham's girlfriend, Hislop murder, the works."

Moxie turned, smiled a little and left.

When Moxie closed his door, Melendez got up and began to slowly pace his office, deep in thought. "What is it...what..." he mumbled to himself. Then he walked out to his waiting area and stared at the poster blow-up of the Beatles' "White Album." He remembered how maligned the album had been when it first came out. "The Beatles have lost their creative touch," the critics had said. Over time, though, the songs became legendary, and the compositions were considered masterpieces.

Be patient. Don't force it. Let the pieces slide together. It's only been a short while. Think. Think. Think.

The financial forensic teams did find something illuminating, even though they still had more work to do to harden up their analysis. They quickly scheduled a joint FBI/SCU team call to present their findings to Melendez and Bruce.

Agent Jackson, as spokesman, began.

"Gentlemen, it's probably best if I give you an example of the kind of thing we have uncovered. I am going to build a flow-of-funds on the right side of the monitor, as I share with you each component on the left.

"Let me start with a contract for a concert performance that compensates Jimi Hendrix and the Experience $15,000 plus expenses, paid separately, for this concert. Now, as you can see," Jackson said, pointing to the right side, "here are two deposits made to Barclays Bank the day after the concert, one for $2,700, which was apparently the expense portion. Now here is one for $25,000, the concert portion," he explained as a tree diagram of component boxes appeared on the monitor.

"Notice the $10,000 difference between the contract and the cash receipts."

"They skimmed it," Melendez pointed out.

"Exactly. Now this is where it gets interesting. Where did that difference go?

"Here are the bank records of three offshore accounts," Jackson said. Three more branches appeared. "One in Saint Lucia, one in the Cayman Islands and one in Bermuda. On the very next day, three wire transfers went out to these banks that totaled $10,000."

"They sent the skimming offshore," Bruce said.

"Exactly. Now, look at what happened a few days later with the Saint Lucia bank. Four wires went out, one to a U.S. based Iowa bank, one to a Canadian bank, one to a Swiss Bank, and one to a U.K. bank."

Melendez and Bruce were speechless. In spite of it being a modest amount of money by today's standards, it was unrecorded revenue, hidden to avoid taxes. That was how the whole scheme worked.

Then Melendez noticed it, the account at the bank in Iowa was for Nevermore Travel. The account at the bank in Canada was for Lexington Records. The tumblers were clicking into place.

"What's the status of these bank accounts?" Melendez asked.

"Unfortunately, all the bank accounts had been closed or inactive for years, except for one," Tanner replied. "The Swiss account periodically wired funds to a community bank located in the Capitol Hill section of Washington, DC. Every six months, a deposit of half a million dollars was made to Red Branch Communications, LLC. This had been going on for more than ten years like clockwork."

"Tanner, what or who is Red Branch Communications?

"Don't know yet. We'll have something shortly."

Washington, D.C.

That afternoon, Brigid Greely once again left the office for the privacy of her car and her burner phone. She dialed an international number and waited.

"Yes?"

"It's me. Are you still in the islands?"

"You know better than that."

"Sorry, we haven't spoken in quite some time."

"Is this important?"

"As important as the proverbial heart attack," she said.

"Shoot."

"I'm very worried. I assume you heard about the FBI agent from our friend, who by the way seems to take it very lightly. I have a subpoena in my hand and there's not much more stalling I can do. The warehouse is history, but there are still a lot of loose ends hanging around out there. Hislop's disappeared, and God knows what he's doing or where he's going. Our conduit is conveniently unavailable. I keep getting a voice mail and no return calls. I need him to take care of this."

Greely's hand was trembling as she glanced around the underground garage she parked in.

"My dear, I'm afraid I agree with our friend. You must remain calm,? said the voice on the phone. "Everything I know from him and from you is purely coincidental. The pieces are too fragmented. Do not overreact. This is why I chose you to handle my legacy, because you're smart, savvy and, I hope, still unflappable. You have powerful friends. Use them."

The phone was silent for a moment.

"Okay. You're right. I just needed to talk it through."

"Good, then. Hang up. Don't want anything traced. I'll talk to you soon. Stay calm and focused. Goodbye, my dear."

Greely knew what she had to do next. She made a series of calls and scheduled a meeting for later in the day.

As she stepped off the escalator and into the bright light of 30th Street Station in downtown Philadelphia, she spotted him sitting at the end of the pew-like benches in a quiet section near the Market Street entrance.

"This is not going away by itself. We are so close to having it all and with you in control of *Rolling Stone*. Now it could disintegrate," she anxiously explained.

Daniel looked at her steely eyed, "I will give Jaeger an ultimatum and get him to explain that this was blown out of proportion by a rouge reporter."

Alex Jaeger was visibly shaken by the call he had just received. He didn't know whether to be scared, angry, or both. An ordinary person would have been intimidated, seeing his business and personal life passing before his eyes, but Jaeger was not an ordinary person. As he sat in his office thinking and staring at the growing pile of RSVP regrets for his wedding, he became more and more upset.

He dialed Melendez.

"Agent Melendez, I just got off a call with the chairman of one of our large media advertisers and a huge benefactor of the Rock and Roll Hall of Fame. He was joined by a representative of the International Record Association," Jaeger said.

"Yes?"

"They were intimating that we were fabricating a story, that we'd spun a fairy tale about dead rock stars! They even said I convinced some 'out-of-touch FBI agent' to spend taxpayer dollars on this escapade. Do you understand what I'm saying?" Jaeger demanded.

"They said it was all absurd, that every company would have skeletons in their closet if they went back far enough, and that this escapade of mine could inadvertently trigger all sorts of legal problems that could go on for years."

"Now, even my partner, Daniel is begging me to call it off. Says it will ruin me."

Melendez kept his silence.

"They suggested that I should think very carefully before biting the hand that's been feeding me for so many years. They even went so far as to intimate that they would cancel certain advertising in *Stone*, unless I called it off. The lawyer suggested that many of their members felt the same way. I wanted to tell them to all go fuck themselves —"

"But you didn't, correct?"

"No, but I came close. I don't like being bullied. No one tells me how to run my business! This is all bullshit!"

"Yes, it is. I know what it feels like to be bullied by the people who pay you."

Melendez's sympathy didn't seem to calm him down.

"Melendez, you don't seem to understand the financial enormity of this. This is my life —this is everything I've spent decades building."

"I understand, Mr. Jaeger, they leaned on you hard."

"Yes, they did, very hard, and right where I am the most vulnerable. Losing your advertisers is the kiss of death. This empire doesn't survive on subscriptions, for Christ's sake. It's all about the advertisers!"

"Let me ask you a question, and I need you to be absolutely straight with me. Are these really murders, or is this all just a wild-goose chase that will end embarrassing all of us?"

Melendez paused for a moment, and then spoke deliberately.

"Mr. Jaeger, I thought originally it might be a wild-goose chase, but with what we have uncovered, I can say unequivocally that this is very real, and was carried out with a sophistication that has stunned our investigators. This is real, Mr. Jaeger."

"Then fuck 'em. Fuck all of them. They can pound sand. I built this company by telling the truth and not allowing myself to be bullied by anyone," Alex shouted. "We'll let the chips fall where they will. I'm seeing this thing through all the way."

"Thank you, Alex," Melendez responded. It was the first time Melendez had called him by his first name.

Melendez had heard all the stories about Alex Jaeger, the good and the bad. But this personal demonstration of his courage when it really counted was one of the most admirable things he had witnessed in a long time. Alex knew what he could lose if this went the wrong way, but he didn't blink. He was laying it all on the line.

Tanner came to Melendez's office later that day.

"We've completed our research on Red Branch Communications," he said with a slight smile.

"Yes?"

"Red Branch Communications is solely owned by one Brigid Greely of Washington, DC."

They let the moment settle in.

"What did you say?" Melendez was stunned.

"Brigid Greely," he answered, smiling.

"Outstanding," Melendez said. "Thank you, Elmer."

"Not at all."

Arriving at FBI headquarters by helicopter twenty minutes later, Melendez had a car and driver waiting for him in the garage and was at Greely and Associates within minutes.

"Ms. Greely, I am sorry to drop in on you unannounced," he said as he opened the door to her office, "but I have something I need to speak to you about."

"Can't this wait, Melendez?" she said. "I am extremely busy today, and quite frankly, I really don't have any more time for this nonsense. Don't you have crooks to catch?"

"Yes, indeed," he replied. "And I think you have time for this." He closed the door.

"Ms. Greely, we have been analyzing the corporate and bank records of a number of companies we believe are related to the management of the rock stars currently under our investigation."

"What does that have to do with me?"

"We believe that a systematic process of profit skimming occurred to avoid the payment of corporate and personal taxes in the U.S. and

U.K. We further believe that the very same accounts were the source of funds to pay for the murder of a number of rock stars."

In the ensuing silence, Melendez watched as a single bead of sweat ran out of her hair and down along the side of her face.

"We further followed a steady flow of funds over a ten-year period out of one of the accounts and into an account at a local Capitol Hill bank, owned by—do you want to hazard a guess?"

Brigid Greely's face had turned stark white.

"Ms. Greely, the facts suggest that you were party to a process of tax avoidance, or to be blunt, tax fraud. The facts also suggest that you may have been an accessory after the fact to murder," Melendez said. "I don't think I need to explain the implications for you personally and professionally."

"Are you threatening me?" She hissed.

"Quite the contrary. I am trying to advise you. And I'm going to be more generous than you deserve. I will give you twenty-four hours to agree that you are going to assist us in this matter."

Without waiting for an answer, Melendez turned and began to walk to the door. As he opened it, he turned back and said, "Oh—and you will be under constant surveillance."

Greely grabbed her telephone in a panic and stabbed in the numbers. Voice mail. All that gibberish about rock & roll irritated the shit out of her.

"Okay. This is my last call, you son of a bitch. I've left four messages. I didn't kill anyone, and I'm not going to be thrown under the bus for this shit! Call me back or I'm going to come over there and cut your fucking balls off!"

It was going on 9:00 p.m. in Quantico, and Melendez was in the clean room with Moxie and Tanner when his cell phone rang.

"Hello, Agent Melendez. This is Detective Jodi Randolph."

"Yes, hello, Detective. What can I do for you. Any news for me?"

"Yes. Did Robert Bruce call you yet?"

"No, was he supposed to?"

"I thought he might. Yesterday, we received some forty-year-old partial fingerprints from London and Paris. They had been lifted from the Jones and Morrison inhalers at my request. I already had McKernan's. On a hunch, I asked that all possible fingerprints be lifted from the St. Albans and Carlton pharmacy bottles in the evidence boxes. There was nothing very useable, with one exception. We got a digital match on the partial print for Morrison and the partial for McKernan—five years and five thousand miles apart."

"Do you have a name?" Melendez asked.

"No, still working on that. So far, they don't match anything that we have in our database or in the international database. Scotland Yard and Police Nationale are looking for a match, as well. I did ask your Quantico forensic scientists to help us try to digitally recreate a more complete fingerprint, so we can make a better attempt to match. It's too early to tell if they will be successful. We need some possible persons of interest to compare to," Jodi said. "We need to isolate the universe of possibilities. This really is a needle in a field of haystacks right now."

"Terrific work, detective. Keep driving it," Melendez responded. "Please make sure Tanner gets you all the people identified in our commonalities work. That is as close as we have to any persons of interest."

"Thank you, sir, he was going to be my next call."

Early the next morning, Moxie rushed into Melendez's office.

"Boss! Brigid Greely's car…it burned in an underground garage in DC. Apparently an explosion."

"Jesus. Was she in it?"

"If she was, there's nothing left of the lady. The explosion took out some of the pylons nearby, fire and police couldn't even get in there till they determined the roof wouldn't come down. So no traces, at least no blood or tissue. But the car was positively identified from a fragment of the vehicle ID number, and her car was still in the garage's computer at the time—meaning it hadn't left the garage. Our agents confirmed they never saw it leave."

"Jesus Christ, who are we dealing with here?"

Four Seasons Hotel, London

Before going down to Dennis's room, Gantry sat thinking, sorting through the possibilities. He was bewildered, even a little scared. He had Hendrix's journal in his possession, and it contained what was very possibly incriminating information—information he thought might help break the case.

Unable to reach Melendez, he was on his own, and had to be resourceful. Should he show the Hendrix journal to Dennis or wait till Melendez saw it? Or just tear out the page? Call London Metro and compromise his undercover role…What?

He jumped when the phone rang.

"Hello?"

"Gantry, I have a great idea," Dennis exclaimed. "I just rented a car for us, a brand new Jag F-Type. Why don't we take a drive down memory lane? We can visit Abbey Road studios. See where some of these stars lived and died. Then we can fly out on the late flight. What do you say?"

"I guess so," Gantry responded, still not sure what to do.

"Terrific, I'll get a porter to help with the boxes. See you out front in fifteen minutes." Then he added, "Hey, by the way, did you take anything from the boxes? I can't find the journal. I remember you had it last, in the garage? I assume you picked it up."

Gantry hesitated. "No, I don't have it. I flipped through it, but I put it back on top of the box."

"Shit," Dennis was irritated. "I don't remember it on top of the box. Are you sure? Shit."

Gantry quickly packed up his bag and went down to the lobby. At the concierge's desk, he inquired, "Can you deliver this today? It's extremely important," as he was writing the address on the envelope.

"Of course, sir," the concierge said, glancing at the address. "It should be there within the hour."

"Thank you very much."

Later that day an envelope containing the Hendrix journal was delivered to *Rolling Stone*'s London office. It was addressed to:

Alex Jaeger
From: Buddy Holly
Useless, Texas
Personal and Confidential.

"Sorry I'm late. You want to drive?" Dennis asked.

"Are you kidding? The wheel is on the wrong side, and they drive on the wrong side of the road. I'd kill us!"

"You used to be a bit more of a risk taker, mate. Let's first go to Abbey Road studios. Being from *Rolling Stone*, you should be able to get us in. Sound like a plan?" Dennis asked. "By the way, I called Chloe, and she didn't see the journal anywhere. The cab company thinks they know what cab it was, and when they check back in tonight, they'll search it for us. Hope we didn't come all this fucking way for some tie-dyed tee shirts!" Visibly angry, Dennis didn't wait for an answer, and changed the subject.

"Isn't this an awesome car? Jaguar did themselves proud with this rocket. Hey, mate, you're not very talkative today, jet lagged?"

"Yeah…tired. I guess the merry-go-round I've been on for the last couple weeks is catching up with me. Need a good night's sleep."

"You can sleep on the plane, my friend."

"Hey, Dennis, where did you live when you were here?" Gantry asked.

"Near Grosvenor Square. I'll drive by there later. "

"Did you work full time for the record company when you lived here? Must have been fun at that time in London," Gantry mused.

"It ended up being full time, but I never intended it to be. Did a lot of grunt work: collections, deliveries, driving stars around. Things like that. Sounded glamorous to the chicks, but actually it was pretty boring stuff."

He pushed the Jaguar around corners at speed and seemed fidgety, glancing in his rearview and side mirrors.

Gantry said, "What's the matter?"

Dennis sped up and suddenly made a left turn. Gantry pulled his visor down and looked behind them. A silver Mercedes was directly on their tail.

"That car has been following us for the last ten minutes," Dennis said.

"Police?"

"In a Mercedes? And the driver is alone. Hold on."

Late that night, Melendez's cell rang. His team had gone home hours earlier, and he was thinking of spending the night in his office as he did in the old days. The caller ID read PRIVATE CALLER. He didn't like answering calls from numbers he didn't recognize, but given all that was going on…

"Melendez."

"Agent Melendez, I only have a minute. I'm being followed."

"Who is this?"

"Let's just say I'm a fan of rock and roll."

The voice was female, deep, sounded middle-aged. And then suddenly he realized who it was.

The caller anticipated his thought.

"Don't use names."

"Where are you? Are you okay?"

"I'm okay, but I won't be for long. They're after me, as I'm sure you know by now."

"Tell me where you are. I'll get two agents there as fast as I can."

"Not until I know I have your assurances."

"Assurances for what?"

"If I cooperate, I need immunity. This is a lot bigger than you think, and you will get nowhere without me—nowhere. There are too many players in too many places."

Melendez knew she was right, but he couldn't unilaterally offer her immunity. The Bureau's general counsel and the district's attorney general would have to approve it, and that wasn't going to happen overnight. But he could bring her in.

"Okay, but I will have to work this over the next twenty-four hours. For now, let me have you picked up and taken to a safe house. You will be protected. You have my word, but you have to tell me where you are."

"Okay."

She gave him an address in Georgetown and a passcode knock.

"We'll be there within twenty minutes. Don't move!"

The phone went dead and Melendez sat down heavily. "This is it. I knew it. I knew she was the key to it all," he said to himself.

His next call was to Agent Lawrence DeHart in the FBI DC office. In spite of the hour, DeHart got on it immediately. Melendez then called the FBI's general counsel and explained the situation. The counsel called their liaison in the attorney general's office in Washington. Melendez had been in contact with them several times throughout the investigation, as was normal protocol. In this case, they had also coordinated with London and Paris to ensure that if warrants were issued, they would come from the most prosecutable jurisdiction, and were ready to be issued immediately.

Brigid Greely would have to be arrested formally before anything could happen, but he could keep her in protective custody for at least forty-eight hours and get a statement from her. He knew she was too smart to give them much until they had a formal deal in writing. And that could take some time.

This could just be the end to all of it. If she could help tie the connections to the wire transfers, the source of funds and the key players, he could do the rest.

Anne Herriot's Apartment

Brooklyn, New York

"Ms. Herriot, I'm Agent Rockwell. I'm the artist you were expecting," the man announced.

He could hear the multiple dead-bolts sliding open one by one, and slowly the woman opened the door.

"Good morning, Ms. Herriot. Is it okay to come in?"

The apartment smelled musty and stale. *Like the windows had not been opened in years, he thought.* Everything in it was dated and in need of upgrading.

"Yes, young man, by all means. Please come in, I've been expecting you."

She gestured to a table near a window and said, "This should work well, a nice north light. I know you artists like northern light."

Rockwell put his case on the table and took out a sketchpad and four or five charcoal pencils.

"Well Ms. Herriot, I will sit here, then. You tell me what the man looked like, and I'll begin to rough out a sketch. As we go along, you can tell me to alter it any way you want: bigger nose, closer eyes, that sort of thing."

"Let's see, he had reddish hair ..." She paused. "But I suppose he might not have that now. He would have to be in his seventies."

"That's all right Ms. Herriot. This is just a start. After we get a good likeness from those earlier days, our computer experts will do what they call an age progression. They'll scan my finished drawing and then apply some techniques that will show us what he might look like today. For example, they'll add wrinkles, weight, changes in the eyes—different aspects of the face that change as we age."

"I see. Well, I remember his face as clearly as I do my own brother's. He was tall—but this is only his face you're doing, correct?"

"Correct. But don't leave anything out."

"He had a thin, oval face."

Rockwell began to draw.

"He had very thin lips and a narrow nose, as well. Nose was a little long, with a little bump in the middle."

Rockwell continued working with Anne Herriot for well over an hour, then together they looked at the finished drawing.

"That's him! No doubt about it. My, you are good, young man!"

"Thank you, Ms. Herriot," he replied. He packed up his materials. "I'll be getting back to you in a couple of days. We appreciate your help."

By midmorning of the next day, the image was finished. Using the original black-and-white sketch, and Rockwell's notes on complexion, hair color, and height, the program was able to produce a full-color image of an intense-looking man in his seventies.

The computer artist rushed the rendering to Tanner's office, but Tanner wasn't there. Leaving the rendering in a manila envelope with the word URGENT written on it, he pulled his cell phone out of his pocket, dialed Tanner but got his voice mail.

"I have bad news," Bruce said to Melendez.

"Damn, I have good news. Give me yours first."

"Gantry is missing. Neither he nor Briganty are in the hotel. But they haven't checked out yet, either. We had our man get housekeeping to open both room doors."

"Maybe they've found a lead, had to go immediately."

"Their bags are gone, too. There isn't a trace that they were even there, nothing. This is not good."

"Jesus," Melendez said. "Maybe they flew home?"

"We already checked. Don't you think Gantry would have called you? My friend, believe me, we are all over this. I have five men out. We sent one of them over to Briganty's girlfriend's house, the girl Chloe, out on the West End. We'll start there."

There was a pause.

"So…what's your good news?"

"We're picking up Brigid Greely. She's in hiding, scared for her life. I'm assuming Tanner told you that the explosion was so potent, we didn't know right away if she was even alive. Now she wants immunity, and she's ready to talk. She'll be in our custody momentarily, and I plan to begin the interrogation personally tomorrow."

Washington DC

Evening

A black SUV pulled up in the dark Georgetown alley next to a heavy steel door. Two agents climbed out. The passenger-side agent, Lawrence DeHart, pulled his 9mm Glock and stood by the front bumper of the vehicle. The other agent knocked three times quickly, but softly, and then twice slowly.

The alley was strewn with overflowing trashcans, liquor bottles and beer cans, and they could hear something in the dark scurrying back and forth.

The agent waited for thirty seconds, then repeated the knock.

The heavy door opened slowly and the agent stepped back.

At either end of the alley stood a black Suburban.

Greely stepped out carrying an oversized purse. Her face was white and her eyes were darting around like a cornered animal's.

The agent by the door glanced around one more time, then nodded for her to climb into the back seat.

She began to cross the three-foot space to the car.

Suddenly a bright flare-like light blazed at the north end of the alley, followed instantly by a penetrating *boom*! The agents at that end whirled toward the sound. Brigid Greely froze—and a zipping *bap*, this time from a sniper's rifle, sounded above them. Greely stumbled, then fell.

She was dead before her body hit the concrete.

The agents regrouped as quickly as they could. DeHart slung Greely's purse into the car and he and the other agent heaved the body in after it. The two other vehicles raced up in unison and agents tumbled out. They knew the shooter was long gone, along with whoever had distracted them, but they reconnoitered the area anyway.

As his SUV sped away, DeHart got on the radio to Melendez.

"We're heading to George Washington. She's dead. They were waiting for us."

"God damn it! Melendez shouted. How the hell did they know what was she was going to do?"

Daniel Culain, dropped his bag in the cabin and calmly slipped behind the pilot's seat, twisted off the cap of his Fiji water and took a long drink. He synced his smart phone to the cockpit stereo and quickly lifted off, fading away in the crisp night sky to the vibe sound of Chick Corea.

The Streets of London

The Mercedes was glued to their Jag.

"Hold on," Dennis yelled. With that, he spun the car in an expert one-hundred-eighty-degree spin and raced off in the opposite direction as the Mercedes kept its forward motion, unable to react fast enough. The Jag took off over London Bridge and zig-zagged through a maze of narrow streets.

Gantry's heart was in his mouth; he'd never seen anyone drive like this in a city. It was like a scene out of *Fast and Furious*, only this was the real thing. He held on to his seat belt with his right hand and the overhead hand grab with the left, set his teeth, and tried to breathe somewhat normally. Though the streets were narrow, he glanced at the speedometer now reading 160 kph. He instinctively looked down at Dennis' hand on the gear shift as he downshifted, and it suddenly registered…the same ring.

"Good thing I remember the back streets, hey, mate?" Dennis said. "I think we lost them, but we do need to ditch this car."

Dennis seemed as calm as a tour guide.

"Dennis, what in God's name is going on?" Gantry shouted. "Where the fuck did you learn to drive like that?"

"It's a long story. Right now we need to get out of this car and get a black hack."

Suddenly, he pulled the car into a covered car park, drove three stories up, turned off the ignition, and opened his door.

"Dennis! What the hell is going on? Is someone after me?"

Dennis hesitated. Then he spoke calmly.

"I need to get us out of here."

"Let's go to the police," Gantry said emphatically.

"No. We have to get out of here as soon as possible. The police can't protect you. Let's grab what essentials we need and leave the rest."

He popped the trunk and grabbed one large case. Gantry followed suit, carrying his valise.

"Leave your suitcase," Dennis ordered.

Gantry grabbed a handful of papers from the Hendrix box and a multicolored scarf and stuffed them into his valise.

"The station is within walking distance. We're going to take the high-speed train to Birmingham, where we'll be safe," Dennis instructed.

"But why? Why there, and why is someone after me?"

Dennis didn't respond. He led Gantry at a fast pace down a side street and into the train station. They bought two tickets and went directly to the gate and boarded the train. Dennis turned to Gantry as they sat down.

"Can Jaeger get us a private plane out of England?"

"I don't know. Why?"

"He's the only one we can trust right now. We need to get out of here as soon as possible. Call him."

Confused and still disoriented, Gantry called Alex, but the call did not go through.

"Take mine," Dennis said, as he handed over his mobile phone.

"Alex Jaeger."

"Alex, Gantry here. I—I don't have a lot of time. Dennis and I need your help. Someone is after me, and we need to get out of here *now*," he said frantically.

"Where the hell are you, and what's going on?"

"I'm really not in a position to talk." Gantry's eyes were darting from side to side.

"Plane," Dennis growled.

"C-Can you get a private plane to pick us up in Birmingham? We will be there within the hour. I need your help," Gantry pleaded.

"Okay. Go to the Eurojet terminal there. That's who I use," Alex replied. "We'll call them now and tell them you're coming. Let me know when you are in the plane and safe."

Jaeger disconnected, then punched in Melendez's number.

"I just got a call from Gantry."

"Where is he? We haven't been able to get in contact with him, and they aren't in their hotel."

"They are on a train to Birmingham and he just asked to get them a plane to get them out of there as soon as possible. He said that someone was after them, and he sounded very scared. Said he couldn't talk. I am arranging for Eurojet to fly them home. It'll be a G-5. They will be there within the hour."

"Nothing more?" Melendez asked.

"No. What the hell is—"

"Okay, I'll notify Scotland Yard. Let me know if you hear from him again."

Fifteen minutes later, Jaeger received confirmation from Eurojet: the plane would be fueled and ready to go within the hour.

Alex's assistant softly knocked on his door.

"Mr. Jaeger, the London office just called and said they got a package addressed to you earlier today."

"Yes. So what?" he replied, a little irritated.

"Well, the reason they called…The package was from Buddy Holly, Useless, Texas," she replied.

Alex jumped up. "Get them on the phone immediately."

In minutes, he was on the phone with security in the London office.

"Please open the package and tell me what's in it," Alex said.

"Yes, sir."

Alex heard the rustling of paper.

"It is a red leather journal. Looks pretty worn."

"Shit, the Hendrix journal," Alex exclaimed. "I want you to have someone take it to Scotland Yard immediately and deliver it to Inspector Robert Bruce. Immediately!"

"Yes, sir. We'll leave right now."

FBI Headquarters

Quantico, VA

"Robert, let's get the team on this now. This has escalated quickly," Melendez said.

Within twenty minutes, the full international team was on a video call.

"Is everyone on?" asked Melendez. "Good. As many of you are aware, the case has taken a number of unexpected turns. We all anticipated that we were dealing with something far more sophisticated than any of us originally thought. That is now confirmed. Angus Hislop, the source of the clues and the creator of the labyrinth of bank accounts and companies, is believed dead. He was shot, execution style, at close range with a .22 caliber pistol.

"Before he was killed, he sent his records to the *Rolling Stone* offices. As many of you are aware, they have proven key in establishing an offshore flow of funds and a tax-fraud scheme that implicated Brigid Greely. Hours ago, Greely was shot by a sharpshooter as she was turning herself in for protective custody."

Gasps and even cries filled the room in response to the devastating facts that were thrown out like machine-gun fire.

"This is what we know so far. I am in Washington with the pickup team, and we are just about to go through Greely's belongings," Melendez explained.

"But one more thing: Alex Jaeger received a call from Gantry Elliot asking if he and Dennis Briganty could be flown privately out of Birmingham. He said they were being followed. We should get confirmation shortly that they are at the terminal."

Bruce said, "Raphael, before you continue, I just received a package from the security office at *Rolling Stone*."

Bruce opened the cover and began to skim through it.

"It's an old journal," he said. "The envelope it came in was addressed to Alex Jaeger from Buddy Holly, Useless, Texas."

"That's from Gantry!" Jodi shouted.

"It's the Hendrix journal," Moxie said. "There was something in there that we picked up on Gantry's video monitor before it gave out. He was focused on it."

"Robert, open the journal and see if you can find what could have made Gantry so nervous," Melendez said.

"It was the pages that looked like there was something spilled on them," Moxie said.

"Let's see," Bruce said.

He read aloud from Hendrix's own hand:

Met my shrink, Dr. Burnham, twice this week. Having trouble sleeping. Am beginning to get scared. They sent that goon down again— pushed me around a little. Asked if I wanted to end up like Jones. Said they own me, and I'm not going anywhere.

Bruce stopped. "It's difficult to read past this. There are stains on the page."

"Any name mentioned?" Melendez asked.

"Don't see anything, Raphael. Sorry."

"Tanner, can we see the age-progression work done on the sketch we got with Anne Herriot?"

The digitally enhanced artist's rendition, age-progressed, appeared on the screen.

"Red hair? Could this be the same guy?" Melendez asked.

Suddenly Jodi said, "That looks a little like Gantry's friend Dennis, at least the Dennis I remember from about eight years ago. Red hair, thin face, piercing eyes—even that bump on his nose."

"Are you sure, Detective?" Melendez asked.

"Well, no, sir, I can't be one hundred percent sure," she responded.

"Okay, team. Keep your schedules clear. This is live and hot!" Melendez instructed.

"That's all that's in her purse? Two phones, cosmetics, and a book on integrative health?" Melendez asked. "She must have held back until she had a deal. Get to her condo and office and grab her hard drives. Also get all her pictures to our advanced photo analytics guys to do a comprehensive facial recognition match. I want a dump of the calls on both phones."

"Sir, one of these is a burner phone," the agent pointed out.

"Let me see it." He looked at the outgoing calls she had made.

"Los Angeles number...New York number...New York number... another New York number, then...a foreign number."

"I'll have them researched for you immediately."

"No need, I'm going to go old school," Melendez replied.

He pressed redial for the first number.

"Thank you for calling Warner Brothers. Mr. O'Brian's office."

Melendez disconnected, then punched redial on the next number. No answer. He tried the next New York Number.

"Sony Music, how can I help you?"

He disconnected and moved to the next New York number.

"Dusty Records. If we don't have it, it doesn't exist. Please leave a message."

Melendez hesitated. The name rang a bell, but too faintly. He moved on.

The foreign number did not answer.

A few minutes later, "Sir, I just looked it up. That last number has a Caribbean exchange, seven-five-eight. Looks like a Saint Lucia country code."

"Got it."

"...And Sir, the unanswered New York number belongs to Daniel Culain."

"Bring him in for questioning," a surprised Melendez instructed.

Melendez needed to think. He went into a darkened office and closed his eyes to help him concentrate as he began to reconstruct the events of the last seventy-two hours. He needed to *become* Brigid Greely, much like a method actor or a novelist who simultaneously creates and inhabits his characters' thoughts and behaviors.

Breathing slowly, he cleared his mind. He then posed the question, imagining Greely with the phone in her hand, who would she call?

All the advanced analytics and sophisticated algorithms melted away, as he inhaled deeply, letting his thoughts rise like smoke. His focus and breathing narrowed.

Suddenly he stood up and turned on the light switch: *The smallest details…the smallest details.*

He called Tanner and then patched in Jodi Randolph.

"Detective Randolph, what is the name of Briganty's record store in New York?"

"Dusty Records."

"That caller ID appeared in Greely's burner phone over the last seventy-two hours."

"Oh my God," Jodi gasped.

"Okay, Tanner, confirm with Herriot that this is the guy."

"Right," Tanner said. "Let me find a current picture. Also check if there is a reception photo at Rolling Stone."

Melendez could see the puzzle pieces fitting together, converging from different directions at once.

"Yes, hang on… Detective Randolph, we need to compare Dennis Briganty's fingerprints to the ones on the inhaler as soon as you can. Tanner, get an agent to his store and get some prints, pronto. And, let's get that to London as well. They have been looking at bank videos near St. Albans Pharmacy from the time of the murders. Compare Briganty to the alias also. And where the hell is that jet?"

"Detective Randolph, do you have any idea where Dennis lived in London?"

"I don't remember him ever mentioning exactly where he lived… somewhere in the West End, maybe? He did talk a lot about a café he liked on Grosvenor Square; it was a place he hung out at with some local music people."

"Tanner, get them that info now," Melendez ordered.

The agent took high-resolution photos of the Briganty prints from his store on Bleecker Street and sent them immediately to the forensics lab in Quantico.

SCU compared the Briganty progression picture to photos for every branch within a two-mile radius of Grosvenor Square for dates preceding the Jones, Hendrix, and Ham murders. They identified what possibly looked like a much younger Briganty twice in the teller line and once at the ATM a week before the murders. The man was thin, red-headed and tall. The Photo Forensics group was doing a facial recognition run to confirm that it was the same person.

Anne Herriot was shown the original sketch and the progression photograph of what Briganty would look like now. She positively identified him as the man she had seen.

Within two hours, Tanner was finished.

"Boss, we've completed our digital examination of the fingerprints of Dennis Briganty and the two inhalers, and we have a match, sir. They are from the same person. No question. We also matched a Rolling Stone reception desk photo of Dennis Briganty to Duluhan."

"Are you absolutely certain?"

"One hundred percent."

"He's the killer," Melendez said.

Birmingham Airport, UK

By the time Scotland Yard arrived, Gantry and Dennis had already taken off.

"Yes, I remember them," the operator explained. "They boarded and flew out on flight 2019 a little while ago. The flight plan destination is Teterboro, New Jersey."

Melendez felt that, for the moment at least, he could breathe. He got up and poured himself a cup of coffee. He put Tanner on the task of contacting the executive airline and Jaeger to see if they could be patched in to the pilot.

A few minutes later, Melendez's cell phone rang.

"Agent Melendez, Alex Jaeger here. Gantry never showed up at the Eurojet terminal. The plane I arranged is still waiting," Jaeger reported.

"But I just got confirmation that they got on a plane together and took off."

"Maybe so, but it wasn't the one I arranged for them."

"Then what plane did they get on?"

"I don't know. Oh my God, someone got to them!" Alex said. "We've got to track that plane."

Within minutes, Tanner alerted the FAA as well as Passur Aerospace, the company that supplies the analytics to support flight planning and destination locations; they'd be able to track the plane's every movement and get an accurate fix on its direction and speed. Then, they could confirm where it might be headed.

An hour later Melendez received a call from the flight agent.

"At first, we thought the plane was headed west, to New Jersey, but the flight plan appears to have changed, and the plane is now headed south traveling at about five hundred fifty knots."

"En route to where?"

"We should know shortly where this flight path will take them, but they are not coming to the states, that's for sure. Based on their trajectory, speed and fuel consumption, the best guess right now is somewhere in the Caribbean."

"Saint Lucia!"

Melendez picked up the phone and called Bruce.

"Robert, The plane has changed course, and is headed to the Caribbean. I think they're going to Saint Lucia. We found a call to Saint Lucia on Greely's phone."

"Are you thinking what I am thinking, Raphael?" Bruce said.

"Yes—the big guy, the brains. That's where the boss is," Melendez replied.

"Raphael, Saint Lucia is an independent country but still part of the Commonwealth. They operate under the British legal system. We have very close ties with the police there," Bruce said. "I will make some calls. We'll have no problem getting extradition, should it come to that."

"Thank you, Robert. I am going to take a team down there immediately and see if our hunch about the big guy is correct. Can you clear the decks for us?" Melendez asked.

"Of course, but I had a plane standing by for our team as well, just in case Briganty rerouted. Will call you from the plane. You will get there before us."

Gulfstream G-5

30,000 feet, somewhere over the Atlantic

Dennis and Gantry did not realize they were not headed for Teterboro. They thought it odd that there were no attendants on board, nor did the pilot explain the flight plan to them.

The plane made a wide, slow turn somewhere over the Atlantic that neither of them felt.

Dennis sat quietly. Looking out the window, he anticipated Gantry's concerns. "I'll explain it all once we land and are safe," he said.

Then he casually closed his eyes to take a nap.

FBI Aircraft

28,000 feet, over the Eastern Seaboard

"Raphael, can you hear me clearly?" Bruce asked.

"Yes."

"I have to say, I have never been on a high-speed chase in a plane," Bruce observed.

"Neither have I."

Melendez had a team of five SWAT agents with him. Bruce had four. Each member was armed with an AR-16 and a .45 caliber pistol, among other, heavier weapons.

"I just spoke to the Saint Lucia police," Bruce said. "They said the plane with Gantry and his friend on board is part of a small fleet owned by a local company and primarily used by a wealthy but reclusive resident. They can't confirm his name, but he has a large, very secure complex overlooking the Pitons," Bruce explained.

"Right. Robert, I have been working on a 'John Doe' arrest warrant for the big boss. We've only used this on rare occasions."

"Not sure I am following you," Bruce said.

"We've used a 'John Doe' when we have determined that the circumstantial evidence, behavioral conclusions and motivations describe a key personality in an investigation. A person who we haven't been able to identify by name. We can arrest and detain the most highly probable person, given the preponderance of evidence, even circumstantial evidence."

"We have something similar. So you're thinking we go for the boss as well?"

"Well, if we're lucky, this could be more than a just a John Doe? Our photo analytics guys have been pouring though Greely's pictures, especially the one's found at her office, and applying our test lab's advanced facial recognition technology to try to match the pictures to anyone associated with the recording industry at that time," Melendez explained.

"Anything hit?" Bruce asked.

"Possibly. One candidate has a characteristic match: Possible ownership interest. Irish. London. Right age range," Melendez explained, " I have sent you the images we have, thus far."

"The only problem is we have very limited info on him. And like Hislop, he seems to have vanished years ago. McMullan was his name."

"Thanks Raphael, just got them. I assume the one picture is from Greeley's office…umm, photo of a meeting…another…was he a priest?" Bruce asked.

"It's only a partial, but it appears to be him in priest robes, doesn't it," Melendez responded. "Our techs say the partial is the same guy."

"No…I see it…no, not a priest. Look at the black Celtic cross on the red vestments. The black hood. Do you know what that is?"

"No. Not at all, "Melendez answered.

"That is the sign of the Knights of the Red Branch. The Christian Crusaders. I remember from my university history work. An extreme sect. Must be from a costume party. Died out at the end of the 13th century," Bruce explained.

"Robert, thanks for the history lesson, my man."

"If we can apprehend Dennis Briganty, he could possibly help to make a positive confirmation of McMullan."

Dennis woke up, looked at his watch and pulled the shade up.

"We should be seeing land by now," he said, looking again at his watch. He looked out the window and saw unbroken open ocean.

"What the hell? This isn't the route to the states."

Dennis suddenly realized what was happening. He jumped up and bolted to the front of the aircraft and pounded on the high-density steel sign that read, AUTHORIZED PERSONNEL ONLY.

"Where the fuck are we going?" he shouted as he pounded and kicked at the door. There was no response.

Then he realized what was going on.

It wasn't Greely who was trying to get Gantry and him.

Vigie Airport, Castries, Saint Lucia

The FBI plane arrived well before the plane carrying Dennis and Gantry. Bruce was still a considerable way out.

Upon landing, Melendez immediately conferred with the Saint Lucia authorities in the small terminal building and began to set up a capture site in the hangar where ground control would direct the plane.

"Here it comes," the Saint Lucia police captain pointed out. "She's coming in fast."

The plane aligned and dropped down quickly to the outer runway, hitting hard. Smoke flew from the tires, and the plane slowed and finally stopped far from the hangar.

Melendez turned at the sound of screeching tires from two SUVs that came flying seemingly out of nowhere, racing to intercept the plane. He knew now that they were in for a real battle, not just a confrontation with Briganty.

"Go, go, go!" he shouted, and his SWAT peeled out in the police Toyotas. At the plane, a handful of heavily armed men jumped out of the SUVs. They were wearing black jumpsuits and carrying assault weapons. They ran up the jetway and popped open the plane door. As Melendez's men raced toward the plane, the men in jumpsuits reappeared, pushing Gantry and Dennis down the jetway. The SWAT team ground to a halt and the agents spilled out, falling into attack position. Gantry and Dennis were hurriedly pushed back into the cabin.

Melendez's team quickly subdued the drivers of the SUVs, then shot out the plane's tires. Melendez told one of the agents to prepare to fire two rounds of advanced tear gas into the cabin, when suddenly Gantry, and then Dennis, reappeared at the top of the stairs, along with their assailants.

Melendez yelled for his men to stand down.

One behind the other, Gantry and Dennis were in line, both held at gunpoint. Comprehending the situation, Melendez communicated with his men through hand signals, holding up three fingers to show that there were three men left to deal with. Two were at the head of the stairs and one was inside the plane. Each of the three agents quickly took positions behind their cars to focus on their targets.

For what seemed like an eternity, no one spoke or moved.

Then the third assailant came out. He spoke loudly and clearly in a British accent. "We will not hesitate to shoot both of these men unless you retreat to the terminal. We will give you one minute."

Why haven't they killed them already? Melendez wondered. That won't happen. Gantry and Dennis must have something the boss needs.

Dennis also assessed the situation and prepared to make his move. Pretending to stumble, he suddenly spun around and placed a hard knee in the groin of the man covering him. In a swift series of moves, he grabbed him by the head and shoulders, spun him around and threw him off the jetway. Before his man hit the ground, Dennis threw his forearm around the other, startled gunman and quickly snapped his neck.

The last gunman, who had ducked back inside the plane, re-emerged in a panic, holding his gun high in surrender. Then, suddenly changing his mind, in desperation he shoved the gun into Gantry's neck and yelled for them to stand down or he would shoot.

In an instant Dennis pushed Gantry violently aside, and the panicked gunman fired two rounds into Dennis's upper torso. The SWAT team members quickly responded and the gunman went down in a blizzard of bullets.

Dennis fell back and into Gantry's arms, his hands clutching his chest. There was blood everywhere. Gantry and team members carried Dennis down the stairway and laid him on the tarmac. Gantry knelt next to him, comforting his friend and whispering something in his ear. Gantry put his ear next to Dennis's mouth so he could hear what he was saying. He slipped the ring off, as instructed.

"Get the medics in here!" Melendez shouted. The drone of the ambulance's siren could be heard in the distance. One of the agents was applying pressure to Dennis's wounds, trying to control the bleeding.

And then, as his position dictated he must, Melendez stood up and said, "Dennis Briganty, you are under arrest for the murder of Brian Jones, Jimi Hendrix, Al Wilson, Janis Joplin, Jim Morrison, Ron McKernan, and Peter Ham. You have the right to remain silent. Anything you say, can and will be held against you."

Gantry was stunned and speechless, unable to comprehend what Melendez had just said.

Robert Bruce and his team rushed to the scene, having just arrived.

Dennis looked at Gantry and tried to whisper something, then his head fell the opposite way as he passed out. The ambulance attendants ran up with a stretcher.

"Two of you stay with him at all times," Melendez ordered, pointing to two team members. "Call Miami right now and get a real doctor down here. Gantry, you go to the hospital with them."

Too stunned to think straight, Gantry could barely get the words out, "Is he going to live?"

"It doesn't look too good," Melendez answered.

"Gantry, what did he say to you...Gantry...what?"

"A name... all he said was a name before he lost consciousness... Ciarin McMullan."

Melendez turned to Bruce. "That's him! The Saint Lucia police captain can take us there."

"Let's go now, Raphael, before McMullan realizes what has just happened here," Bruce said.

They commandeered the SUVs and headed north.

The Saint Lucia police captain in the lead car directed them over rutted, unpaved roads up the mountain. When they came to the gates of the estate, they crashed through and raced up to the house. The combined SWAT teams quickly spread out and surrounded the compound, firing two rounds of tear gas into the building. Three agents burst through the front door.

Melendez and Bruce waited behind the cars as gunfire ensued. Then, as quickly as it had begun, it was over.

"Clear!" a SWAT team member yelled from the doorway.

Bruce and Melendez ran into the mansion, waving away the dissipating fumes.

On the far side of the room, an old man stood propped on a cane. Two men, apparently bodyguards, stood at his side; they'd been disarmed quickly.

The old man looked to be in his eighties, and very fragile.

Melendez took the lead. "Ciarin McMullan?"

The old man nodded as Melendez and Bruce approached.

"Ciarin McMullen, you are under arrest as an accomplice to the murder of Brian Jones, Jimi Hendrix, Janis Joplin, Al Wilson, Jim Morrison, Ron McKernan, and Peter Ham. You are also under arrest for evasion of taxes and committing tax fraud against the governments of the United States and the United Kingdom."

Rock and Roll Hall of Fame, Cleveland, OH

November

Gantry had arranged a private tour of the Rock and Roll Hall of Fame for himself and Melendez through his old friend and former colleague, Jim Henke.

As they walked the halls, they lingered at the Rolling Stones exhibit and stared at Brian Jones's first guitar. Gantry pointed out the recording of the Rice Krispies jingle Jones had written. They stopped at the exhibits of all the dead rock stars. These had now become almost shrines, as flowers and messages were placed in front of each one by fans from around the world who never forgot them.

Emotions ran high for both men.

"These are the first editions of *Rolling Stone* magazine." Gantry pointed out, as they stopped at one of the landings. "Looks like a tabloid, doesn't it?"

"Yeah, you guys have come a long way," Melendez smiled.

They stopped in front of the Kurt Cobain and Nirvana exhibit, then sat down on a bench near the display.

"You know what, Raphael? There have been a lot of emotions flowing through all of this—the stars, the era, the stories, us meeting and working together, and Dennis...I've been reliving those days of Aquarius vicariously, as I'm sure you have. Now it's time to write the story. Not just for me or Alex or *Rolling Stone*, but so the world will finally have the truth."

"You're a good man, Gantry. It has been a true and unique privilege working with you," Melendez said, shaking Gantry's hand with both of his. "I also have to give your boss credit. When Greely put his *cojones* in a vice, he did the right thing. That is a rare virtue in this day and age."

"Yeah, that's why I stayed with him all these years. In the end, each of us fought the fight that our dead heroes needed each of us to do," Gantry answered. "How about you, now that Mayflower's no longer on your weekly radar and you're almost officially retired? What are you and Lucia going to do?"

"Well, oddly enough, after our little visit to the islands, I took her back down there. The police captain showed us around. It's absolutely gorgeous, and it's very cheap in comparison to here. We decided not to go to Palm Desert, and we bought a little *casita* in Saint Lucia—me and Lucia in Lucia.

"And you, Gantry? The world's gonna be your oyster when this story breaks in *Rolling Stone*. You wouldn't consider taking some time off would you, like, permanently?"

"Hell, no. The party's just starting," Gantry laughed. "If Mick Jagger and Keith Richards can still crank it out, no reason I can't! I'm a pup compared to them. The kids at *Stone* all want my advice now!"

Gantry turned serious and said, "What's going to happen now?"

"Well, the case against McMullan is more than enough to keep him in prison for the rest of his life, which may not be very long. The families and estates of all the murdered rock stars have filed a myriad of civil suits to compensate them for the loss of those brilliant careers cut so short by that madman. The forensic accounting teams have been working with the banks and have uncovered dozens more accounts. In fact, with the information that Hislop provided us, we eventually tied some of the large insurance drafts to dummy companies that, in turn, flowed the cash through the same offshore process we previously pieced together.

"I expect that criminal charges in Europe and the states will be filed soon. There is talk of conducting them remotely, from his prison hospital room, because of the political pressure to get this going."

"How about Daniel Culain. Have they found him yet?"

"No trace," Melendez curtly answered.

Gantry looked at him and was about to say something.

"Oh, and you'll love this," Melendez added. "Mayflower tried to muscle in on the positive PR that the agency was getting, trying to make it look like he was behind the scenes, driving the investigation. What a joke. But the Director got a direct order from the attorney general to back him off. What the hell," he said, laughing, "I never knew that Tanner was the attorney general's nephew!"

Gantry high-fived him.

"So Gantry, you didn't answer my question, what are you going to do?"

"Well, that's why I asked you to meet me here in Cleveland. The Rock Hall came a-callin' and they want me on the board. I think I'm going to accept. They also want to give me a lifetime-achievement award at the next induction ceremony. But of course, I'll keep writing. It's all I know, really, as long as Alex will keep me.

And...Jodi and I are spending next week together in San Francisco." Jodi walked up to them and gave Gantry a kiss.

"Hello detective, fancy meeting you here?" Jodi laughingly said.

"Congratulations, you two! You deserve it. Wow, on the board of the Rock and Roll Hall of Fame. And you get the girl, too? Not bad.

"May the sun always shine on your window pane," he said as he hugged both of them, "I'm proud of both of you."

"Anything's possible. We're both a lot wiser now," Gantry answered, smiling. "Well, I won't claim wisdom. But all of this—everything that's happened—it all made us think about what we'd been doing, and who we are, and what we are to each other."

"Yes, anything is possible," Melendez said. The two men laughed, then they got up and walked toward the exit. As they opened the door and a flood of late November sun spilled across the floor at their feet, Melendez reached out his hand, smiled at Gantry and said, "Pardner, you keep in touch. Don't wait another thirty years to call me."

Gantry nodded, and felt a lump come up in his throat. Reaching out, he hugged his friend, then took a deep breath and said, "Raphael I need to show you something", as he pulled out a new iPhone.

"A smartphone?" Melendez said sarcastically. Gantry's expression stopped his joking.

"I received this video file late last night. It's from Hislop."

"Hislop. That's not possible…"

"Just watch this," He coldly interjected.

A video of Hislop sitting behind a desk appeared on the screen.

What I am going to tell you will be hard to believe, but you will discover that it is true.

Ciaran McMullan is a Red Branch Knight. As were his father, grandfather, great-grandfather…all his known lineage.

The Knights of the Red Branch are an Irish off-shoot of the Knights Templar, the Protectors of Jesus. They look to Cuculain, the warrior saint of Ireland, as their founder and patron. As legend has it, Cuculain died in a fierce battle, tied to a tree in order to die on his feet. He was twenty-seven years old.

In Red Knight culture, the age of twenty-seven was a sacred time of transition from manhood to knighthood. It was the age that Cuculain went from warrior to legend. To McMullan, the age symbolized a time of perfection. In Knight lore, it was more than that; an inflection point of total dedication to the Knights. So total, that legend has it that if a prospective Knight failed, he was not just alienated from the Knights, but eliminated to preserve the sacred secrets that had been entrusted to him.

That sacred trust went all the way back to the time of Jesus and his ultimate betrayal by Judas. Well documented in the Bible is Judas' betrayal of Jesus for thirty pieces of silver. His guilt built to the point that he committed suicide by hanging himself. A scene so iconic in the Christian Religion that the very variety of tree he hung himself from has been forever called the Judas Tree, known for its blood red coloring.

The Knights of the Red Branch believed something different and protected that knowledge for centuries. They protected the ancient archive that documented not only the crucifixion of Jesus and the betrayal by Judas, but the revenge murder of Judas by the followers of Jesus. An outcome so diametrically opposed to Jesus' message of forgiveness, that they committed from the time of Cuculain, to protect that knowledge with their lives.

In fact, the very tree that Judas hung from…the Judas Tree…the Red tree, begot their name…Red Branch. Judas was hung from a red branch to revenge Jesus' death.

Judas was 27 years old.

Melendez and Gantry looked at each other.

…To McMullan, his rock stars were perfect in a different way. They commanded huge audiences who followed their every action and song message. They were legends. They were his own special Knights and he expected their full loyalty.

To a megalomaniac like McMullan, their lewd behavior and their disloyalty infuriated him. He saw them as almost god-like and perfect. Legends to be worshipped.

Their behavior at twenty-seven years old, made him go berserk with a consuming rage. Not only was it a blasphemy on the sacred age of Knight transition. But it was the age Judas made the ultimate betrayal.

He saw them as publically betraying the loyalty he entrusted in them and failing in their transition to legendary perfection.

In his mind, he had no choice but to eliminate them.

With that, the video ended and the two men stood speechless staring at each other.

Was it possible that the Myth of 27 was explained as the work of an insane businessman? A crackpot whose maniacal distortion of Irish myths led to murder?

"Dennis asked me to keep this, right before he died," Gantry slowly spoke, as he reached into his pocket and took out a Celtic cross signet ring in a red stone setting.

"This looks just like the ring we took off McMullan when we arrested him," a surprised Melendez answered, "It was the only jewelry he wore. Unmistakable."

"Raphael, I recognized it in the Bill Wyman picture in Greeley's office we both stared at," added Gantry.

"After I got the video last night, I googled Knights of the Red Branch. This is their symbol. A Celtic cross set in red. Its origin goes back to their founder," Gantry explained as he showed Melendez the image on his phone. "They must have all been Knights of the Red Branch...including Dennis."

Gantry looked at Raphael with an empty look that belied the internal emotion within him.

"Raphael, we need to..."

Without speaking, Melendez waved his hand to stop Gantry as he shook his head and began walking to the parking lot.

He was done.

Gantry instinctively started to go after him, but Jodi grabbed his arm and pulled him back.

"It's over, sweetheart," she said, "It's all over. Let him go. You all brought justice. You did it, baby."

Gantry turned and exhaled a deep breath. Then he smiled.

It was time to move on...tell the story...rewrite history.

Lake Erie magnified the dusky sun reflecting off of I.M.Pei's iconic glass pyramid, illuminating a wide pathway on the entrance promenade, as the wafting lyrics of "Crystal Ship" poured out of the outdoor speakers like a warm musical sauce.

"Cosmic," as Jodi put her head onto Gantry's shoulder and whispered into his ear, "Cosmic."